THE SERIAL KILLER'S WIFE

THE SERIAL KILLER'S WIFE

ROBERT SWARTWOOD

RMS PRESS

For Holly

Just as in Eden, where Adam was manipulated by Eve, I believe that Edward Piccioni was manipulated. Not that he did not viciously rape and murder those women—he did do that without a doubt—but he was manipulated into doing so by his own Eve: Elizabeth Piccioni. He was the puppet, she the puppet master.

—Clarence Applegate,
The Widower Maker

PART I
CHILDREN OF CAIN

1

They were discussing the different ways to kill the child molester.

Or rather Chad Cooper was discussing the different ways, sitting at his place at the lunchroom table, slicing an apple, while the rest of them stared at him in stunned silence.

"Drowning him might not be the best idea," he said, his focus on the apple, "as it raises the question of just *how* you get a chance to push and then keep his head under water. Maybe a hit-and-run would be better. No, you know what would be best? An icicle. Don't they say that's the perfect murder weapon?"

He paused, suddenly noticing the palpable silence, and looked up. He was in his forties, his brown hair thinning, his potbelly beginning to grow more pronounced by the semester. A social studies teacher for eleven years, he was known for being one of the students' favorite teachers in the middle school. He always incorporated movies into his lessons and would sometimes bring in his guitar and play popular songs whose words he'd change around to help the students remember certain vocabulary words and important dates and places that would appear on their tests.

"I'm sorry"—his voice now suddenly gruff—"did I say something inappropriate?"

How the conversation had even turned to Reginald Moore nobody could begin to guess, but they all knew Chad's frustrations, what with the convicted sex offender having moved into his neighborhood just a few weeks ago.

"Chad," Eileen Peters sighed, an English teacher for fifteen years, the eighth grade team leader who seemed to always have her auburn hair in a bun, "we all know how you feel—"

"No you don't. Especially you, Eileen. You don't even have kids."

The silence that followed this was even more palpable. Eileen's face had begun to redden. It was true, she had no kids, because, according to gossip, she was barren.

Chad, who normally had a cheery disposition, didn't even seem fazed by the fact Eileen now looked like she was about to cry.

"And the worst part?" He shoved an apple slice in his mouth. "They let him move into a house less than three miles away from the elementary school. I mean, seriously, what the fuck is that?"

Nobody spoke. Nobody moved. Nobody even looked at Chad now as he chewed his apple slice and shook his head. He scanned the table, trying to find supporters, somebody to back him up with just a simple nod, but none of his colleagues would meet his eyes. And so it made sense that, after having exhausted the normal route, he would turn to her.

"What about you, Sarah?"

Lunchtime on Fridays had always been a treat for her, the

Oakville Middle School eighth grade teachers winding down after a stressful week, the men going without ties, the women wearing jeans, happy to know that in only a few hours the weekend would start and it would be another two days off before they had to come back in on Monday and do it all over again. They'd sit around the three long tables pushed together to create one large table, their brown-bagged lunches placed in front of them. During the week one or two teachers might work at one of the half dozen desks set up around the room, grading papers or prepping tests. But not on Friday. No, Friday was a time when everyone shared lunch together, joking, laughing, telling stories.

She found herself clearing her throat in a demure sort of way. "I'm sorry?"

"You have a son. He's what—five, six years old?"

She gave a cautious glance around the table. "Five."

"So then how would you feel if a registered sex offender moved in right down the block from you? Wouldn't you be a little, oh I don't know, upset?"

For the first time in a long while she reminded herself that she wasn't supposed to be here. She was a teacher's assistant, yes, but this room, this table, was for the teachers. Those men and women who had taken four years of college to earn their education degrees, some who had gone on to earn their master's, who applied and interviewed and were eventually hired as first-year teachers, always the toughest job for any teacher, having to prove your worth not just to the faculty and staff and school board but to the students, to yourself.

Where she should be right now was in the cinder-block room connected to the cafeteria, a sterile place filled only with the continuous buzz of the Coke machine in the corner, of myriad conversations from the seventh and eight graders out beyond the door propped open with a makeshift wooden stopper. There she should be with the other teacher assistants, the other substitutes, but over the past two years she had slowly stopped eating her lunch in that room and transitioned to this room, with the real teachers, the place that felt more comfortable, and they had welcomed her with open arms and she had enjoyed every moment of it, every moment except this one.

"Well?" Chad said, chopping off another slice of apple much harder than was necessary, his focus on her turning into a glare.

"I imagine I would not be happy about the situation, no."

That glare continued, but only for a moment, and then Chad grinned, gave one of those half-laughs, and turned back to the rest of the table.

"See? Even Sarah wouldn't be happy about a child molester moving in next door. And the truth is, none of you would either."

"Chad," Dick Cummings sighed, a Phys Ed teacher of fourteen years who had no choice but to endure his name, "none of us said—"

"*I don't want to hear it,*" Chad snapped. He'd brought up the paring knife so it was pointed toward Dick, held it there for a second or two before he noticed the expressions on everyone's faces. Pulling himself together, he quickly lowered the knife, placed it on the table beside his napkin and the remains of his apple, and stood up. "I'm ... sorry. I think I just need to take a walk."

And then before anyone could say a word he was gone, the door closing behind him with the finality of a period, and at once everyone released a breath at the same time.

The phone on Eileen's desk rang.

As Eileen got up and went to her desk, everyone else started talking.

"The ironic thing?" Gail Costello said, an Art teacher. "He considers himself so liberal. Always about pro-choice this, no death penalty that. I mean, I wouldn't be happy if that pervert moved in down the street from me either, but don't be a hypocrite."

This was followed by nods of agreement, more murmuring, and before she knew it Eileen called her name.

"Sarah? You have a phone call."

She frowned as she met Eileen at her desk, wondering who would be calling her at this extension. Maybe Todd if he had a free period that coincided with this lunch hour. Anybody else would have her cell phone number and would try her there first, and when she didn't answer they'd leave a message if whatever they wanted to discuss with her was important enough. Then again, that was doubtful too, as pretty much *nobody* had her cell phone number.

Eileen gave her a forced smile, one that reminded her she wasn't supposed to be here in the first place, was just a lowly teacher's assistant whose lunchtime was meant to be sequestered to that cinder-block room just outside the cafeteria with the rest of the non-faculty.

She took the phone with her own forced smile, then waited until Eileen had started away before placing the phone to her ear and saying hello.

"Elizabeth Piccioni?" said a dark robotic voice on the other end.

She let only a moment pass before saying, "I'm sorry, I think you have the wrong person."

"Elizabeth"—that dark robotic voice having no emotion whatsoever—"how would you like me to kill your son—fast or slow?"

2

She was in the hallway, headed directly toward room 218—Mary Boyle's Earth Science—when Chad Cooper came out of the men's room and stood directly in front of her.

"I want to apologize."

Her body was shaking, blood was pounding away in her ears, that for an instant she didn't hear him—didn't even see him standing there—and automatically went to step around him.

He moved to the side so he was standing in her way again.

"Sarah, please. I acted like an asshole back there, and I wanted to—"

"I have to go."

"What?"

"Chad"—speaking between clenched teeth—"get out of my way."

"But—"

She pushed him, much harder than she intended, catching him by surprise and knocking him off balance. He stumbled backward, tripping over his own feet and falling to the floor.

"What the fuck?" he said loudly, then quickly shut his eyes and raised his shoulders, hoping no student (or administrator) was nearby.

She was already walking past him, ignoring him as he called her name, asking what was wrong, what her problem was, then, under his breath, calling her what sounded like *crazy bitch*.

That last bit almost stopped her, her body shaking even more, the blood so loud in her ears she could hardly hear her own thoughts. The idea of turning around, stomping back toward Chad, slapping him across the face appealed to her in a way she knew was wrong. She even paused for an instant, considering it, then continued forward, passing different Art projects taped to the walls, one of them having pulled away from the wall and hanging limp, like it would fall down at any moment.

She hurried around the corner, came to the room, tried the door but it was locked just as she knew it would be. Fumbling then in her pocket, bringing out the keys, she thought briefly of Eileen, thinking that she wasn't a *complete* non-faculty because at least she had a room key. As she opened the door she could hear her cell phone vibrating in her bag located beneath the shelf behind the teacher's desk.

A minute, that terrible voice had told her, she had one minute to answer her cell phone, and as she sprinted past the desks to the front of the room, tore open her canvas bag, she knew that Chad Cooper had caused her to miss her deadline, that when she found her phone the sixty seconds would be up.

The phone was still vibrating when she pressed the TALK button and held it to her ear.

"Three seconds left," the voice said. "I didn't think you were going to make it."

So far—from leaving the lunchroom, to her encounter with Chad Cooper, to entering room 218—she had managed to hold back the tears. Now they sprang freely, running down her face.

"Why are you doing this?"

"Do you know what I find interesting? You denied being Elizabeth Piccioni only once. Then I mentioned killing your son and you immediately dropped the pretense. Why do you think that is?"

"Please"—clearly sobbing now—"I don't know what this is about."

"I also find it interesting that you ended back up in a school. Only you're not a real teacher now, are you? What's the proper word for someone like you?"

Her legs had become much too weak so she pulled out the chair and sat down and propped her elbow on the desk and cradled her head with her free hand.

"Elizabeth? I asked you a question."

"Teacher's assistant," she murmured. "I'm a teacher's assistant."

"What does that pay—barely minimum wage? Do you even get health benefits?"

"Please ... let my son go."

"Okay."

She paused, holding her breath.

"I mean, you present such a solid argument. Plus, you asked nicely. Why shouldn't I let your son go?"

She stared down at the desktop, at the tests spread out before her. They were the ones she had graded only a few hours ago, Mary reviewing them before she added the scores into the computer.

"Elizabeth?" When she didn't answer, the voice said, "Elizabeth, answer me."

"What?"

"If you haven't figured it out by now, I'm not going to let your son go. I will promise you this, though—if you do exactly what I tell you to do, you will get him back alive and without a scratch."

Steeling herself, taking shallow breaths, she said, "What do you want from me?"

"We'll get to that. First, let's go over the usual bullshit. No police. No talking about this to anyone. I'm keeping tabs on you, and any slight indication you've broken my simple rules, your son dies."

She was silent, staring down at the test on top of the pile, a quiz about volcanoes and earthquakes that was scored a 63%. It belonged to Dillon Bockian, a sweet boy but not very bright, whose parents she was pretty sure paid him hardly any attention at home.

"Elizabeth?"

She'd been sniffing back the tears, wiping at them, but one managed to escape and flee down her cheek. It paused on her chin and hung there for a second before it fell, splashing on the red ink marking Dillon's test.

She whispered, "Who are you?"

"You can call me Cain."

"The world's first murderer."

"Well, that's open for debate. If anything, I think he was just a troubled, misunderstood individual. Now, Elizabeth, listen carefully, because I'm going to say this only once."

3

Leaving school wasn't as easy as she had thought it would be.

Just as Cain quit giving her instructions and disconnected, the bell rang, signaling the end of lunch. A moment later the door opened and in came Mary Boyle, her long gray hair trailing behind her, Mary's lips pressed tightly together in a strange kind of smile as she approached the desk.

Elizabeth said, "I have to leave."

Mary ignored this statement completely, striding right up to her and gently squeezing her arm. "He shouldn't have singled you out like that in there—believe me, we all agree on that—but you really shouldn't have pushed him down like you did. He was attempting to apologize, after all."

"What?"

Before Mary could respond, the sound of frantic footsteps filled the hallway outside the door, sneakers squeaking against the linoleum, and then the door opened and the students began trickling in, first Roxane Leonard, her dark hair wrapped in a tight braid, followed by Kevin and Justin Humphrey, twins identical in every way except a slight birthmark on Justin's left ear.

More of the children entered the classroom, one after another, and though Elizabeth tried not to—though she tried to keep her mind as blank as she possibly could—she saw Matthew's face in each of their faces, his eyes, his ears, his nose, even his crooked smile, and then Dillon Bockian came in and the tears threatened again, Elizabeth wanting to rush to him and take him in an embrace and tell him that he didn't have to be scared of anything, he was a bright boy and would always be bright.

But no, wait, she couldn't do that, because some psychopath had taken her child, someone who had given her instructions, a deadline, and that deadline had been for five minutes and now how many precious seconds had she wasted here with Mary Boyle?

"I threw up."

Mary turned to her, raising an eyebrow. "I beg your pardon?"

For an instant her hands clenched into fists, the nails digging into her palms, Elizabeth wondering what kind of idiot still said *I beg your pardon?* these days. Mary Boyle, that's who, and while Elizabeth had heard her say it countless times before—mostly during class when a student mumbled an answer to a question—the fact that this woman would say those four words now, to her face, while her child was some-place unsafe...

"I vomited. I've been sick all morning. Something I ate for breakfast, I think."

"You know," Mary Boyle said, turning toward her desk to start tidying up the scattered papers, "food sickness usually isn't the very last thing you ate. Most people think that it is, but ... Ms. Walter? Ms. Walter, where are you going?"

Elizabeth, her bag hanging off her shoulder, headed straight for the door. She had to pause as a few more students straggled into the classroom, each of them smiling at her and waving and saying, "Hi, Ms. Walter," but she ignored them all and then was through the door, her pace increasing with each step.

How many seconds had passed, turning into minutes, how many of those minutes had expired so far? Cain had only given her five, no more, and she had wasted them on Mary Boyle.

"Sarah?" said a voice behind her, what sounded like Eileen's, but Elizabeth kept walking, headed for the nearest exit, deciding she wasn't going to check out first with the office, why should she? Yes, normally she would, but this wasn't a normal day, far from it, and besides—thinking this as she pushed through the exit door, took in a deep breath of the crisp fall air—a half hour ago she had been Sarah Walter, a teacher's assistant, but now she was Elizabeth Piccioni, a person she thought she would never be again.

Her phone began vibrating as she reached the parking lot. She hesitated, then started running, her sneakers slapping against the macadam as she rushed for where her car was parked.

But the phone would vibrate only four times before going to voicemail—she knew this for a fact—and she couldn't let that happen, not to Cain, who had promised extreme violence against her son in the event she failed to comply with his instructions.

On its third vibration she pulled the phone from her bag and placed it to her ear, nearly shouting, "Yes, I'm here."

"Are you in your car yet?"

She suddenly stopped running, not wanting the sound of her footsteps or her ragged breathing to give away the fact that she had not yet made it to her car.

"Yes," she said, as calmly and coolly as possible.

"I don't believe you."

She closed her eyes, started forward, walking as quietly as she could. "But I am."

"Then beep the horn."

Her eyes snapped open and her head twisted back and forth on her neck. Vehicles surrounded her but none were unlocked—at least none that she knew of—and none had their windows down.

Elizabeth said, "But won't that draw attention to me?"

"What do you care if attention is drawn to you?"

"I just left school without permission. Honking my horn in the parking lot might not be the wisest decision."

"Are you seriously questioning me?"

She turned to the closest car, a blue Saturn, and tried the door. Locked.

"No," she said. "But I—"

"Beep the goddamn horn or else I'll kill your son right now."

She hurried to the next car, an aging Buick, and tried the door knowing it wouldn't open. It did. She leaned in and pressed down on the center of the steering wheel, convinced for an instant that the car's horn was broken—that it wouldn't even give off a pathetic little toot—but there it sounded, just as strong as she had hoped, breaking the fragile silence of the day.

"There," she said. "Happy?"

Cain didn't answer for the longest time, and she worried that she had somehow lost him, and that in losing him she had lost Matthew. Then he said, "The elementary school, you have fifteen minutes to get there," and clicked off.

She stood for a moment, still leaning into the Buick, noticing for the first time that Mardi Gras beads hung from the rearview mirror. She didn't want to move, didn't want to break whatever little luck she had managed to grasp. Because not only had she beeped the horn when Cain requested it, but she had inadvertently proved that he wasn't close by watching her. Keeping tabs on her all the same, yes, but he couldn't see her.

Which, she quickly realized, wasn't necessarily a good thing.

Because if Cain wasn't close, that meant Matthew wasn't close either, which meant the two of them could be anywhere.

Elizabeth sprinted for her car.

4

Cain had given her fifteen minutes to make it to the elementary school, but Elizabeth managed to make it in ten.

Only pausing through stop signs, making every traffic light except one, she was doing nearly fifty in a thirty-five zone when she came around the bend of the development that led to the school and saw the fire trucks, ambulances, police cars.

The sudden salvo of so many flashing lights caused her heart to skip. She pressed down on the brakes so hard the tires screeched as her Corolla came to a halt. A horn blared behind her and a car swerved past her, its driver shouting at her in frustration.

She glanced in the rearview mirror, conscious now that she wasn't alone in the world, especially on this street. There was a car farther back coming her way and she hit the gas again, pulling over to the curb.

Her hands shaking, her heart pounding, she turned off the car and got out and hurried toward the large group of mostly children fanned out on the soccer field. Teachers were circulating among the students, and there were a handful of police officers and firemen talking to each other and into radios.

Elizabeth came up to the closest teacher—a young man named Mr. Daniels—and said, her voice a little too rushed, "What happened?"

He stood with his arms crossed, hugging a clipboard. He glanced at her, glanced away, then glanced back when he recognized her as a school parent. He looked past her, as if what he had to say was completely confidential, before whispering, "Bomb threat."

The school itself stood maybe two hundred yards away, all that brick and mortar and glass much too close in the event a bomb really did detonate. There was nothing here to protect the children, nothing at all, but Elizabeth reasoned that there wasn't a safe place to take them, not here in the middle of this neighborhood, not to shield over five hundred children from an explosion.

"I'm looking for my son."

The young teacher uncrossed his arms, looked down at his clipboard. "What's your son's—"

She was moving before he could finish the question, having spotted Joyce Gibbons, her son's teacher. Weaving in and out of children, some sobbing, some laughing, she noticed that Joyce was talking with Mrs. Ross, the assistant principal. Mrs. Ross holding the standard school-issue radio in her hand, a big black bulky thing, saying something to Joyce as she pointed across the field toward a row of newly developed houses.

They must have heard her coming, or sensed her, or maybe Mr. Daniels had a radio of his own and warned them of her arrival, because they turned simultaneously, their bodies shifting to greet her.

She said, breathless, "Where's Matthew?"

The teacher and assistant principal glanced at each other for a moment, long enough for a look of exhaustion to pass between them, Elizabeth no doubt the first in a very long line of parents who would be arriving with demands to see their child.

Then Mrs. Gibbons, a plastic smile on her face, said, "He's here."

Relief flooded her at once, her eyes closing, her shoulders lifting as she took in a large gulp of air and released it. She wanted to drop to the ground, scream her frustrations and happiness into the grass, but she managed to stay on her feet, a smile creeping on her face, as she said, "Where is he then? I need to see him."

Mrs. Gibbons lifted her clipboard, began shuffling papers, Elizabeth noticing from where she stood it was a list of the entire elementary school. Beside each name was a perfectly formed checkmark in blue ink, the pen of which rested in the crook of Mrs. Gibbons's right ear.

As Joyce Gibbons flipped through the attendance, her posture changed. A slight scowl formed on her face. She glanced up at Mrs. Ross, glanced back at the clipboard, then said to the assistant principal, "Maybe he's with Clark?"

The relief that had so quickly flooded her now dissipated, leaving her dry and hollow, and before Mrs. Ross put the radio to her mouth and asked Clark (the school's principal) if Matthew Walter was included in his group, Elizabeth knew why Cain had given her the extra time to make it here. He'd wanted her to see the fire trucks and ambulances and police cars, have another panic attack as her imagination threw its worst at her. Then, just as he had planned, she had dived into the sea of students, searching for her son, maybe finding a teacher who would tell her that her son was fine, safe, here with the rest of the students, and that the blessed relief she'd felt for only an instant would pour into her until, when she asked for her son, demanded he be brought to her, she would receive the answer he had known she would, the one that Mrs. Ross, having listened to the radio, now looked at her with just a glance that told her the whole truth:

Her son was missing.

5

The phone in her pocket vibrated just as she made it back to the car. Tears in her eyes, her body shaking again, she whipped the phone out and didn't even bother looking at the display screen before she answered.

"Goddamn it, what have you done with my son?"

"Sarah?"

The voice wasn't robotic, was quite far from that dark demented thing calling itself Cain.

"Hello?" said the voice, the voice that belonged to Todd, and hearing his voice now Elizabeth realized this wasn't some terrible dream, a silly notion she had just put in front of her mind because trying to make sense of the truth was just too much to take.

She glanced back over her shoulder at the cluster of teachers and police officers that had quickly formed, a few of them watching her. She opened the car door, got inside, started the engine. Cain had said no police—of course he would say that—and the last thing she needed right now was to speak with a cop.

"Hi, Todd," she said as she pulled away from the curb. She wiped at her eyes. "How are you?"

"Sarah, are you okay?"

"Me? Yeah, I'm fine."

"You don't sound fine. In fact, the first thing you did was yell at me. Said something about Matthew?"

She drove past the fire trucks and ambulances and police cars, their bright lights still flashing, for some reason convinced now that one of the cops would hop in his ride and chase after her.

"What?" she said, forcing a smile, hoping he would hear it in her voice. "Are you serious?"

"Sarah."

"Shouldn't you be teaching or giving a test or sitting behind a desk reading a book?"

Todd was a substitute at the high school and middle school. That's how they had met, always running into each other in the hallways, always smiling and nodding hello, until one day Todd stopped and struck up their first of many conversations. Now they'd been seeing each other (dating wasn't quite what it was, not really) for almost six months. She had been leery of bringing him around the apartment, not wanting Matthew to get too attached to him in case it fell through.

He said, "This is a prep period. I'm standing in an empty classroom, talking on my cell phone, because they're saying..."

She came to a stop sign. Stared across the street at the line of houses. Thought about the families inside, all the families in the neighborhood who would never be in a position like the one she was now in.

Todd cleared his throat. "They're saying you hit Chad Cooper."

She wiped at her eyes again, wanting to laugh out loud at the absurdity of the statement.

"Sarah?"

Before she could respond the phone beeped. She pulled it away, saw on the display screen she had an incoming call. The number wasn't listed, unlike Todd's, but that was okay— she knew exactly who was calling.

"Todd, I have to go."

"They said you left the school, too. Are you okay? Did you" —he cleared his throat again—"hear about the bomb threat at Matthew's school?"

The phone beeped again in her ear.

"Todd, really, I have to go."

"But what's going on? Are you okay?"

"Yes, I'm fine. Look, I'm driving now and need to get off the phone. I'll call you later."

She disconnected before he could say anything else, switched over to Cain.

"Your son wasn't there, was he?"

Despite the poor timing, Todd's call had helped calm her down. She was still shaking, tears were still in her eyes, but her heart rate had slowed.

She said, as calmly as she could, "What do you want?"

"I want you to drive to a certain location. Do you think you can do that?"

"Will my son be there?"

The robotic voice seemed to sneer. "You'd probably hope not."

"Where?"

"Take a left."

She tensed at once, realizing he was nearby watching her. Or had something nearby that he could watch her with. Or …

well, she couldn't guess what, but it was clear now he knew her location.

Without speaking she made the left through the intersection.

"Good," Cain said. "Now keep going for the next five blocks. When you come to that intersection, take a right."

A minute later she had made the right and said, "Now what?"

"See the blue house on the left?"

Her voice was barely a croak: "Yes."

"That's where I want you to go next. Park along the street, then enter through the back door. It's open."

Cain clicked off but she barely noticed. Her car was still drifting forward, hardly even a crawl, and she barely noticed that either. Her entire focus was fixated on that blue one-story house with the rose bushes in the front yard, a house she had found herself checking out within the last couple weeks, just like any other parent of small children would, because, suddenly, this house had become tainted in ways nobody wanted to imagine.

Once sweet and happy grandparents had lived there—at least Elizabeth liked to think so—but now it had been corrupted by the child molester Reginald Moore.

6

Elizabeth didn't remember exactly how she had first heard about Reginald Moore. It wasn't like word of a convicted sex offender moving into town had been broadcast on the evening news, or even mentioned in the newspaper, but within days it seemed everyone in town knew about him. She'd overheard teachers—much like Chad Cooper—whispering their outrage that a man like him was allowed to live not only among everyone else, but within miles of the elementary school. Of course, there were those who said that he had paid his debt to society (how many years in prison, she didn't exactly know) and that he was now a changed man and everyone should give him a second chance.

The man hadn't been as much of a threat to Elizabeth as he had been to Chad Cooper and others who shared his same viewpoint. Sure, she wouldn't want to live next door to Reginald Moore, not with Matthew still so young, and even if Matthew were older—in middle school, or even high school —she probably would still have had reservations. Even if they shared the same block she might have felt nervous, and as she opened her car's trunk and extracted the tire iron, she wondered what distance would dispel such worries.

The day was still cool, the metallic sky still clear, and the shade of the elm trees caused a chill to race down her back as she purposefully strode up the driveway. Besides a few birds chirping in the trees, the neighborhood was quiet.

Was Matthew really in this house? Was Cain—the owner of that awful robotic voice—Reginald Moore?

She knew on some internal level the answer to both questions was no. Reginald Moore had been convicted and sentenced for molesting children—and even the details of that were sketchy—but he couldn't orchestrate something like this. And besides, what would be the point? This was all too elaborate, all too complex for a man who preferred children over adults.

The cement back porch was empty. She climbed the two steps and walked to the door. There wasn't even a mat in front of the door to wipe off dirty shoes.

The door was already open, just slightly. For some reason she had assumed when Cain said it would be open he meant unlocked, but no, here it was, already open and waiting for her to enter.

She hesitated, working this out in her head, trying to figure out who Cain could be and why he was doing this. Obviously he knew about her past—this was evident from his very first words, calling her by her old name—but what was it about her past that would cause him to go to such lengths?

Though she expected Cain to call, tell her to quit messing around and enter the house, the phone in her pocket remained still and silent.

She waited another moment and then stepped forward, pushing the door open. Here was the kitchen, pots and pans stacked on the counters, cardboard boxes dotting the floor.

Reginald Moore had moved in only two weeks ago and still hadn't completely unpacked all of his things.

The floor was linoleum—one of those old ugly square brown patterns—and she walked cautiously, not wanting her footsteps to make a sound in the silent house.

Staring up at her on the floor, only a few feet away, was a large photograph. She took another step forward, her legs starting to lose strength, as she recognized the child captured there.

Matthew.

She bent, meaning to pick the photograph up, but decided it best not to touch it. Still, her body began to shake again as she stared down at the picture of her son, taken from a distance. It was black and white and showed Matthew on the playground at school. Other children were around him, boys and girls alike, but it was clear the focus of the photograph was on him.

She placed a hand to her mouth, tasting bile in her throat for the first time. Before it was her imagination that had flung nasty thoughts and images at her, but now, right here in front of her, was evidence that this was real.

But it wasn't the only one. There was another photograph a few feet away leading into the dining room. This photograph didn't feature her son, but rather another child her son's age, taken at the same playground, possibly even at the same time. A pretty girl with dark hair in pigtails, a girl that Elizabeth thought she recognized, and it disturbed her to realize she didn't feel the same disgust looking at this photograph as she had at the one of Matthew.

A few feet beyond this photograph was another, then a few feet past that one another. Like following a trail of breadcrumbs—because that's what they were, she knew, that's what they had to be—she moved as carefully as she could through the house, the tire iron gripped tightly beside her. Through the dining room, into the living room, then down a hallway where the photographs stopped in front of a door.

Lifting the tire iron above her head, she reached out with her other hand, gripped the knob, and quickly pulled open the door.

Stairs stretched out in front of her, leading down into the basement. Lights were already on down there. On every other step leading down were more photographs, each showing a child from the elementary school, captured while they were busy with their innocent play.

Elizabeth started down the stairs.

7

The basement, like the rest of the house, hadn't been completely moved into yet. It was a finished basement, with carpet and fake wood paneling, and off in the corner around a partition were the washer and dryer. Cardboard boxes were stacked against the wall. On top of one of those boxes was an alarm clock, showing five o'clock instead of the correct time.

None of that interested Elizabeth, though. What interested her instead was the man tied to a chair in the middle of the basement, surrounded by hundreds of those black and white photographs. A man whose ankles were bound to the chair legs, whose hands were tied behind his back. A man who wore a strange sort of collar around his neck and who had his mouth taped shut by a large piece of duct tape.

He was conscious, his eyes going wide when he saw her, making a kind of mewling noise as he tried shouting through the tape.

She didn't move. She just stared, surprised by the fact that this man—this Reginald Moore, this child molester, this monster—appeared quite handsome.

He looked to be in his mid-thirties, maybe a few years

older than her, but he had a clean complexion, deep blue eyes, a healthy head of hair. He was dressed only in a pair of boxer shorts, and his legs were trim, his chest nicely toned, only a little gut around his middle. Had she seen him anywhere else —at the grocery store, at the gas station, even at the school— she would have acknowledged him with a quick smile, nothing more than that, maybe waited to see what would happen if he approached her.

She didn't know what she had expected, exactly—some overweight pale man with thick glasses, a complete stereotype—but Reginald Moore looked almost normal.

His eyes still wide, still shouting through the tape, Reginald Moore started twisting his shoulders back and forth. She guessed his attempt was to tip the chair over, though she doubted it would work. The chair looked too solid, as if its legs had been bolted to the floor.

Elizabeth expected the phone in her pocket to start vibrating at any moment. She wanted to move forward, rip the tape off Moore's mouth, ask him who had done this to him. If he could describe the person in any passing detail, maybe she could figure out who was doing this to her. Somebody from her past, obviously, from the life she had run away from. Somebody who had managed to track her down, abduct Matthew, and bring her to this house.

But why?

It took her seven strides before she reached him, conscious the entire time that she was trampling on photographs of children. As she approached he stopped twisting, watching her come up to him, then watching as she took one end of the duct tape and ripped it off.

He let out a pathetic cry, his voice hoarse from shouting, and said, "Please, please, untie me."

She stepped back. That close she had been able to smell

his sweat and fear and shampoo, all mixed together, and it had caused her stomach to churn. The tape stuck to her fingers and she had to flap her hand a few times before it came off and fell to the floor.

"Where's my son?"

"Please, I'm begging you, untie me."

"*Where's my son?*"

The intensity at which she spoke, the shrillness of her voice, shocked even herself. Reginald Moore paused, his mouth open, his eyes widening at first in fear, then confusion.

"Listen," he croaked, "I don't know what you're talking about. There's nobody here."

It occurred to her that he didn't speak like a child molester, which was a strange thought because a child molester was just like a serial rapist or murderer—on the outside most of them appeared like normal human beings.

She looked down at the photographs spread out around him, tasting that bile once again in the back of her throat.

Noticing her noticing the photographs, Reginald Moore said, "Those aren't mine."

"Then whose are they?"

"The guy that did this to me."

Her breath caught. "Who did this to you?"

"I don't know. It was just some guy. I'd never seen him before."

"Can you describe him?"

Before Reginald Moore could answer, the phone in her pocket began to vibrate.

She looked down at her jeans, looked back up at him, then pulled the phone from her pocket and answered it.

Cain said, "So what do you think?"

"Why did you bring me here?"

"He looks pathetic, doesn't he? Certainly not like a man who molests children."

Reginald Moore's face had paled. He mouthed, *Who is that?*

Elizabeth said, "Give me back my son."

"Not yet. First I want you to see something."

"What?"

"Ask him why he did it. I know you took the tape off his mouth. I watched you do it. Ask him why he liked to touch children in their private parts."

The basement had begun to spin. She closed her eyes.

"No," she whispered.

"Yes, Elizabeth. If you ever want to see little Matthew again—or should we call him Thomas?—you will ask Mr. Moore that question."

She opened her eyes again. The basement hadn't stopped spinning but it was slowing down.

She said to Reginald Moore, her voice dry and monotone, "Why did you like to touch children in their private parts?"

The man reacted as if her words had slapped him across the face. He actually flinched, looked embarrassed, glanced away from her as he murmured, "I don't know."

Cain said, "Make him repeat it."

"Say that again," Elizabeth said, her gaze darting surreptitiously around the basement in search of the hidden camera.

"I don't know," Reginald Moore nearly sobbed, fighting back tears. "I don't know what's wrong with me."

"He's lying," the dark robotic voice of Cain said.

Elizabeth said, without knowing why, "You're lying."

"I am not!" Clearly sobbing now, tears running down his face. "Please, I'm ... I'm ... I'm troubled. I know that. I've been taking medicine, seeing doctors. I'm trying to be normal!"

Cain said, "Tell him he now has five minutes."

"What?" Elizabeth asked, frowning now, but immediately she knew what he meant. She turned toward the stack of boxes against the wall, to the alarm clock resting on top. It still read five o'clock.

Until it suddenly began to count down.

8

"What is it?" Reginald Moore asked. "What's wrong?"

Elizabeth stood motionless, transfixed by the bright red numbers that had quickly begun to count down on the alarm clock.

4:57 ... 4:56 ... 4:55 ...

In her ear, Cain said, "In less than five minutes Reginald Moore will die. There's no changing that. The collar he's wearing is filled with C-4. Do you know what C-4 is, Elizabeth?"

She had been gripping the tire iron tightly, but now her fingers relaxed and the makeshift weapon fell to the floor. Her gaze shifted back to Reginald Moore. She just stood there, completely frozen, watching him as he bucked in the chair, jerking his head back and forth as if that might release the collar around his neck.

"Elizabeth, do you know what C-4 is?"

"It's a bomb."

Her voice hardly sounded like her own, too hollow and small.

Cain seemed to chuckle. "A simple way of saying it, but

yes, it's a bomb. Wrapped around inside that collar is enough plastic explosive to kill both of you right now."

She glanced back at the clock: **4:26 ... 4:25 ... 4:24 ...**

"I know what you're thinking, Elizabeth. You're wondering if it's possible to take the collar off him without bringing harm to either of you. It's a noble thought, but the answer is no."

A tear fell from her eye, sloped down her nose, over her cheek, held in place on the end of her chin for an instant before falling to the floor.

She whispered, "Why are you doing this?"

4:01 ... 4:00 ... 3:59 ...

"To give you an example."

"An example?"

"Yes. Of what's to come."

Despite his efforts, Reginald Moore could not move the chair even an inch. Apparently it had in fact been bolted down, Cain keeping in mind the animalistic way humans will react when faced with death. Only Moore wasn't faced with death so much as embraced around the neck by it.

"Please," he whimpered, his face covered in tears. A wet spot suddenly appeared on the front of his boxer shorts. "Please, help me. Just don't stand there. Help me!"

Cain said, "He is a disgusting creature, isn't he? Any man or woman that molests children should be killed outright."

Elizabeth had that strange sense of being outside her own body. Floating on the edge of existence, watching it all from a safe and secure distance. Close enough to smell Moore's urine and sweat and fear, but at the same time so far away that none of it fazed her.

"What about you?" she whispered. "If he's a disgusting creature, what does that make you?"

"And what am I?"

"I don't know. You tell me."

3:34 ... 3:33 ... 3:32 ...

"What about your husband, Elizabeth? What about Edward Piccioni? Is *he* a disgusting creature?"

She still saw herself from a distance, just standing there only feet away from Reginald Moore who continued to sob and scream and buck in the chair. Trying to do whatever he could to free himself, knowing in his heart and soul and mind that nothing he did would work.

"Do you know why I call myself Cain? It's because we're not descendants of Adam and Eve. Each and every one of us are children of Cain, all of us with the dark desire in our hearts to watch things die. You know you feel the same thing, too. That's why you haven't left the basement yet. Though, I must warn you, if you don't leave in three minutes, you too will die. And if you die, your son dies."

Unconsciously she started backward, one slow step after another. "That's not my name."

"What?"

"My name isn't Elizabeth. It's Sarah."

"Please, I thought we were done playing those silly games. You must realize by now I know everything there is to know about you. Why deny it?"

3:01 ... 3:00 ... 2:59 ...

"Ask him one more time. Ask him why he molested children. Maybe now that he knows he's going to die he'll be truthful."

But she couldn't ask the man anything, not now that he was so close to death, bawling like a baby, begging to her to please please please help him, that he was sorry for what he'd done, that he was a bad person but *please* he didn't deserve this.

One backward step after another, she said, keeping her voice calm, "What have you done with my son?"

"He's safe. And he'll remain that way as long as you continue to do what I tell you."

2:41 ... 2:40 ... 2:39 ...

"Now ask him. Ask him why he did what he did."

Before she knew it she disconnected the call, sprinted forward, placed a hand on Reginald Moore's shaking shoulder. "Reginald," she said, then shouted, "Reginald!" and smacked him with her open palm across the face.

He went still, stunned, and slowly looked up at her. He whispered, "I don't want to die."

"I know," she said, and despite all the terrible things she knew about this man and what he had done she felt true sympathy for him, wishing she could do anything to free him from this awful mess. "But I'm sorry, there's nothing I can do."

"Please"—his voice cracking as he started sobbing again —"please, I said I was sorry. I did my time in jail. I've ... I've ... I've *changed!*"

2:07 ... 2:06 ... 2:05 ...

The phone in her hand started vibrating.

She said, "Describe the man who did this to you. His height, his hair color, anything you can remember."

Shaking even harder now, his face scrunched up, Reginald Moore sobbed, "I'm so sorry, I'm so, so, so sorry."

The phone vibrated a second time.

"Reginald, please, tell me anything you can."

"My parents hate me. They ... they ... they think I did what I did to spite them. But I didn't. I ... I ... I ..."

The phone vibrated a third time.

She slapped his face again, much harder this time, shouting, "Reginald, goddamn it, tell me!"

But it was clear he wouldn't, that he couldn't, and before the phone vibrated a fourth time she pressed the TALK button.

Cain said, "Never fucking hang up on me again."

She looked at the alarm clock.

1:36 ... 1:35 ... 1:34 ...

"Elizabeth, I'm not sure if it's obvious to you yet or not, but I can detonate that collar whenever I wish."

"Please, please, please," sobbed Moore.

"All I have to do is press a button here on this remote switch and ... well, I'm sure you get the picture."

Moore, rocking back and forth, staring up at her with tears in his eyes, begging, "Please, just help me, you've gotta help me..."

Cain whispering in her ear with that dark robotic voice, "Elizabeth, you do get the picture, don't you? Because I'm about to press the button right now."

Elizabeth, holding the phone to her ear, slowly backing away from Reginald Moore, back toward the stairs.

"Ten seconds, Elizabeth."

1:08 ... 1:07 ... 1:06 ...

"Seven seconds."

"Please," Moore sobbed, "*please!*"

No, she wanted to say, no it's not fair, none of it's fair, but then she heard Cain's voice once again in her ear—"Five seconds"—and she turned her back on Reginald Moore and fled for the stairs.

9

She reached the top of the stairs, slammed through the door, and ran only four paces before the collar exploded.

The house shook, a mini-earthquake, enough to knock her to the floor. She hit her chin against the carpet, bit her tongue, instantly tasted blood. She scrambled to her feet, her stomach churning even more, that bile in the back of her throat fighting to make an exit.

Down the hallway, through the living room, the dining room, the kitchen, and then out the back door and she jumped over the two steps, went sprawling into the backyard just as the bile forced its way out. At first the stream of vomit was healthy but then it dissipated and all Elizabeth could do was dry-heave.

How long she lay there in the grass and fallen leaves, tears in her eyes, vomit ringed around her mouth, she didn't know. Ever since she had been young, the sight—even the thought —of blood had nauseated her. Her mother had worked as a dental assistant, and sometimes she would come home and there would be spots of blood on her uniform and little Elizabeth would become lightheaded. A few times she had even fainted. Once when she was twelve she had scraped her knees badly on the playground and had gotten blood on her hands and had screamed and screamed until she passed out.

She hadn't seen any blood, but she could imagine it. Even now, lying here in the grass, she could still see Reginald Moore twisting and turning and bucking to get out of the chair, the bright red digits on the alarm clock counting down, nothing either he or she could do to stop them.

It's not fair, she had thought there in the last few seconds of Reginald Moore's life, and it was true. According to the clock, he should have been given another minute before the C-4 detonated. But no, Cain had decided to prove just how powerful he was, accelerating the man's death even if it was just by sixty seconds.

Still, she wondered what might have happened in those sixty seconds. Would Reginald Moore have come to some kind of understanding for the life he'd led? Would he have made his peace with God if he hadn't already?

She didn't realize she was still holding her cell phone until it started vibrating again.

Elizabeth picked her head up off the grass, squinting at the phone in her hand. She hated the thing. She'd gotten it because it made no sense paying for a landline and now here it was, a device linking her to this madman.

Climbing to her feet, she answered the phone, listening for Cain's voice but hearing a distortion instead.

"What?" she asked.

Then it hit her. The explosion—it had been loud enough to cause her ears to ring, only she hadn't realized it at the time, not with the taste of blood in her mouth and the bile rising and her need to get outside.

She put her finger to her ear, pressed down on it, then tried the phone again.

Cain was saying, "... don't you think?"

"I couldn't hear you. My ears were ringing. What did you say?"

"I said that must have made quite an impression on the neighborhood."

At once she became conscious of the fact that she was still in a neighborhood, a quiet place where the only normal noises were the birds singing in the trees and the occasional car driving down the street. Anyone within one hundred yards or more could have heard the explosion and probably did, and she wondered how many of them were right now calling 911. Maybe someone across the street, or right next door, a concerned neighbor who despite the fact the house belonged to a child molester was still worried that something awful had just happened.

And something awful had just happened indeed. A man had died brutally. It didn't matter that he was a child molester. Nobody deserved to die like that. Except, she thought, maybe Cain.

"Why did you do that?" she asked.

"I told you. To give you an example of what's to come."

"Where's my son?"

"Home, Elizabeth. He's waiting for you."

She was running before she knew it, back down the driveway, under the shade of elms, toward the side of the street where she'd parked her car. She was inside and had the engine started a moment later, the tires squealing as she sped away.

It hit her much too late that she should have taken her time, that her squealing tires would draw attention to her, but then she figured what did it matter—at the moment she had no control over the events at hand, was merely a game piece being moved around at will, and the only thing that mattered right now was her son.

Her foot never once touched the brake, the needle of the speedometer rising steadily with every second. She had no choice but to stop at the intersection on the main drag.

The light turned green and she made the left, punching the gas. Here it became two lanes and she whipped past the other cars. Their apartment was less than ten minutes away; she thought she might be able to make it in seven minutes. Not that it made much difference in the larger scheme of things, but after just witnessing a man having been denied his extra minute of life, sixty seconds had become a tangible concept.

The speed limit here was forty-five miles per hour, strip malls and car washes and chain restaurants on both sides, and the speedometer's needle was at fifty-five, working its way toward sixty, when she saw the cop car.

Parked in the same spot as it always was when running speed trap, just waiting for that careless driver who was in a hurry for no good reason, it didn't move for a couple of seconds—Elizabeth's gaze transfixed on the rearview mirror —but then, predictably, its roof-lights started flashing as it rolled out into the street.

Her fingers tightened against the wheel, her foot lifting off the gas. The phone was silent and still, Elizabeth for the first time wishing Cain would call because he would know what to do. Or would he? It didn't matter. What mattered was that a cop was coming up behind her, the car growing larger and larger in her rearview mirror, and one of the things Cain had told her was she couldn't talk to the police.

For an instant the idea to try to outrun the cop popped

into her head, but she immediately dismissed it. That would only make things worse, at least as worse as things could get, and besides, the cop was right on her tail now so there was no thinking he was after anyone else. She had no choice, so she pulled the car over and waited.

10

"License and registration."

She already had it ready for him and handed it out through the driver's-side window as calmly as she could.

The officer took them and glanced at both, then glanced back at her. She could see her face reflected in his sunglasses and tried guessing whether or not she looked guilty.

"Do you know why I pulled you over?"

Always deny, the man who'd once been her husband had told her, because if you admitted fault then you were automatically guilty. She didn't know why she thought this now or why she went along with it, but she did.

"No."

Studying her license as if it were a rare baseball card, he said, "I clocked you doing fifty-eight in a forty-five zone."

"Really?" Her voice surprisingly steady. "I wasn't aware I was going that fast."

"We normally give about a five mile per hour cushion, but—"

"There was a bomb threat."

"Excuse me?"

"At my son's school. I just got a message about it and was on my way there. I, well, as you can imagine I'm sort of freaking out and didn't realize how fast I was going. I mean, I know it's no excuse, but ..."

She let it hang there, surprised that the lie came out so smoothly, wondering at what moment Cain would call and ask her just what the hell she thought she was doing. Except for what happened in the middle school parking lot, he always seemed to know where she was, what she was doing. Was he following her in a car? If so, where had he gone now that she had been pulled over?

"Yes, I heard about the threat." The cop had been studying her license and registration again but now glanced up at her. "But the elementary school is in the opposite direction."

She just stared back at him, at her reflection in his sunglasses that had suddenly begun to look more than guilty. She thought about Matthew, how according to Cain he was waiting for her at home, and she wanted to tell the officer this, tell him how her son had been abducted and how Reginald Moore had been blown to pieces and how she had thrown up in his backyard.

Remembering this last bit, she quickly reached up and touched her mouth, hoping that no vomit residue was there.

"Ma'am?"

She shook her head. "I'm sorry."

He stared at her for a long moment, saying nothing, and then finally nodded and said he'd be right back.

It took him five minutes before he returned with her ticket, another minute for him to explain the details of the ticket, and then, with a sort of flourish, he ripped it off his board and handed it to her.

She took it from him, feeling like a volcano about to erupt. She should already be home, should already be with Matthew, but instead she was here with this cop staring down at her with eyes she couldn't even see.

"How about we slow it down a little," he said. "If you plan accordingly, there's never any reason to be rushed."

11

Not even ten seconds after she had pulled back onto the road, the cell phone vibrated.

Cain said, "What the hell was that?"

"I was pulled over for speeding."

"You told him about me, didn't you."

"No."

"I don't believe you, Elizabeth. You're a liar. You've been living a lie for the past five years."

She glanced at the rearview mirror. The cop was still parked alongside the road, finishing up his paperwork.

"I just want my son."

"And you'll get your son. If you'd just listen to me, you'd know that by now. My intention here is not to harm you or your son unless I'm given no other choice."

"You killed that man back there."

"He killed himself."

"You were the one that put that collar around his neck."

"From the moment he touched a child—no, from the moment he *thought* about touching a child—his fate had already been sealed. Besides, I did him a favor. I did the entire town a favor."

She came to another major intersection, the traffic gods taking pity on her and favoring her with a green light. She made the turn, her apartment complex less than five minutes away.

"What is it that you want?"

He ignored her. "Would you believe it if I said I admired your husband? Or should I call him your ex-husband? You never got an official divorce, did you? How could you have after you disappeared like you did?"

Her fingers tightening once again around the steering wheel, she repeated, "What is it that you want?"

"I want you to hurry home. I want you to see your son. Only then will you truly understand the gravity of this situation."

The gravity of this situation—she didn't like those words, didn't like them one bit, but before she could ask him what he meant Cain clicked off.

She tossed the phone on the passenger seat and kept driving. Her complex was now less than a mile away. It was a low-rent place, one of the cheapest in town, and while she could have afforded something nicer she had thought it best to keep a low profile.

The large wooden sign at the entrance said **SUMMER RIDGE**. It was a peculiar name for an apartment complex, seeing as people lived there year-round and was located nowhere near a ridge, but again, the rent was cheap, only six hundred a month for two bedrooms.

After she parked and grabbed her cell phone, she hurried for the stairs leading toward her apartment. She took the steps two at a time, gripping the railing for balance, because now that she was this close her body had begun to shake again.

She came to her apartment door, the key already prepped to be inserted in the lock like this was just another day coming home from work or the grocery store. She paused, thought a moment, then gripped her keys in her fist so three of them poked out between her fingers. She stepped to the door, reached out with her other hand, gripped the knob.

It should be locked—she had locked it herself this morning—but it turned easily in her hand.

She pushed the door opened. It creaked. She didn't move.

"Matthew?" she called.

There was no answer.

She started forward, slowly, holding the fist full of keys by her side. If Cain was here—if anyone other than her son was here—she would aim for their face, try to poke out one if not both of their eyes. There would be blood, yes, but she would manage. She would have to.

Despite her better judgment, she called out again.

"Matthew?"

Still no answer.

One slow step after another, taking her down the hallway past the table where she always placed her keys and the mail. A picture sat on the table, a photograph of her and Matthew taken last year at the Six Flags in St. Louis, the place her son had first been introduced to the marvel of roller coasters. He'd been too young and small to ride on them, but he loved watching them and they planned on returning this summer for his first ride.

The first room she came to was the kitchen. It was empty. She continued on to the living room. Her body had stopped shaking. Her breathing had slowed. She was suddenly calm and didn't know why. She took several more steps and came into the living room and then all at once stopped.

The TV was on. Matthew was on the screen. He was tied down to a bed. Tape was over his mouth. A blindfold was over his eyes. And around his neck, just like Reginald Moore, was an explosive collar.

12

The sound that emerged from Elizabeth's mouth was neither a scream nor a yell nor even a shout. It was a primitive noise, going all the way back to the beginning of time, the type of sound a caveman would have been familiar with. It started deep down in her soul and worked its way through her heart, into her lungs, and then out of her mouth in an animalistic cry she had had no idea she could even produce.

She rushed toward the TV, fell to her knees, placed her hands on the screen as if by doing so she would somehow reach through the glass, grab hold of her son, and pull him to safety.

She thought about the day he was born, how he had entered the world with the umbilical cord wrapped around his neck, and despite her exhaustion she had immediately sensed the panic in the room, knew before anyone else that something terrible had just happened to her baby. She had tried getting up, moving from the bed, wanting to do *something* to help her son, but the nurses held her down while the doctor unwrapped the cord, severed it, and took her baby away into another room, the entire time Elizabeth screaming to him to bring her child back to her. Ten minutes passed before word came that her son was okay, that he had started breathing again, and for Elizabeth those ten minutes were the worst she had ever had to endure. Not even the day the FBI had come to take Eddie away, when she had learned the horrible truth about her husband, could compare. Those ten minutes when she was convinced the life she had just given birth to was now dead was the absolute worst.

That was until today.

A phone was ringing. Elizabeth was faintly aware of this but wasn't sure what it meant. Her cell phone was still in her pocket, set on vibrate. It would be the only phone in the apartment, as they didn't have a landline.

So what did it mean?

Elizabeth blinked, realized the ringing was coming from the top of the TV, and quickly stood up.

It was a BlackBerry. On the screen were the words UNKNOWN CALLER.

She wiped at her eyes, hesitated, then answered it.

Cain said, "So how are you enjoying the program so far?"

"You sick son of a bitch. Give me back my son!"

"Not quite yet. First I want you to help me."

"Help you do what?"

"If you don't help me, your son will die just like Reginald Moore."

"Help you do what?" she repeated, nearly shouting now.

"Before I tell you, Elizabeth, I want you to understand this is nothing personal. I have nothing against you or your son. But, unfortunately, to get what I want, I need you."

"Let me talk to him."

"What?"

"Let me talk to my son. Right now. I won't help you do a goddamn thing until I hear his voice."

There was a silence on Cain's end, and then he said, "Hold on."

Elizabeth stepped back so she could see the television screen. Her son just lay there motionless, like he was dead, and she wanted to look away, turn it off, but she feared that by doing so she would never see him again.

For the longest time nothing happened, and then a black-gloved hand appeared in the left-hand corner of the screen. The black-gloved hand became a black-shirted arm as it reached toward Matthew's mouth and pulled the tape off. Then, before she knew it, Cain's other black-gloved hand was holding a phone to Matthew's ear.

"Hello?" her son said in a tiny and terrified voice.

Elizabeth wiped at her eyes again, holding back more tears. "Honey, it's me. It's Mommy."

"Mommy?"

"I'm here, baby."

"Mommy, I'm scared."

"I know. I know you are. But it's okay. I'm going to make sure everything's okay."

On the screen Matthew's body was jerking as he sobbed. He went to say something else, but Cain pulled the phone away and placed the tape back over his mouth.

"Happy now?" that dark robotic voice asked.

"You better not lay one fucking finger on him. I swear to God, I will kill you."

"A little overdramatic, wouldn't you say?"

"What do you want from me?"

"That's quite simple."

But before Cain could continue there was a sudden knocking, hard and frantic, coming from the apartment door.

13

Through the peephole she could see Todd standing on the other side of the door, still dressed in khakis and collared shirt from substituting, his tie hanging loose around his neck. He leaned forward with his left hand placed flat against the doorframe, using his other hand to bang urgently on the door.

"Sarah?" he called. "I know you're in there. Please, let me in."

In her ear, Cain said, "Who is it?"

"Nobody," she whispered.

"It doesn't sound like nobody."

Todd banged on the door again. "Sarah, please, open up. I'm not leaving until you do."

"A friend," Elizabeth whispered.

"Will he eventually go away?"

"I don't think so."

"I see," Cain said. "Then this will make it harder for you."

"What will?"

"Killing him."

Through the peephole she watched Todd step back from

the door, loosen his tie even more. He looked both ways down the hallway, stepped close, began banging on the door again, calling her name.

Elizabeth whispered, "You're joking."

In her ear Cain chuckled a dark robotic chuckle. "I am. Just make him go away. Do not let him in the apartment and do not hang up on me. I want to hear everything you say."

Elizabeth closed her eyes, thought for a long moment, though Todd's constant banging on the door and calling her name wasn't helping her concentrate. Finally she opened her eyes, engaged the door chain, and opened the door.

"Hi, Todd."

He looked surprised, his fist suddenly frozen in midair. Immediately he said, "What's wrong?"

"Nothing's wrong."

"When I called you earlier, you hung up on me. Then when I called you back, you didn't pick up."

She tried remembering the excuse she had given him. "My battery was really low. It went dead right after I'd talked to you."

His fist was still frozen in the air. He lowered it to his side, frowning at the chain. "Can't I come in?"

"Now's not a good time."

"Why?"

"Matthew's sleeping. He was really worked up about what happened at school."

"I'll be quiet."

"You mean quieter than you just were?"

"Sorry about that. I was worried."

Elizabeth stood with her face looking out through the narrow gap, the BlackBerry in her left hand behind the door.

"I appreciate that," she said, forcing a smile. "But Matthew's fine."

"I'm sure he is. I was talking about you."

The forced smile faltered. "What do you mean?"

"About what happened between you and Chad Cooper."

"What are you talking about?"

"The word is you knocked him down to the ground. Which I don't blame you for doing one bit. The guy can be a jerk and no doubt deserved it."

She wondered briefly how many other variations of the story were circulating around the middle and high schools, teachers and other school staff always being ones to love good gossip, but the BlackBerry was suddenly heavier in her hand and she knew she had to make Todd leave.

"Thank you for your concern," she said, "but everything's fine. I'm going to go lay back down with Matthew now."

Todd just stood there on the other side of the door, looking confused. He was almost ten years older than her, a divorcee with two children, his wife already remarried to a contractor in Arizona. She wasn't in love with him but was falling for him, despite her better judgment, and every time he visited she invited him in, even if Matthew was asleep.

"I'll call you later," she said.

Todd didn't say anything but nodded dumbly, looking lost.

Elizabeth said goodbye and closed the door softly. She looked back out through the peephole and waited for Todd to leave. He didn't at first, just standing there, running the conversation through his mind, probably wondering what he had said or done wrong. Finally he turned and walked away, and Elizabeth waited ten full seconds before placing the BlackBerry to her ear.

"He's gone."

"He sounds like he cares about you," Cain said. "Is it just a schoolboy crush or are you lovers?"

She returned to the living room but immediately stopped when she saw the television. "What is that?"

"What is what?"

"Above Matthew's head."

"You see that now, do you? That's because originally it wasn't turned on."

"What is it?"

"You're a bright woman, Elizabeth. You tell me."

On the screen everything looked the same as it had before: Matthew tied to a bed, tape over his mouth, a blindfold over his eyes. What had changed were the bright red numbers hovering above his head:

100:00:00

"Don't do this," she whispered.

"You have one hundred hours to get me what I want. Every hour a picture will be sent to the BlackBerry. It will show your son and the time. If you don't get me what I want before those one hundred hours elapse, I will detonate the bomb. The last picture I'll send will be your son's remains."

Staring at the screen, at those bright red numbers, she whispered, "What do you want?"

"Your husband's trophies," Cain said.

And the numbers began to count down.

14

The first thing she did after Cain disconnected was rush into the bathroom. She made it to the toilet just in time before the dry heaves. Nothing came up—not after she had vomited back at Reginald Moore's house—but she still stayed there for several minutes, trying to get that image of her son out of her mind. Thinking it never should have come to this. How did it come to this?

At some point she stood back up and went to the sink. She washed her hands, her face, even rinsed her mouth out with Listerine. She dried her mouth and face with a towel, started to turn away but paused as she caught a glimpse of herself in the mirror.

This morning—less than eight hours ago—she had stared into this same mirror as she applied her makeup and did her hair and the thought that had gone through her mind was that she hadn't lost it, at least not yet. Almost thirty-five years old, the starting of crow's-feet around her eyes, she had managed to keep her looks while the rest of her body—her stomach, her thighs, her ass—had begun to grow more than she would have liked. Not that it wasn't her fault, no longer working out, not even following along to one of those yoga DVDs she had ordered from Amazon, all her attention focused on Matthew and work, work and Matthew, and now Todd, that she just didn't have the extra time.

Thinking of Todd now, how she had pushed him away, forced him to leave when she needed him most, she touched her stomach, could feel the scars through the fabric, the strange patchwork that—

No, stop it. She didn't have time to think about that. The clock was literally ticking, right above her son's head. She had to hurry.

Back out in the living room, she stared one last time at her son on the screen—doing her best to ignore those red glowing digits—before turning the television off.

She went into the kitchen and opened the junk drawer. She sorted through the clutter and pulled out a Phillips head screwdriver. She wished she had a gun, some kind of weapon, but the closest thing would be one of the steak knives in the other drawer, and even those were pretty dull. She realized she had nothing to take with her other than the BlackBerry right now in her pocket (she'd ditched her own cell), so she grabbed her keys off the floor and hurried toward the door.

A glance through the peephole told her nobody was in the hallway. She disengaged the chain, opened the door, checked both ends of the hall. Nothing.

She stepped out, locked the door behind her automatically, and then hurried toward the stairs leading to the parking lot.

As she approached her car, she kept an eye out for anything suspicious. She doubted Cain would be here in the parking lot, watching her, but she didn't want to put it past him. She even glanced around for Todd's Prius but didn't see the hybrid in its regular visitor space.

She didn't have time to worry about people watching for what she had to do next. As Cain had explained before hanging up, it was surprisingly easy to clone cell phone numbers nowadays, and when the police tracked down the originating number of the bomb threat, it would appear as if it came from her phone. Also, now that Elizabeth had brought it to the elementary school's attention that her son was missing, the police would definitely want to speak with her, so she had to make sure they wouldn't be able to find her car.

It took her only a minute to take off her license plate. Cupping the two screws in one hand, holding onto the screwdriver and license plate with the other hand, she surveyed the parking lot, deciding which vehicle to choose. She settled on a pickup truck that had been backed in to its parking space. There was cover there by the bushes, enough that she had no worry of being seen as she took off the pickup's license plate and replaced it with her own.

Then it was back behind her car again, the new license plate in hand, and she had just begun to tighten the first screw when a voice spoke behind her.

"What are you doing?"

15

Elizabeth froze. At once she had the childish thought that if she didn't move, didn't make a sound, nobody would see her.

"Sarah?"

She blinked, recognizing the voice, and, knowing she had no choice, stood up and turned around.

Todd was standing only a few feet away, a confused expression on his face. He held a bouquet of tulips at his side. Behind him was his Prius, parked in its usual space.

Elizabeth said, "Are those for me?"

"What are you doing?"

"You know tulips are my favorite."

"What are you doing?"

"Especially the yellow ones."

"Sarah."

She was quiet for a moment, then said, "It's not what it looks like."

"It looks like you're switching license plates."

"Okay, then it is what it looks like."

Todd shook his head as if to clear it. "What's going on?"

Now what was she going to do? Before she'd had a door to hide behind. Here she had nothing.

"Sarah?"

"It's complicated," she said, but before she could say anything else, the BlackBerry began to ring.

Todd's gaze shifted down to her pocket. He waited for her to pull out the phone, and when she didn't, he said, "Aren't you going to answer that?"

Elizabeth didn't move.

He frowned at her. "What's wrong? What are you hiding?"

Elizabeth wanted to keep standing still but she knew she had no choice. She withdrew the BlackBerry and placed it to her ear.

Cain said, "Have you reached the highway yet?"

"No."

"Why not?"

"I got a slow start."

"A slow start? Elizabeth, that is not the answer I was hoping to hear."

Todd said, "Who are you talking to?"

Elizabeth closed her eyes just as Cain said, "Who was that?"

"Nobody."

"*Nobody?*" Todd said, taken aback.

"Who's with you?" Cain asked.

She hesitated but realized the last thing she should do was lie to this madman. "It's my friend from earlier."

"I thought you sent him away."

"I did. He came back."

"Why?"

She glanced at the bouquet of tulips at Todd's side, the petals drooping toward the ground. "To bring me flowers."

"Well, isn't that sweet. A nice gesture that has now sealed his fate."

Todd took a step forward. "Sarah, who are you talking to?"

"What are you talking about?" Elizabeth asked Cain.

"I've spent a lot of time putting together this plan. It must go on as scheduled, and nothing—absolutely *nothing*—is going to ruin it. Do you understand me?"

Elizabeth said nothing, staring back at Todd.

"You have no choice," Cain said, "not if you want to save your son. Your boyfriend there? Kill him."

16

Besides her husband—or the version of her husband she had fallen in love with—Todd was the gentlest person she knew. From the very beginning she had sensed this. He always had a smile on his face, always able to look on the positive side, no matter how dark it appeared. He read books—mostly nonfiction—and was even in the middle of reading *James and the Giant Peach* to Matthew. While she had not yet allowed him to spend the night, Todd would come over in the evenings, about an hour before Matthew's bedtime, and he would play board games with Matthew and help him with his homework while Elizabeth cleaned the dishes or did the laundry or tidied up the apartment. Then, at bedtime, they would sit on either side of Matthew in his bed, and all three of them would take turns reading, a round robin exercise that Matthew really seemed to love. Matthew was even seeming to love Todd, the man who Elizabeth had finally admitted was her boyfriend despite the fact they hadn't slept together yet, the man who almost never said anything negative about anyone, who was as non-confrontational as could be. The man who right this instant was standing in front of her with a bouquet of tulips at his side, his eyes filled with fear.

"No," Elizabeth whispered into the phone.

There was a pause, and then Cain said, "No?"

"I need him. He can help."

"How?"

"It's a long drive to Pennsylvania, and you haven't given me much time."

"I think I've been very generous with the amount of time I've allotted you."

"Besides," Elizabeth said, keeping her gaze focused on Todd, "killing him would bring too many complications. There's the chance I could get caught. How would you expect me to get you what you want then?"

There was another pause, this one much longer.

"I don't like this."

"Neither do I, but right now neither of us has a choice. I need him. He's coming with me."

Cain was silent for another long moment. Finally he said, "If you fuck this up, your son dies," and disconnected.

Elizabeth realized she was still holding the screwdriver. She set it on the trunk of her car as she slipped the BlackBerry back into her pocket.

"I need your keys," she said, starting toward Todd.

He immediately began walking backward, shaking his head. "Stay away."

The parking lot was blessedly deserted, at least from what she could tell. She took another step toward Todd, and he took another step back.

"I need your keys," she repeated.

"What's going on? Who was that on the phone? What did you mean, 'killing him would bring too many complications'?"

"Do you care for Matthew?"

This made him pause. "Well, yes, of course I do. But what does—"

"If you don't help me, Matthew will die."

"What are you talking about? I thought you said Matthew was taking a nap."

"Your keys, Todd. Give them to me."

She had backed him up against the Prius, just another testament to his gentle nature. He said he'd bought it the week after he watched the Al Gore documentary on global warming, just doing his part to help keep the world spinning a little bit longer.

Todd glanced past her at the apartment building. "So ... he isn't napping?"

"No."

"Where is he?"

"I don't know, but I intend to find out. That's why I need your help."

"My ... help?"

"Yes."

"But I ... I don't understand."

"That's okay. I'll explain everything. Just please, give me your keys."

She was bullying him, forcing him up against his own car, and she hated herself for doing it. But she had no choice. She was doing this for his sake now, too. Otherwise she would have to do what Cain wanted—she would have to kill him— because right now she was going to do whatever it took to get her son back.

Todd hesitantly reached into his pocket, brought out his keys. He stared down at them as if they possessed the knowledge of the universe, and then looked up at her.

"I'm ... scared," he said quietly, and placed the keys in her open palm.

17

"We have to call the police."

"No."

"Sarah, from what you've just told me, a madman kidnapped your son and is holding him ransom. There's no arguing here. We have to call the police."

She'd told him just the basics—about Cain, about what he had done to Matthew, about how he wanted something from her—but that was it. They had left Oakville, were now on I-70 headed east.

"If we go to the police, he'll kill Matthew. He has a bomb strapped around my son's neck, for Christ's sake."

Todd shook his head. "I don't buy it. The guy's definitely crazy but he's not that crazy. He wouldn't actually kill anybody, especially a little boy."

She glanced briefly at him in the passenger seat but hesitated in speaking.

"What?"

"He's not bluffing."

"What makes you say that?"

"He's already killed someone."

"*What?*"

"This guy, Cain, he sent me to Reginald Moore's house."

The mention of the child molester's name caused a deep furrow in Todd's brow—the two of them, concerned parents, had discussed Moore before—but that deep furrow quickly changed to confusion as he said, "What are you talking about?"

"Reginald Moore is dead. Cain killed him."

"How?"

She told him about the pictures scattered on the floor of Reginald Moore's house, how they led her down to the basement where she found the child molester tied up to a chair, an explosive collar around his neck. She told him how the alarm clock began to count down, and how Cain had detonated the bomb.

"Jesus Christ." Todd shifted uncomfortably in his seat. "And this psycho has one of those things strapped around Matthew's neck, too?"

She nodded, glancing for the first time at the speedometer and realizing she was going much too fast. The last thing she needed was to be pulled over again for speeding, especially now that the police would be looking for her.

Todd said, "You need to call the police."

She tightened her grip around the steering wheel, shook her head.

"Then I'll call them for you."

He pulled out his cell phone from his pocket.

"Todd, please, don't do this."

He ignored her, began dialing the three numbers that would connect him to the police, and before she knew it she had ripped the phone from his hand, lowered her window, and threw it out.

"What the heck?" Todd shouted. He was more incredulous than angry. "Why did you do that, Sarah?"

"For starters, my name isn't Sarah."

"Say that again?"

"It's Elizabeth. Elizabeth Piccioni. My husband is Edward Piccioni."

The incredulity on Todd's face quickly turned to confusion. He shook his head as if to clear it. "Wait. Slow down. Your name's not—"

"Edward Piccioni was arrested and convicted five years ago for raping and murdering six women. The man who abducted Matthew, he wants the things my husband took from his victims."

"What things?" Todd asked, his voice soft, but before Elizabeth could tell him the BlackBerry dinged.

She had set it on the middle console so it would be easy to grab when Cain called. This was how Todd was able to grab it before she could. He now had a determined look on his face as he pressed a button and stared down at the screen. But soon that look of determination faded, and his face began to pale.

"My God," he whispered.

"What? What is it?"

He hand visibly shaking, he tilted the BlackBerry so she could see the picture on the screen: Matthew, again tied to the bed, again with the tape over his mouth and the blindfold over his eyes, the bright glowing digits above him now reading **99:00:00**.

18

Just before they reached St. Louis, they stopped for gas.

They hadn't spoken a word since the first picture of Matthew was sent—the BlackBerry dinged one hour later, as promised, with another picture—but when Elizabeth pulled up next to the pumps, she asked Todd if he had his ATM card with him.

"Of course."

"And your credit cards?"

"Yes. I have everything."

"Use the credit card to pay for the gas, then take out as much money as you can with your ATM card."

Todd had opened his wallet and was staring down at the loose bills and credit cards. Now he looked up at her. "Why?"

"Because when the FBI gets involved, they'll be able to track our movements with your credit card."

"How would they even know I'm with you?"

Elizabeth shrugged. "I'm just trying to cover all our bases."

She was hesitant to let him out of her sight, fearing he might try to call the police while inside. But she trusted him, and she had seen the look in his eyes when she explained what had happened to Matthew, how his life was in danger, and she knew Todd would do whatever it took to get him back.

Todd returned two minutes later with a filled plastic bag showing the gas station's logo.

"I got you a Diet Coke," he said. "You know, in case you're thirsty."

She didn't realize until they were back on the road just how thirsty she really was. She drained the soda in nearly five swallows. Todd offered his bottle of water but she declined. He took something from the plastic bag and opened it and immediately the car was filled with the smell of coffee.

"What is that?"

"Coffee beans. Breakfast Blend." He placed one in his mouth. "You want one?"

"You're *eating* them?"

Todd shrugged. "My dad chewed coffee beans when we went on road trips. He said it was healthier and cheaper than smoking. He'd let me try some and I eventually came to love them. Now when I drive long distances, I can't do it without chewing some kind of coffee bean. What—you look surprised."

"I'm just surprised that gas station actually had coffee beans."

"They did, and they were expensive, too. Are you sure you don't want one?"

"I'm sure."

There was a silence. Elizabeth felt unnerved by the exchange. It seemed too conversational for the situation at hand. Still, they had a long drive ahead of them, and Elizabeth didn't want Todd to feel more uncomfortable than he was already, so she said:

"You know, you never mentioned your father before."

"I haven't?"

"Not once since I've known you. I always just assumed he was dead."

She flinched when she said that last word.

Todd said, "Are you okay?"

"I'm fine."

"We don't have to talk about this."

"No, really, it's okay. What were you going to say?"

Todd studied her for a long moment before speaking. "My father, he might as well have been dead. When I was in high school he ran away with this woman he met at the gym, she was like ten years younger than him. He left me and my sister to take care of my mom. She had MS."

"I'm sorry," Elizabeth said, at once thinking of her own mother. "You never mentioned that either."

Todd produced an ironic smile. "What can I say—I don't like to be a downer."

They drove for another minute in silence.

Elizabeth said, "My father died when I was very young. He was healthy, kept himself in shape, but he still had a heart attack. It was a strange case, but the doctors admitted that it does happen."

"You know," Todd said, "that's the very first time you mentioned your father."

"I know."

"I'm assuming you're talking about your real father."

"Yes."

"What about your real mother?"

"Breast cancer. She found a lump one day and decided not to do anything about it. Apparently she had been in a kind of depression ever since my father's heart attack. She wasn't suicidal, per se, but just didn't have the will to continue living. So she found the lump and let it go and it wasn't until one of her regular checkups did the doctor find it. He wanted to start treatment immediately, but she refused."

"So what happened?"

"In the end the doctor did something he probably shouldn't have done: he called me. Right after that I got my brother involved and we pretty much forced her to start treatment."

"I didn't know you had a brother either."

"Jim," she said. "I never even had a chance to say goodbye to him. He was in Africa when the FBI came for my husband."

"Africa?"

"He was in the Peace Corps. He called me up, apologizing, saying it was all his fault."

"His fault?"

"He and my husband were college roommates. That's how we met. Jim set the two of us up together, and Eddie and I immediately hit it off."

"Eddie is your husband?"

She nodded. "Edward Piccioni."

Todd was quiet for another moment. "So your brother blames himself for you marrying a serial killer."

"Pretty much."

"Do you blame him?"

"Of course not. How was he supposed to know? I was closer to Eddie—had been close for almost seven years—and even I didn't know."

Todd reached into the bag of coffee beans between his legs, plucked out a bean, went to put it in his mouth but paused and offered it to her.

"Sure you don't want one?"

She shook her head. "No thanks."

"Are you positive? They're not that bad once you get used to them."

"I drink coffee, Todd. I don't eat it."

He popped the bean in his mouth, chewed it like a mint, and said, "So what about your mother?"

"What about her?"

"You said you and your brother forced her into treatment."

"Yes."

"And?"

"And what?"

"Fine," Todd said. "If you don't want to talk about it, we don't have to talk about it."

Elizabeth stared out at the highway in front of her, watching the oncoming night. She had begun to feel unnerved again, thinking it wrong that they held a conversation like this while Matthew was somewhere tied to a bed with an explosive collar around his neck. But talking was good. She would have to explain everything to Todd eventually. There was just so much that it was impossible to tell all at once. She would have to tell a little at a time, piece it out like that, so she might as well get started.

"I don't really know what happened to my mother. I'm assuming she's dead. In fact, I'm positive she is. When I … when I left, she was still alive. Barely holding on, but still alive."

Elizabeth shook her head, wiped at her eyes even though there were no tears.

"I'm sorry," Todd said softly.

"Thank you."

There was another brief silence.

Todd said, "Who do you think this guy is?"

"I have no idea."

"But don't you have a, like, suspect?"

Elizabeth said nothing.

"I recognize your husband's name."

She still said nothing.

"I sort of remember his trial, too. It was all over the news."

Still nothing.

"And I remember a couple people on TV—I can't remember who now—making these, you know, speculations on why you disappeared."

"That speculation started with just one person," Elizabeth said. "His name was Clarence Applegate. He thought I was an accomplice."

"Clarence Applegate," Todd said slowly. "Why does that name sound familiar?"

"He was one of the victims' husbands. He ended up writing a book about my husband, and about me. He called Eddie 'The Widower Maker.'"

Now it was Todd who said nothing.

"I wasn't, you know. His accomplice."

He glanced at her, already nodding. "Yeah, I know that. It never even crossed my mind."

"Sure it did. The whole thing was so bizarre, why not have the wife be part of it?"

"No, none of that—"

"I left because I ... well, I was a coward. That's basically it. I just couldn't stay there. I couldn't go through the whole ordeal of the trial. I couldn't sit in that courtroom and act like his wife anymore. I thought about what our lives would become—mine and Matthew's—and how if we stayed they would be forever ruined, so I just ... left."

Those were all reasons she had left, yes, but another

reason—the most important—was something she could never tell Todd. Something she could never tell anyone.

"How did you get away without anyone knowing?" Todd asked.

"I had friends."

"What kind of friends?"

Before she could answer, the BlackBerry dinged. They both glanced down at it on the middle console, the notification light blinking red. Todd reached for it.

"Don't."

He froze and looked at her.

"Just don't," she said, and pressed her foot down even more on the gas, driving them deeper into the oncoming darkness.

19

At some point after they crossed over the Indiana state line, Todd had begun to doze.

They hadn't spoken in hours, and the night had worn on, and eventually Elizabeth became aware of Todd breathing heavily through his nose. He was slouched down in his seat, his head tilted back on the headrest. Good for him, she thought. At least one of them was getting some rest.

The speed limit here was seventy, and she set the cruise control to seventy-five, her urgency to get to Pennsylvania so strong that she found herself with lead in her foot, the needle rising and rising, but reminding herself that getting pulled over by the police a second time was not in their best interest.

The BlackBerry had dinged five more times. Like that second time, she had refused to look at the pictures, fearing she might lose it. The only evidence they were there at all was the notification light blinking red for several minutes before it stopped.

She tried to concentrate on who Cain might be and why he was doing this. There had only been two people back home who knew about her escape, because they had been the ones who helped arrange it. Sheila, her best friend, and Mark Foreman, their family lawyer. Both had had a hand in helping her slip out from public view, start a new life, but both, she was certain, were trustworthy. No, wait. She was *more* than certain neither of them had anything to do with this, and the fact that she even considered the possibility was a testament to just how clueless she truly was when it came to figuring out the identity of Cain.

At one point she tried one of the coffee beans, grew nauseous after the first bite, had to roll down her window and spit out the remains, the wind whipping at her hair and face. As she powered the window back up, Todd stirred in the seat beside her, asked if everything was all right.

"Chewing coffee beans is disgusting," she said.

He smiled, his eyes still closed, repositioned himself in the seat, and began snoring almost immediately.

A half hour later the lights of Indianapolis began to rise on the dark horizon, and for the first time today Elizabeth felt the smallest flare of hope spark in her soul.

She knew there was no guarantee Van would still be in the city. There was always the chance the police or even the FBI had gathered enough evidence on him to finally make an arrest. Only she doubted that was the case. Men like Donovan Riley did not go quietly into the night or even the day. He was a survivor, just like her, and right now he was the only person she could trust.

Like a baby, Todd was soothed by the constant motion of the Prius, so when she eventually found her exit, slowed and took the off-ramp, he stirred again, yawned, wiped at his eyes.

"Are we there already?"

"Not yet."

Todd sat up straighter in his seat, his arms crossed, squinting out the window. "Where are we?"

"Indianapolis."

"Why are we stopping here?"

"For one, we could use a quick break to stretch our legs, use the bathroom, and get something to eat."

"And two?"

"There's someone here, an old friend, I need to see."

Todd didn't ask any more questions, just sat silent as she navigated the hybrid through the city streets. It had been over three years since she had been back here, and for some reason she thought she would be lost, the street signs and buildings all looking foreign to her. But she found her way without any problems, leading them downtown.

"Um"—Todd shifted nervously in his seat—"are you sure you know where you're going?"

"Yes."

"Good. Because ... well, this doesn't look like a safe part of town."

"It isn't."

This part of the city became more broken down, gang-bangers hanging out on the street corners, souped-up cars passing them with their rims glowing neon and their basses set to the highest decibel.

The closer she got toward where she hoped she was going, the more she realized it wouldn't be there. Either that or she had lost her way, had brought them down into the middle of the worst part of the city, where almost every street soldier carried a weapon.

And then there it was, Riley's Pub, the three-story building looking the same as it had the day Elizabeth first saw it. The parking lot was half empty, as she had expected it to be, the bar not filling up with its regulars until after midnight.

"An Irish bar," Todd murmured, "in the middle of ... *this*?"

Elizabeth pulled into the parking lot. "They have a loyal clientele."

"And how, exactly, do you know this?"

She found an open spot near the door and parked the Prius. She turned toward Todd, forcing a smile. "I'll be right back." Her expression became all at once serious. "Make sure to lock the doors."

20

The bouncer just inside the door was big, almost seven feet tall, and he was heavy, maybe three hundred and the bulk of that muscle. He was bald, too, wearing black pants and a black T-shirt, and to complete the ensemble he wore wrap-around shades.

"ID?" he said, already holding out his hand.

Elizabeth said, "I'm here to see Donovan Riley."

"I'm sorry, ma'am, but Mr. Riley isn't here tonight."

The *ma'am* didn't surprise her, as neither did the *mister*. Van trained all his employees to be respectful, no matter how deviant they might be. Here now in this bar, hearing the din of voices and laughter and music, she remembered once two bouncers had to break up a fight, the entire time the bouncers calling the guys fighting *sir*, as if that excused their behavior.

"I know that's not true," Elizabeth said. "It's Friday night. He's always here Friday night."

The bouncer's hand didn't move. "If you'd like to enter, ma'am, I'm going to need to see some ID."

"Do I really look like I'm not old enough to be served?"

"Ma'am, all I'm asking for is your ID."

She took a breath, gazing past him into the bar. Van had rearranged the place since she was last here, but it was still basically the same set up of tables and chairs, four billiards tables near the back, the stage area beside it.

Elizabeth took another breath, counted to ten in her head, and said, "Listen, I know you're new here. Van always puts new guys on the door. But believe it or not, I used to work here. Right there behind the bar, I used to serve drinks."

"That's nice, ma'am."

"No," she said, "what's nice is that I also know exactly what kind of man Van really is. And I don't mean that he's gay; everybody knows that. What I'm talking about is the stuff the FBI would just love to get their hands on."

The hand finally lowered, went back to the bouncer's side. He said, "Ma'am, if you're threatening Mr. Riley, I'm going to have to—"

Elizabeth pushed past him, headed into the bar. He reached for her, grabbed her arm, and she spun around him, lifting up the back of his shirt, pulling the Glock he had concealed at the small of his back.

Digging the gun's barrel into his ribs, she said, "I also know that everybody here carries, even the bouncers. I always told Van it was stupid to have bouncers carry, especially the guy on the door, but it seems he never took my advice. Now, if you would be so kind, I would very much like to see him."

The bouncer didn't move. He didn't even breathe. He just stood there without a word, and it occurred to Elizabeth that he would continue standing there until she was forced to shoot him. That was how Van liked them, after all, his employees willing to die for anything. Elizabeth had been the exception, and she had told him that up front and he had always said that was what he liked best about her.

She said, her teeth clenched, "You have no idea what I've

gone through today. I don't want to shoot you, but I will if you don't let me see Donovan Riley in the next minute."

This last was something she shouldn't have said, not with a gun jabbing the bouncer in the ribs, because it came off much too threatening toward the man's boss. She realized this a second too late, but by then the barrel of another gun was placed gently against the bottom of her skull.

"Easy now, Elizabeth," said a voice behind her, "step back and hand me the gun."

Without moving, without even turning her head in the slightest, she said, "Harlan?"

"That's right, E."

"I'm here to see Van."

"I figured as much."

"It's important."

"I'm sure it is. First though, you need to step back and lower Jerry's gun."

Harlan's own gun still kissing the back of her neck, Elizabeth took one step back and lowered the bouncer's Glock.

"Good," Harlan said. Then, "Turn around slowly, Jerry, and take your gun back."

Jerry did as he was told, turning and taking his gun back.

"Now thank Elizabeth here for not killing you."

The bouncer said nothing.

"Jerry," Harlan said, his voice growing dark, "don't make me repeat myself."

"Thank you, ma'am, for not killing me."

The barrel against the back of her neck disappeared, and next thing she knew Harlan was taking her arm and leading her deeper into the bar. His grip tight, walking quickly, he said, "Are you crazy?"

She decided it best not to answer that and kept pace with

him past the tables and chairs, then through the door that led into the kitchen. Through another door, then up a flight of stairs, they came to the second floor and there was another man wearing all black standing in front of a closed door.

"You know," Harlan said, releasing his grip on her arm, "you could have saved yourself some time and hassle and just asked for me first. I am Mr. Riley's right hand man."

She turned to face him for the first time, this small man wearing a dark suit, a pair of horn-rimmed glasses on his scarred face.

"Honestly? It never even crossed my mind."

"Mr. Riley is in a meeting right now. Do you mind waiting?"

"That depends."

"Depends on what?"

"The psychopath that's kidnapped my son."

Harlan's scarred face twitched slightly, which for Harlan was the same expression he would give to being shot in the chest. He glanced at the door, took a breath, then stepped forward, nodded at the man who stepped away. He knocked twice, entered, closed the door behind him.

Thirty seconds passed—she counted them down in her head, imagining them as bright red digits—and then the door opened again and two men appeared, both white. They gave her a once over before the man standing guard outside the office motioned them to follow him down the steps.

The door remained open. Through it was the office, and at the desk sat Donovan Riley.

When Elizabeth stepped into the room, she shut the door behind her. Then she just stood there, staring back at the man who had helped her escape her past life with the promise that she would never return to it.

"So," Van said, his elbows on the desktop, his hands folded in front of him, "just what kind of trouble have you gotten yourself into this time?"

PART II
THE WIDOWER MAKER

21

Within minutes of abandoning her old life—Foreman and Sheila now miles behind her—Elizabeth knew she had made a terrible mistake. Just what was she thinking? Running away from her troubles, from her husband's sudden bad name, yes that was all true, but how was she going to do it? There had been a plan, but a weak plan, and it had mostly come off way too spontaneous, Elizabeth deciding that it was now or never and her friends had gone along with it, given her the help she needed, and now here she was, her baby asleep in the backseat, the rising sun shining down on his head, and what were her friends going to say when she had no choice but to return?

But she couldn't do that—she just couldn't—and so she kept driving west, across the state, glancing in her rearview mirror every minute certain that a state trooper would appear, the cruiser's lights flashing. By now someone would know she was gone—the police, the FBI, the media—and word would spread quickly, and an APB would be put out for her like she was a fugitive, a criminal, which she guessed she now was because she was on the run.

Then again, what if nobody noticed or even cared?

The first week was the hardest. She had no direction in mind, no destination. She stayed at the cheapest motels she could find, the ones with the not-so-clean sheets, and she would hold her baby and cry and tell herself that he was not like his father, that the evil inside her husband had not been brought into their child and so she did not have to kill him.

After that first week she realized her money was running out faster than she thought it would. She needed to find a job, something that would pay under the table and not ask any questions. She needed to stop staying at these cheap motels whose management never cleaned the bathrooms and allowed mildew to form on everything.

Just outside of Pittsburgh she found a rooming house run by an old Jewish woman. The rent was, unbelievably, eighty dollars a week. The woman, Mrs. Mesika, wasn't going to take her in at first—it was clear she smelled trouble—but Elizabeth convinced her that she was on the run from her abusive husband and just needed time to get back on her feet. He was a cop, she explained, which was why she couldn't call the police on him, because he had cop friends everywhere.

In the end Mrs. Mesika took pity on her. She even agreed to watch the baby while Elizabeth looked for a job. She found one in two days, working at a truck stop diner along the Interstate, the owner willing to pay her under the table by hardly paying her anything at all. Most of her money came from tips, and she smiled more than she had ever smiled in her life, trying to be friendly with the patrons no matter how rude or perverted or slimy some of them might be.

Two months passed and Elizabeth knew she had to move on. Despite working nearly every day she was making no money. The tips were okay, just keeping her afloat, but still she hadn't even left the same state she had decided to escape, and she was certain—very certain—that at some point the police would recognize her. Every time the state troopers came in for breakfast, her heart always beat a little faster, and though she had cut her hair short and dyed it, wore glasses with nonprescription lenses, she always feared that one of them would give her a second glance.

When she was ready to leave, Mrs. Mesika embraced her and whispered into her ear, "Take good care, Elizabeth. I understand why you are doing what you are doing. I think I would do the same thing in your position."

She had never told Mrs. Mesika her real name, having given an alias, and when Elizabeth looked at her, the old woman gave her a knowing sad smile and said, "God be with you."

Next she and Thomas had ended up just outside of Canton, Ohio. A few more cheap motels before she found another boarding house, this one run by a woman with three kids who agreed to watch Thomas for thirty bucks a day. That plus rent was just under the amount she ended up making at another diner she found, another place where the owner agreed to pay her under the table, the wage again barely a respectable wage.

How, she wondered, had women lived two hundred years ago? How had people traveled across this country in wagons and lived in tents and hunted for their food?

It was here in this diner that she first met Donovan Riley. He was accompanied by Harlan, and they were just passing through like everyone else. She hadn't even been waiting on his table, but before the two men left Donovan had made it a point to walk past her and smile and nod and ask how she was doing.

She had only smiled back, said fine thank you, and that had been that until the very next day when Donovan and

Harlan came in again. This time they sat at a table in her section. She had waited on them, expecting the man to try to make more small talk, but he hadn't. And for the next week they came in, always dressed in suits, always sitting in her section, until on the very last day he left a one hundred dollar tip and a note that said if she wanted a better job, a better life, to give him a call. He had left his number but she had thrown it out immediately, thoughts of prostitution and pornography being the first two things that entered her mind.

The two men did not show up again. A week went by, then another week. She started to think she would never see them again until, after leaving work one day, she returned to the boarding house to find the pair waiting for her.

"My name's Donovan Riley," he said, holding out his hand.

She didn't shake it, just stared back at him and asked him what he wanted.

"I wanted to let you know my offer still stands. I can tell you're a woman in trouble. I can also tell you're practically working for free. I'm willing to change all that."

"I'm not interested."

"I didn't even tell you about the job yet."

"I'm not a whore, either."

"I never said you were."

She started to walk past him. "If you don't leave me alone, I'm going to call the police."

"A bartender," he said.

She paused but didn't turn back.

"I have a place in Indianapolis, a bar there that could use a good bartender. Don't ask me why but I think you would be perfect for it. No funny business, either. You just serve drinks, keep the place clean, that's it. I'll pay you well for your time and also set you and your boy up with a place to stay."

As far as she knew she had never told this man she had a son, there was absolutely no way he should have known it, but instead she said, "What's the catch?"

"The catch is you've got to make your decision. Right now."

Everything in her gut told her to just say no, walk away, call the police. Instead she turned around, slowly, and crossed her arms over her chest. "How much an hour?"

The bar was located in downtown Indianapolis. It was three-stories, the top floor an open apartment. This was where Donovan allowed her and Thomas to stay.

"While you're working, I'll have one of my guys watch after your son. Don't worry—they look tough, but they're gentle."

The situation was beyond bizarre but at the moment she didn't have that many options.

She was trained how to bartend, and it was difficult at first. She had to shamefully admit that she had never thought it would be hard, pouring drinks and beer, but when you were waiting on a dozen people at the same time, trying to keep all the recipes separate in your mind, you begin to realize it takes a special personality to tend bar, one she wasn't sure she had. Still, after a couple weeks she got the hang of it, though sometimes she still screwed up orders and let a renegade glass or two slip through her fingers and shatter on the floor.

She figured out quickly that Donovan Riley was homosexual, just as she figured out that he was mixed up in some shady business. Not drugs exactly, but weapons or something else just as dangerous. Every time she wanted to leave she remembered how well he was taking care of her and her son, the money he was paying her (nothing great, but nothing terrible either), and how he never asked for anything in return except for her to tend the bar.

After a couple months, when she had become adjusted, he began to spend more time with her. He said as a single mother she should learn how to protect herself. He had a karate instructor come to the bar, work with her in the apartment while Thomas watched from his crib. She learned how to defend herself from a mugger, what to do if someone were to come at her with a knife. Sometimes Van took her to the shooting range, saying that every woman should know how to shoot a gun, and while she was scared at first (just the thought of touching a weapon made her nauseous) she began to look forward to going to the firing range and emptying a magazine into a paper target.

At times she was reminded about her husband. After all, there would occasionally be an article in the paper about his trial, about his conviction. Articles about the victims and their families. Even articles about her and her sudden disappearance.

It was during these times that she would think again about the evil inside her son. How one day he would grow up to be just like his father. How she should not only do the world a favor, but herself, even her son, and end his life. And how every time these thoughts passed through her head, she would cut herself. Just a little slice along her stomach or chest, not where anyone would ever see it. She would do this as a punishment to herself for even *allowing* the thoughts to enter her mind, because she knew they were just as evil as the possible evil inside her son. After a time, though, she would cut herself for no other reason than she liked the moment before the blade touched the skin, the anticipation of the numbness.

One time she cut herself so deeply she wasn't even aware of it and blacked out. When she awoke, she was tied to a bed and Donovan stood over her.

"You're troubled, Elizabeth, you know that?"

Her throat was parched, but she managed to croak, "That's not my name."

Van shook his head. "So very troubled."

It was Harlan who had found her unconscious, Thomas crying from his crib. They had called a doctor they knew to be discreet who came over and helped revive her. In the process they found the rest of her scars, over one hundred of them, like patchwork covering her stomach and chest.

After two days of being tied to the bed, Elizabeth said, "You can let me go now."

"Are you sure?"

"Yes."

Van nodded at Harlan to untie her.

She rubbed her wrists and ankles, glaring back at Van. "How did you know my real name?"

"Well," Van said, "there's sort of a funny story involved in all that."

As it turned out, Van, among everything else, had a fascination with serial killers. Though he said he knew it sounded vulgar, it was really quite innocent. Just as men followed sports and women collected shoes, Van liked to study the psyche of killers.

"Just like snowflakes, no two serial killers are alike. They're disturbed, obviously, but in many ways they're also brilliant."

He showed her his collection. It was in a room just off his office, an overlarge closet she had always known without being told was off limits. Books and DVDs of serial killers filled shelves. Trading cards with the pictures of serial killers on the front and their stats—where they were born, where they went to school, how many people they murdered, what murder weapon they used—were protected in thick plastic sleeves and stored in shoe boxes. There were even items supposedly owned by serial killers, such as a letter from Ted Bundy written to Van when Van was young and his fascination began to grow. Van wouldn't let her read the letter but said it wasn't anything too bad, just the man talking about his time in prison. He sounded, Van said, rather normal.

Elizabeth said, "You knew who I was the moment you saw me, didn't you?"

Van admitted that he had. The reason he wanted her to come work for him was because he wanted to help her and her son, but also—selfishly—he wanted to learn more about Edward Piccioni. There hadn't been many serial killers recently who had gotten so much attention. Van wanted to know what the man was like. What kind of cereal he liked to eat, what type of television programs he liked to watch, the type of shoes he wore. Everything.

Elizabeth said, "I think it's time Thomas and I left."

Van said he didn't blame her. He was sorry if she felt lied to but he knew if he had come right out with the truth to begin with he would have scared her off.

"I can help you," he said. "Start a new life, I mean. As you've probably figured out, I'm not what you would call an honest citizen. I do have certain connections that could benefit you."

She asked him what he was talking about.

"How much savings would you say you had in your bank account before you left?"

Elizabeth shrugged. "Maybe thirty thousand."

"And that money is probably still sitting there. It's not going anywhere. Your husband certainly can't do much about it. Well, until legal fees are paid for, but I've always said screw the lawyers."

Van explained that he knew a couple computer-savvy

individuals who could hack into her account, clean out the money, transfer it to a number of offshore banks. The money would be bounced from account to account to account where it would eventually disappear. The authorities would never be able to trace it.

"And where would it go?" she asked.

"Half to you, half to me and my people for our troubles."

She let only a few seconds pass before she nodded and said, "Do it."

A week later he produced a duffel bag full of old twenties and fifties as well as new identification for both her and Thomas.

"From now on your name will be Sarah Walter. And your son here will be Matthew Walter."

She stared down at the birth certificates, the social security cards. "What happened to them?"

"Don't worry about it. Let's just say that where they are now they won't be needing them."

She swallowed, tried holding back tears. "Thank you."

"Don't thank me. But, Elizabeth—I mean, Sarah?"

She looked up at him.

"It's been nice knowing you. I wish I hadn't lied to you but I'm sure you can understand by now why I did what I did. And..." He sighed. "And, well, after everything you've told me about your husband—truthfully, he doesn't sound like a killer to me."

"Is that supposed to make me feel better?"

"No." He placed a hand on her arm. "It's supposed to remind you that he's human, just like you."

She embraced him and Harlan, thanked them for everything. They both took Thomas—now Matthew—and kissed his forehead.

"Where should I go now?" she asked.

"That's up to you. But, Sarah?" How strange Van was able to say that name like it was really hers.

"Yes?"

"Do me a favor and promise me that you won't ever come back here. Not that I wouldn't love to see you, but if you ever came back here I'll know something terrible has happened, and I don't want that to ever happen. Okay?"

She promised.

22

"No idea?"

"None."

"You haven't noticed anything suspicious in the past week? The past month?"

Elizabeth leaned forward in her seat. "If there was anything suspicious I would have noticed it immediately. You know that."

"So this whole thing"—Van waved his hand in the air—"came out of nowhere this afternoon."

"Just like I told you, yes."

Van still sat behind his desk, slouched now, his elbows on the armrests and his hands folded in front of his face. He was still a handsome man, tall and broad shouldered. While Harlan stood off to the side, while Todd sat on the leather couch by the door, while Elizabeth sat right here in the middle of the room, Van stared back at her with his dark, intelligent eyes.

"So why did you come here?"

"You know why."

"I don't."

"We need help."

"That's obvious."

"I can't go to the police with this. Cain said he would"—Elizabeth swallowed—"do something bad if we did that."

"Of course he would say that."

"You think he's bluffing?"

Van sat another moment with a thoughtful look on his face, then shook his head. "No, I don't. But tell me—what do you *want*?"

"For starters, weapons would be nice."

"Weapons aren't a problem. Harlan?"

Harlan stepped forward from his place against the wall. He walked toward Elizabeth, withdrawing his gun, turning the gun around in his hand so it was extended to her with the grip out.

Elizabeth stared at it for a moment, then said, "I'm not taking that."

"What's wrong with it?" Van asked.

"Nothing's wrong with it. But it's Harlan's."

"You think that's his only one? Take it."

Elizabeth took the proffered weapon.

"Now that that's out of the way," Van said, "what are you really here for?"

"You know people."

"I know a lot of people."

"I was thinking maybe you would know people who could trace those texts." She motioned at the BlackBerry on Van's desk. "Like, find out where the signal is coming from."

Van picked up the BlackBerry, began scrolling through the pictures. Elizabeth had already forced herself to look at them. All of Matthew, all with him tied to that bed. There really wasn't much difference in any of the pictures except that the bright red glowing digits above his head kept decreasing by one hour.

"There's no guarantee these pictures are even real."

"What do you mean?"

"This guy could have already taken one hundred pictures, just changed the time on that countdown clock and snapped away. He keeps sending you pictures every hour, you keep thinking your son is still alive when he's really not."

This wasn't what she wanted to hear but she had to admit the thought had crossed her mind.

"I spoke with him, though. He's still alive."

"Eight hours ago he was, yes. When this Cain calls you back, ask to speak to him again. Make him give you proof of life."

Elizabeth was silent, thinking about that morning, what felt like a thousand years ago, packing Matthew's lunch, pouring him a bowl of cereal, dropping him off at school.

Van said, "Those people you mentioned, I might know a couple."

"Where are they?"

"Not here."

"Van."

"It's going to take some time."

"How much time?"

"How the hell should I know? Depends on who I can contact first. Maybe an hour. Maybe two."

"We can't stay here long."

"Yes," Van said, nodding slowly, his gaze shifting past her at Todd on the couch. "Now let's run over this again, shall we? This guy—this Cain—wants your husband's trophies. Which, I'm assuming, are the ring fingers of the last four women he killed. Maybe the rings themselves, too, but I'm guessing this guy is fixated more on the fingers. Fair assessment?"

Elizabeth said nothing.

"And so this guy, he obviously knows what he's doing. He's planned this thing out to the very last detail. Except your boyfriend over there, that wasn't according to plan."

Behind her she could hear Todd shift on the couch. When he spoke, his voice was strained. "What are you trying to say?"

"Me, I'm not trying to say anything. If Elizabeth says you have nothing to do with this, then you have nothing to do with this."

Elizabeth said, "Are you actually insinuating that—"

"Look," Van said, "I just sat here and listened to what you told me. I don't know what you've done in the past three years. I don't know that man other than his name. So right now, right here, I'm questioning everything. Do you have a problem with that?"

The question was directed at Elizabeth but it was Todd who answered, his voice still strained. "I was just bringing her flowers, that's all. She was in a bad mood and I thought leaving flowers outside her door would cheer her up. If I'd known this was going to happen, I never would have ..."

But he didn't finish the thought; he didn't have to. Elizabeth knew very well what he had meant to say, and she couldn't blame him for it.

Van sat silent for a long time, staring back down at the BlackBerry. Finally he nodded and stood up and said, "Elizabeth? I'd like to speak with you alone."

23

The first thing Van did when they got to the apartment on the third floor—the same apartment she and Matthew had stayed at when they were last here—was turn and take Elizabeth into an embrace, hold her head to his chest and whisper, "I'm sorry."

She let loose then, the tears from before nothing close to the ones she shed now, her entire body racking with sobs as she took the expensive fabric of his shirt in her fingers and balled her hands into fists.

They stood that way for several minutes, Van simply holding her as she cried, until Elizabeth calmed down, wiped her eyes, and stepped back.

Van said, "You know what this means, don't you?"

Wiping at another stray tear, Elizabeth nodded.

"I can't even imagine how you're going to get in to see him."

"I'll find a way."

"How? You've been gone nearly five years. You expect to just show up at the prison asking to see your serial killer husband and they'll let you in?"

"Look, I don't know how it will happen, but it will happen. It has to."

"You hope."

"I don't have much else keeping me going right now, Van. My son..." She looked away, shook her head. "You need to help."

"I am helping. I already sent out an encrypted email to two of those people we spoke about. They're probably already on their way."

"How long?"

"Like I told you, it could be an hour, it could be longer. But the real question you need to ask yourself is what will you do if it works?"

"What do you mean?"

"Say we are able to trace where the texts are originating from and determine this guy's location. What then?"

Elizabeth said, "You and Harlan go kill him and bring back my son."

Van smiled. "As much fun as that would be, let's be realistic here for a second. Say we can't trace those texts and you're forced to continue. What if there are no trophies?"

"Excuse me?"

"Your husband cut off those fingers but what if he didn't save them? Cain's doing all of this on the assumption that these things are saved somewhere, somewhere easy to get to. But what if they're not?"

"I don't even want to consider the possibility."

"But you have to."

Elizabeth forced herself to take a deep breath. "Don't you think I know that already? Don't you think I've been thinking about it for the past eight hours?"

She turned away from him, started toward the couch—the

same pull-out couch that had once been her bed—but then redirected herself toward the window overlooking the street. She stood there, her arms crossed, staring out through the blinds. She remembered staring out them years ago, knowing that while she was in this building she was safe, that nothing out there on the street or in the city or even in the entire world could hurt her.

Van came to stand beside her. When he spoke, his voice was just above a whisper.

"You have to accept the fact that Cain does not plan on returning Matthew. Most likely he's going to kill him and you, and now your boyfriend, too."

"You don't know that."

"But I do know that, and so do you. And once you understand it and accept it, then you'll have an advantage over him. Right now he thinks you're a woman who has everything to lose, but in actuality that's not the case."

She turned her head just slightly, frowned at his shoes. "Are you insane? I'm not gambling my son's life away."

"But don't you get it? You don't have a choice. Right now Cain wants something, and to get to that something he needs you. *You*, Elizabeth, you have the power."

There was a knock at the door.

Van turned slightly, called, "Come in," and in came first Harlan, then Todd.

"Is everything all right?" Todd asked.

Van said, "Harlan, why don't you take the boyfriend here and get us all some food. Grab us some pies and some cheese steaks from Gino's."

"I'm not leaving Elizabeth," Todd said.

Van smiled again, only this time it was without mirth. "That's very noble of you, but right now we're not in your house, you're in mine."

Elizabeth watched a shadow of fear cross Todd's face. He lowered his head, nodded, and turned toward the door.

After Todd and Harlan left, Van said, "Not much of a backbone."

"He's a great guy. He shouldn't be here right now."

"Neither should you."

"What does that mean?"

"Just how the hell was this guy able to track you down? I'm assuming of course you did as I told you and never contacted anybody from your old life."

She hesitated only a moment before saying, "Of course I didn't."

"Right."

They stood there then in silence, staring out the window at the street below, that safety Elizabeth had once felt in this room now completely gone.

24

Harlan and Todd returned with food twenty minutes later, Harlan carrying two pizza boxes, Todd with a large brown paper bag.

Todd set the bag down on the table, pulled out a Styrofoam container. "I got you onion rings. I know how you like them."

Elizabeth felt a familiar pang in her chest at his thoughtfulness, even at a time like this. Their first date hadn't been at a fancy restaurant but at a pizzeria, not Todd's idea but hers because ... well, she couldn't remember the reason anymore. They'd ordered a pizza, she had ordered onion rings, and when the rings arrived Todd had crinkled his nose.

"What's wrong?" she had asked.

"Onion rings. I'm sorry, but they're just so disgusting."

"Oh really. And have you ever even tried one?"

He had tilted his head from side to side, shrugged, and admitted he hadn't.

"You're like my son," she said. "He doesn't like to try new things either."

"Well," Todd said, reaching toward the basket, "I can't let you think I'm not open to new things, can I?"

Now, less than six months later, Todd forced a smile at her as he pulled two cheese steaks from the bag. Harlan set the pizzas down next to the container on the table, then turned to her.

"Where is Mr. Riley?"

"Back in his office, I think. You know him—all business, all the time."

Harlan said, "Well then, I will leave you alone to enjoy your meal," and left without another word.

When the door closed, Todd said, "That guy weirds me out."

"Who—Harlan? He's harmless."

"I don't know. Something tells me he could probably kill me with his pinkie."

Elizabeth came away from the window, met him at the table. "Not with his pinkie. His index finger, though ..." She forced a smile that quickly faded. "I'm sorry."

"For what?"

"All of this. Getting you into this mess."

"It's my fault. I should have just gone home and watched *SportsCenter*." He forced a smile of his own. "I hate to admit it, but I'm starving."

They opened the food. Two large pizzas, one with pepperoni, one with extra cheese, two cheese steaks, and the onion rings.

Elizabeth took a bite of an onion ring, widened her eyes. "Hot," she said. Then, "You want one?"

"No thanks."

"Oh, come on."

"Hey, I tried it that one time, didn't I?"

"Yes, because I guilted you into it."

"Well, you're a woman. Guilting men into doing stuff they don't want to do is what you're good at."

A slight grin played on his face, and Elizabeth found herself grinning, too. It felt good to produce a smile that wasn't forced, to find some joy, no matter how small, in this situation. But then, just as quickly, their grins faded when they remembered where they were and why they were here and where they needed to go next.

Todd said, "So."

"So."

He looked around the room again. "You, what, lived here once?"

"For a while, yes."

"What did you do? I mean, as a job."

"I tended the bar."

"Seriously? Like mixing drinks and stuff?"

She nodded.

"Huh," Todd said. "I never would have pictured that."

Elizabeth didn't say anything, letting the silence remind him there was a lot he would probably have a hard time picture her doing.

Todd turned to the table, grabbed a slice, held it for a moment before setting it back down.

"So this guy, Donovan Riley, he's what—a drug dealer or something?"

"Not quite. He doesn't deal drugs. In fact, he detests drugs."

"But he's, like, connected somehow, right?"

"Honestly, it's best if you don't even think about it."

Not thinking about it, though, was something Todd couldn't do. She knew that, just as she couldn't stop thinking about this place herself. How she had lived here and worked here and then, with thoughts of killing her son swarming in her head, had begun cutting herself here. She thought she could even feel the scars now, almost tingling, as if they too sensed this place was where they had been born.

Todd turned away, picked up his slice again.

Elizabeth watched him, thinking about her scars and why she hadn't let her intimacy with Todd continue more than it had. They had kissed, yes, had even made out several times, but every time Todd tried taking it to the next level, she always pushed him away. She couldn't explain why—telling him about the scars would then prompt even more questions, like where they had come from and what brought them on— and she was certain he wasn't going to put up with it much longer. But, surprisingly, he had remained patient with her, and that made her care for him even more.

She opened her mouth, wanting to tell Todd something (what, she wasn't even sure), when the door opened.

"Look at you two," Van said as he approached them, carrying two books, "you couldn't even wait for your host before you started filling your faces."

Elizabeth said, "Hey, you snooze, you lose."

Van opened a pizza box. "Ah, extra cheese. My favorite."

Another thing she had forgotten about Donovan Riley— he was a pseudo-vegetarian.

"Are those what I think they are?" she asked, meaning the books in his hand.

"Yep." Van pulled up a chair, placed the books on the table, grabbed himself a slice. "I figured you might want to catch up on some light reading."

Todd craned his head to read the titles. "*Never Coming Home: The Edward Piccioni Murders* and *The Widower Maker.*" He glanced at Elizabeth, frowning, then back at the books. "Wait. Isn't that one by—"

"You guessed it," Van said, chewing his slice. "The one and only Clarence Applegate."

Elizabeth sighed, shaking her head.

Van said, "Elizabeth here isn't much of a Clarence Applegate fan. The truth is, the guy is a god-awful writer. He thought of himself as the next Ann Rule but he didn't even come close. Of course, now he keeps that blog of his, and has thousands and thousands of followers on Twitter. He does for serial killers what Perez Hilton does for celebrities."

There was a long silence. Elizabeth sat very still, staring down at her plate. She didn't want to think about Clarence Applegate, about the book he had written and the crusade he had taken to try to track her down.

Van took a large bite of his slice, chewed loudly (another thing she had forgotten), and said, "This is the best pizza you'll find in the city, hands down." Then said, "Hey, Todd, you curious to know what Elizabeth was like when she worked here? Well, have I got some stories for you."

25

It felt wrong, it really did, the three of them sitting around the table eating pizza and laughing, like this was poker night and her son wasn't held captive by a madman, a bomb strapped around his neck.

But there they were, laughing despite themselves, Todd the loudest of the bunch, Van telling stories about Elizabeth when she worked here, the kind of trouble she caused.

"I swear it's true," Van said, taking a swig of bottled water (he was a steadfast teetotaler), "she kneed him right in the balls."

Elizabeth couldn't help herself, she was laughing, too, though it was a kind of embarrassed laugh.

Todd raised a Miller Lite bottle to his lips, paused, gave her a look. "In the balls?"

She gave an innocent smile, shrugged.

Van said, still laughing, "I wish I had it on video. This fight starts up by the pool tables, all my guys go over there to break it up, and this guy—this greasy skinny brother—starts flirting with E. Guess he sees his chance, that nobody's watching, so as she's trying to make her way back to the bar he keeps stepping in her way, trying to talk to her. E, she's being professional about it, just trying to do her job." He glanced at her. "All true so far, yes?"

Elizabeth, now taking a sip of her Diet Coke, only gave a slight nod.

"Right, so he keeps trying to talk to her but she keeps trying to walk around him, until this guy, he starts to get angry. He says something to her, something rude, and he grabs her arm. E's holding her tray at this point, has glasses and bottles stacked on top, but she doesn't lose her cool. Remember what you told him, E?"

She stared down at her plate. The laughter—at least her laughter—had all of a sudden vanished. It had been a nice reprieve, a couple of minutes to actually feel some joy, but now reality was shoving itself back in her face, reminding her of what was at stake.

"Elizabeth?" Van said, and the smile was gone from his face, the light from his eyes, his voice worried. "You okay?"

"Yeah. I'm fine."

"Do you remember what you said to that guy?"

She said, "I told him if he ever wanted to walk right again, he should remove his hand."

Van snapped his fingers. "Hell yes, you did. And this guy, he doesn't believe her, thinks she's just this helpless white girl working in a big bad black bar. So he keeps his hand on her arm, starts to say something else to her, and E here, she doesn't hesitate."

Todd, a look of awe in his eyes, turned to her. "You're kidding me. You really did that?"

Again she shrugged, though the innocent smile she'd given before was now gone.

"Right there in the balls," Van said, taking another swig of water, "and you want to know the best part? She didn't drop her tray. She didn't even tip over any of the glasses or bottles. E's got perfect balance, I used to say, and it was true." He squinted at her. "You think that's true now?"

Elizabeth started to speak but yawned instead.

"Don't do that," Todd said, yawning himself.

Van said, "Maybe you two should lie down, rest for a couple of hours."

"We'll be fine," Elizabeth said.

"E—"

"When are those guys getting here?"

"They'll get here when they get here." Van's phone vibrated on the table. He picked it up, read what Elizabeth assumed was a text message, and sighed. "I have to head downstairs. I'll come get you when they arrive." He nodded at the books on the table. "And when you get the chance, you might want to freshen up on your history."

And then he was headed toward the door, walking backward, saying, "Todd, have E tell you about the time she sliced a guy with a beer bottle. Smashed it right across the table and held it at his throat."

Todd gave a half-laugh, glanced at Elizabeth with another look of awe. "Now that one can't be true. Can it?"

Van laughed as he left, shutting the door behind him.

Elizabeth yawned again, louder this time. "I don't know what's come over me. My eyelids are starting to get heavy."

"Do you want to lie down?"

"No. Once those guys get here, I want to be awake."

"Why? They can work on the trace without you looking over their shoulders."

"I just want to be there."

Todd said, "So is it true?"

"Is what true?"

"What he said. About you breaking a bottle and stabbing some guy."

"First of all, I didn't stab him. It was just a little cut. Second of all, what does it matter?"

"It doesn't. I'm just ..."

"Yeah?"

"Impressed. Well, I'm also sort of intimated. Actually, I'm very intimated. And"—here he lowered his voice—"kind of turned on."

"Don't."

"What?"

"Just don't."

"Sorry." Todd went to take another sip of his beer but set it back on the table. "I'm such a lightweight. Shouldn't even have had that one."

Elizabeth yawned again. She couldn't help it.

Todd yawned too, said, "Come on, you have to stop that," and yawned again.

"Maybe you should lie down."

"Are you sure?"

"I'll wake you when they get here."

"Then what are you going to do?"

"I don't know." She motioned at the books Van had left. "Freshen up on some of my history, I guess."

Todd looked hesitant, but then he went over to the couch and lay down.

Elizabeth stood up and went to the window. She stared down at the street, at the cars driving past, at the gangbangers on the corner, and she found herself yawning again, too.

She told herself no, she couldn't sleep, not even for a few minutes. Because what if something were to happen in those few minutes she was asleep? What if Cain tried calling? What would he do if he couldn't get hold of her? Would he take it out on Matthew?

Todd seemed to be right on the brink of sleep when she brushed a few loose strands of hair from his forehead. He took a deep breath, opened his eyes slowly, peered up at her.

"Yeah?" he murmured.

"Do you think I can get in here, too?"

This woke him up a bit more, and he lifted his feet, swung them off the couch, and sat up straight.

Elizabeth sat beside him, and he put his arm around her. She snuggled into him and rested her head on his shoulder, thinking she would only close her eyes, just for a few minutes, nothing more than that, and then when she opened her eyes again this nightmare would be over and she would find Matthew asleep in his bed, safe and sound.

A few minutes, just a few minutes, she thought, and she closed her eyes, saw a long black river in front of her. She tried fighting the current the best she could, until she had no strength left and let it take her whichever way it pleased.

26

The dream was more a memory than anything else. She knew it at once, the exact time and date and location: Elizabeth in the kitchen making breakfast, little Thomas asleep in his crib, Eddie at the kitchen table reading the newspaper. A TV was on in the corner, a small nine-inch thing that sat on the counter and which was mostly used for background noise. This morning it was the local news, the feature story about a fatal accident that happened in the middle of the night, a drunk driver having entered the off-ramp to the highway, going the wrong way, and colliding head-on with another car.

Elizabeth had been standing at the sink, cracking eggs into a bowl—she had never perfected her egg-cracking skills, no matter how hard she tried—and when she heard this she gasped.

Eddie turned the page of the newspaper. "What is it?"

"Aren't you watching this? It's terrible."

Three men, the newscaster said, on their way to work in the wrong place at the wrong time. Three men with families of their own. All three men now dead. The only survivor was the drunk driver herself, who walked away with only a few minor bruises.

Elizabeth's attention was fixated on the screen and the newscaster's words so much that when Eddie came up behind her, placed his hands on her shoulders, she jumped.

"Oh my God, you scared me."

He pulled her to him, kissed her head. "It's okay."

She could already feel the tears welling in her eyes. This was something that always happened, her crying after seeing or reading a tragic news story. And while the story itself was always tragic, in her mind she found herself thinking about the spouses and the children, about their loss and how their lives were forever changed because of one simple (and often-times stupid) mistake.

"Shh," Eddie said, holding her closely now, rocking her back and forth.

Thomas continued to sleep peacefully in his crib, something she was grateful for, because even though he was a baby and would never remember—or even notice—she hated the thought of her son seeing her cry.

The segment had ended, the camera now showing the two newscasters in the studio. Before one of them could speak, Eddie turned off the television. The kitchen suddenly went silent. He turned to her, opened his mouth, and that was when the doorbell rang.

He frowned. "I wonder who that could be."

She wiped at her eyes, turned back to the sink, picked up another egg. She had tapped the egg against the rim of the bowl when she heard Eddie open the door. She had tapped it again, hard enough to break this time, when she heard the voices. With her fingernails she tried to pry the egg apart, something she knew she shouldn't do, and the result was the yolk running into the bowl along with a few tiny pieces of shell.

"Shit," she muttered, dropping the shells into the trash and turning to the sink to wash her hands. The voices continued, deep authoritative voices, and she shut off the water, wiping her hands on a towel, stepping into the hallway to see Eddie standing at the end of it, three men in suits outside.

Eddie was turning around, placing his hands behind his back, staring at her with a look that said this wasn't a surprise at all—he wasn't surprised, so neither should she be.

Only here was where the memory changed, because around his neck now was an explosive collar. An alarm clock just like the one in Reginald Moore's basement sat on the table beside the door, the bright red numbers counting down.

0:10 ... 0:09 ... 0:08 ...

Elizabeth felt it around her own neck, another explosive collar, and she touched it like she would a priceless diamond necklace and glanced up just as the numbers on the alarm clock went five ... four ... three ... two ...

She opened her eyes, immediately reaching for her neck, but of course there was nothing there. The room was dark, much darker than it should have been, and she sat up at once.

Todd shifted beside her, his breathing heavy with sleep. He'd had his arm around her but now it slipped down to his lap.

She stood up. Went directly to the kitchenette, the only place where there was a clock, telling herself it couldn't be, that it was impossible. But right there on the microwave she got her confirmation: it was nearly four o'clock. She had been asleep for almost four hours.

"Damn you, Van," she whispered. She remembered how Van had been so adamant about them resting. He didn't want them on the road and be completely exhausted, which she guessed made sense. Only while one drove, the other could sleep. It was that simple, sure, but then you had to figure in the fact they still had to wait on those guys Van had contacted.

Van had promised to come back once they arrived. Had he come to the room, saw they were sleeping, thought it best not to wake them and shut off the lights?

Possibly. Still, she knew Van. She knew that despite his insistence that they rest, he wouldn't purposely put her behind schedule.

She considered waking Todd but instead headed for the door. Down the hallway, down the stairs, she came to Van's office expecting to find one of his boys standing guard outside.

There was no guard, which meant Van wasn't inside.

She went down to the next floor, came out into the bar. It was dark here, too. The distant mixed scent of alcohol and perfume and cologne and cleaning materials hung in the air.

Elizabeth thought of the time again. Would this place be completely cleaned up and dark by four o'clock in the morning? Sure. Except it was a Friday, and Fridays were always the busiest here. Or at least they had been when she worked behind the bar.

She returned to the second floor, confused now. She stared at Van's office door. If Van was in there, a guard would be outside. It didn't matter that it was after hours; one of the rules was a guard was always stationed outside the door.

Elizabeth didn't know why, but she expected the knob to be locked. It wasn't. It turned easily in her hand, and then the door swung open revealing the dark room inside.

Only it wasn't completely dark.

The computer monitor was still on, creating some light. The screensaver had been activated, a theme that required a good portion of the screen to be black, so there wasn't much light but just enough to confirm that Van was there at his desk, leaning forward with his head down.

A man as busy as him, she wasn't surprised. He worked hard every day in whatever it was he did (she never really did find out the entire truth), and he should have gone home by now. Except maybe he was still waiting on those guys. Maybe the guys hadn't arrived and he had dozed off, not wanting to leave her and Todd alone even for a few minutes.

"Van?" she whispered, stepping into the room.

He didn't move.

Five paces took her to the desk, another five paces took her around to the other side. She had never decided who had been calmer, Harlan or Van. Harlan was certainly more stoic, that was a no-brainer, but calm, well, calm was another thing completely. Van had always claimed he was never surprised, that he never could be surprised, and a few times Elizabeth had tried doing something that would surprise him, like hide behind a door and shout boo when he turned the corner. It had been juvenile, yes, but she had been okay with that. Van was, in his own way, like an older brother to her, one she would never be able to one-up.

Now she came around the desk, quietly, stealthily, walking on the balls of her feet, and she reached out toward Van, smiling now because she knew she would finally surprise him.

Her hand bumped the mouse on desk, taking the screen-saver away, creating light, and for an instant before she grabbed Van's shoulder, she looked up and saw Harlan on the floor against the wall. His legs were splayed out in front of him, his head tilted to the side, his glassy eyes staring at nothing. Her eyes shifted toward the couch by the door and she saw two men slouched there, just as dead as Harlan. By then she had touched Van's shoulder, enough to cause him to move, his head rolling on the desk toward her, the light of the monitor illuminating the bullet hole in his head and the dark blood dried to his face.

27

Todd was slow waking up, groggy from a deep sleep, and it was clear he misunderstood her because at first he only frowned, his eyes squinted, and murmured, "Bed?"

"*Dead*," she whispered harshly, shaking him harder now, "they're *dead!*"

Why she was whispering, she didn't know. Maybe she feared Cain was still somewhere in the building. Or maybe it had to do with the fact she hadn't turned on the lights, and it was just a normal human reaction to keep your voice low when the lights were off. Still, she was shaking, that nausea that always attacked her at the sight of blood still fresh, and the room continued to spin, though slowly.

Suddenly understanding her, Todd sat up straight on the couch. He wiped the drool from his mouth, started to stand up, stayed seated, shook his head. Finally he managed, "What are you talking about?"

"Van and Harlan and two others." Still whispering. "They're down in the office. They've been shot dead."

This was enough for Todd, finally waking up enough to

put the pieces together. "Holy shit. Do you think he's still here?"

"I don't know."

"If he killed them, why didn't he kill us?"

That answer was obvious, at least to her, and she thought after a few moments Todd would get it, too. They didn't have time to talk, not like this, not with four dead men (and possibly more) downstairs.

"We have to leave," Elizabeth said. The room had finally stopped spinning, and she didn't need to hold onto anything to keep her balance anymore. "Now."

Five seconds, that's all it took for Todd to get his bearings straight, and then he was up and headed for the door. He paused and turned back to her.

"Where's that gun Harlan gave you?"

She already had it in her hand, having grabbed it the moment she reentered the room.

"Do you ... want me to take it? To, like, go first?"

She appreciated the gesture but knew Todd wouldn't be able to handle a gun, not if it came to the point where he actually had to fire it.

"That's okay," she said. "You can carry the books instead."

They went down the stairs, pausing on the second floor, staying still and quiet and listening for any sound.

"Stay here," she whispered.

"Where are you going?"

"I forgot something."

The screensaver hadn't come on yet and Van's office was still illuminated with that bright artificial light. She could see Harlan and Van and the two men on the couch more clearly now despite the fact her nausea threatened to return. Elizabeth managed to keep it down, though, and strode right up to Van's desk and grabbed the BlackBerry.

Back in the hallway, Elizabeth took the lead again. They went down the stairs, then through the kitchen to the door that led into the alley where Todd had moved the Prius earlier.

"Give me your keys," she said, holding out her free hand.

He shook his head. "I'll drive."

"You don't know these streets like I do."

Without anymore objection, Todd reached into his pocket, dug the keys out, handed them to her. They were in the hybrid moments later, the engine started, Elizabeth throwing the car in gear.

"Hold on."

She punched the gas, jerking them forward, taking them down the alleyway. Out onto the street, not slowing at all, an oncoming car having to swerve out of the way and blaring its horn at them.

"Slow down," Todd said, gripping the caution bar, but Elizabeth didn't slow down, swerving between the little traffic that was out on the street at this time of night.

Todd said, "You don't want us to get pulled over by the cops, do you?" and that was what reminded her that she was in a major city, fleeing from a murder scene.

She lifted her foot off the gas. She hadn't been in this city in years, but suddenly she remembered every street, every alleyway, every shortcut.

They made it to the highway five minutes later. They took the onramp headed east. The sky was still dark but beginning to show light off on the horizon.

"Son of a bitch," Elizabeth said suddenly. She began smacking the steering wheel with every word. "Son—of—a—bitch!"

"Elizabeth," Todd said quietly.

"He was right there. He was right fucking there. Which means Matthew was there, too."

"You don't know that."

"But I do. I feel it."

"Feel what?"

And that was when the BlackBerry rang.

28

"Despite what you may think," Cain said, "I did not enjoy doing that back there."

Elizabeth was conscious of Todd watching her from the passenger seat, his body tense. "Doing what back there?"

"Don't be coy. If you didn't know what I was talking about, you wouldn't be back on the road like you are now."

"You didn't have to kill them."

"You're right, I didn't have to. But you forced my hand."

"How?"

"You went there and got them involved. I suppose when I told you no police, I thought you would be smart enough to know that meant no anybody."

"They were no threat to you."

"But they were. At first I didn't understand why you had gone there, but after some quick research, it all made sense. Donovan Riley wasn't the most upright citizen, as you no doubt already know."

"That was still no reason to kill him."

"What about those hackers? What purpose were they going to serve?" When she didn't answer, Cain said, "Exactly.

If you don't want to play our little game fairly, then there is going to be consequences."

"I want to talk to my son."

"No."

"Yes. You want those trophies, I want to hear my son's voice."

"You want to hear his voice? Okay, then. Listen."

There was a pause, and then she heard movement, the sound of tape ripping away from skin. She heard Matthew but just barely, his voice faint, only it quickly grew stronger as he began to scream.

"No!" she shouted. "Don't!"

Todd was visibly shaking beside her, his eyes wide.

Matthew's screaming went on for only a few more seconds but to Elizabeth it felt like days. Then the screaming suddenly ceased, and Cain spoke again.

"There, you wanted to hear your son, you heard him."

"You bastard."

"I don't know what kind of game you think you're playing here, Elizabeth, but it's not going to work. I will teach you not to fuck with me."

She hesitated, then said, "Clarence, please don't do this."

"Shut up! You say one more word and I will make your son scream again."

Elizabeth bit her lip hard enough to draw blood. Tears had begun to well in her eyes, blurring the highway in front of her.

"I'm beginning to think I'm giving you too much leeway. I thought one hundred hours was more than kind, but it seems you have decided to take advantage of my generosity."

There was another pause, this one much longer, Elizabeth at first thinking that either Cain had disconnected or else she had lost the signal. She heard a beep in her ear, pulled the phone away, and saw there was a new text message.

"There," Cain said. "That should motivate you a little more, don't you think?"

Then he did disconnect and Elizabeth immediately clicked on the icon to show her the picture.

Her foot instantly lifted from the gas pedal. Her hand fell away from the steering wheel. Her body was weightless and she was just sitting there, staring at the image on the screen.

"Elizabeth!" Todd shouted, grabbing the wheel and trying to keep the car in their lane.

Elizabeth barely paid any attention. Her entire focus was now on the image on the BlackBerry's screen: her son still tied to that bed, still with the tape over his mouth and the explosive collar around his neck, the bright red digits above his head now reading **70:00:00**.

29

By the time they passed over the Pennsylvania state line it was almost noon. Todd was driving now, Elizabeth in the passenger seat paging through the two books. The sky was clear and the sun was bright and Todd wore his sunglasses. He didn't have an extra pair for Elizabeth but she didn't care, keeping her head down and her gaze focused on the pages.

For the past seven hours they had barely spoken. Three times Elizabeth had cried, both for her son and for what had happened to Van and Harlan. There was a time when those men had been the only family she had, and now because of her they were dead.

Every hour the BlackBerry dinged, and Elizabeth would glance at the picture and then quickly set the phone back down on the middle console. She felt like one of Pavlov's dogs —every time she heard that familiar and innocuous ding, she started to tremble.

At one point she was paging through *Never Coming Home: The Edward Piccioni Murders* and sighed heavily, shaking her head.

"What's wrong?" Todd asked.

She didn't answer for the longest time, just staring down at the book. Finally she said, "There's a chapter in here about how me and Eddie met. Only it's half right. I'd completely forgotten it was in here."

"What part did they get right?"

"Basically that we were in college. This author, he interviewed some people we went to school with but who weren't even close friends."

"So the author was being a lazy reporter?"

"Either that or he just didn't give a shit. To be honest, I can't blame him. Besides Eddie, who was to say he didn't have it right? As far as anybody knew, I was gone and never coming back."

There was a silence, and then Todd said, "Can I ask you something?"

"What?"

"Why did you bring them with you?" Meaning the books.

She glanced down at the paperback in her lap. The other was on the floor by her feet. The gun—Harlan's gun—was locked tight in the glove box.

"Like Van had said, I need to freshen up on my history. I never thought I'd go back home. Not even once did the idea cross my mind. And now we'll be there in"—she glanced at the dashboard clock—"probably four hours or so, and I don't remember what happened."

"You don't remember?"

"I remember bits and pieces, but for the most part I forced myself to forget. It was just ... a different life. It wasn't my life anymore. I kept telling myself I had nothing to do with it, that I would never have to think about it again."

"So then reading those books—at least, that book—it helps?"

"It brings some of it back. Most of it's bullshit, though."

"Like what?"

"Just the stuff they say about Eddie. Like one time in high school he had gotten suspended for pulling some prank. The author says his teachers should have seen the signs then. I mean, he wasn't the only one. The prank—and the author doesn't go into detail about what kind of prank it was—it involved two other kids. The author doesn't even mention them. So apparently Eddie's teachers shouldn't have considered the possibility there would someday be trouble with them, just Eddie."

Todd had begun his ritual of chewing coffee beans again. He started to place another one in his mouth but paused, his mouth hanging open.

"What?" Elizabeth asked.

"Nothing."

"It's clearly not nothing. What is it?"

"You mentioned the author talking about warning signs. You never noticed any yourself?"

She slumped in her own seat, staring now out her window. "No, I didn't. For the longest time I asked myself how that was possible. I mean, I was with him the most. We shared a bed together. We shared a bank account together. I should have seen the signs, right? I should have noticed something was going on. In a way"—and here she wiped at her eyes, her voice breaking—"in a way, I'm responsible for those women's deaths. In a way, I killed them, too."

"Don't do that."

"Don't do what?"

"Blame yourself. It's not your fault."

"But what if I'd been more observant? What if I noticed the signs right away? I could have done something."

"Like what?"

"I could have called the FBI myself. Had him taken away."

Todd started to say something but shook his head instead.

Elizabeth said, "When these books first came out, I wanted nothing to do with them. But my curiosity got the better of me. Every time I went into a bookstore, I managed to find at least one of them. I'd flip through a dozen other books on the shelf before picking up that one. And then I'd read a page and get angry and want to tear the book in half."

"Did you read the one by Clarence Applegate?"

"Unfortunately."

Todd hesitated again in speaking.

"What is it?"

"Before, after we left the bar and Cain had called, you called him Clarence. What did he say to that?"

"He didn't say anything."

"So he didn't deny it?"

She looked at him. "Go ahead and say it."

"You think Cain is really Clarence Applegate."

"At this point, I'm not ruling anybody out."

"But ... he was a husband of one of the victims, right? I mean, I know he wrote that book and everything, but why would he do this?"

Elizabeth stared back out her window. She hadn't been back to this part of the country in five years. She'd forgotten just how beautiful this region was, especially during the fall. The fields and the mountains and the trees with their yellow and orange and red leaves.

"Do you really want to know about Clarence Applegate?" she asked.

"Yes."

"Okay. Then the first thing you need to know—the only thing, really—is the guy is a complete psychopath."

30

Clarence Applegate hadn't always been a psychopath. Not in his formative years, those in middle school and high school and even college. He was bright, confident, and, despite his unfortunate name, surprisingly good-looking. He married his high school sweetheart, though they had broken up after school and had gone their separate ways during college, both attending different universities. It was by chance that they ran into each other two years after graduation, both having just dealt with recent breakups, that they decided to get together for dinner and reminisce about old times. A year later they married. Three years after that Elizabeth's husband raped and murdered Clarence's wife.

"How do you know all that stuff?" Todd asked. "You know, about high school and college and when they got married."

"It was in his book."

"He wrote every single detail like that?"

"Well, yeah. What do you expect? The man's not only an opportunist, he's a narcissist."

That's not all Clarence Applegate was. He worked as a

loan officer at a prestigious banking firm in Atlanta. That was his day job, but what he really wanted to do—his ultimate goal in life—was to become a published author.

Ever since middle school he had been writing stories. He kept sending them to magazines—places ranging from *The New Yorker* to *Ellery Queen's Mystery Magazine* to small literary journals that paid only in copies—but nobody would take his work. Mostly all he received were form rejections, though sometimes a generous editor would scratch out a short note with words of encouragement. He knew the road to publication was not an easy one. Some people got lucky. Mostly everyone else had to work their asses off and even then they weren't guaranteed a spot in what he regarded as Publication Heaven.

But that didn't keep Clarence Applegate from dreaming.

Every morning he would wake up early and write for an hour, and every evening, before bed, he would sit at the computer and write for another hour. He was relentless, and kept more consistent hours than most professional writers (a claim he had no basis to make but one he liked to use to break the ice at social gatherings), but despite all that, he still was never able to sell any of his work.

And then his wife was murdered, and all media attention was focused on him—Clarence Applegate, Grieving Husband Extraordinaire—and something in the back of his mind (this part Elizabeth admitted was her own speculation) whispered a helpful reminder: *All publicity is good publicity.*

Within a week he had come up with a book proposal about life seen through the eyes of a husband whose wife was murdered by a serial killer. A week later he had managed to secure an agent for the project. At first there wasn't much interest from publishers, but then months later a team of FBI agents arrived one Saturday morning to the home of Edward and Elizabeth Piccioni, and suddenly the idea of Clarence Applegate's book wasn't so uninteresting. Within days a small bidding war took place between a handful of publishers for a book not even written yet.

Todd said, "So how much of his book has to do with your husband?"

"Very little. Clarence mostly talks about himself, giving anecdotes from high school and college, and how his dream was to become a writer. About halfway through he actually starts talking about the murder. How his wife was away on a business trip. How she didn't call him one night and when he called her she didn't answer and he got worried. After a day when he didn't hear anything he became extremely worried and started making calls. Eventually he got the police involved."

"So what," Todd said, "he also thought of himself as a detective?"

"The book makes you think that. He goes into a lot of detail about the initial investigation. But I remember reading online from some of the real detectives involved how he played a very minor role. Actually, if I remember this right, one of the detectives said Clarence acted more like an annoying gnat than anything else."

"I still don't get it."

"Get what?"

"How you become involved. I mean, to the point where he would do ... *this*."

Elizabeth produced a mirthless grin. "This is the part of the story where the psychopathic nature of Clarence Applegate really begins to shine."

As expected, once the FBI had come for Edward Piccioni, the media began its circus. This was when Clarence's agent began shopping around the proposal again. Clarence by that point began studying serial killers. He knew not all of them had to have nicknames—in fact, the only ones who seemed to have nicknames were those never captured—but he thought the public loved a good villain, one with a good moniker, and so he came up with The Widower Maker.

It wasn't a good nickname. Many thought it was stupid. But Clarence fought to have it brought into the mainstream. He argued that Edward Piccioni had raped and killed only young married women. And by doing that, he left only widowers behind—children, too, but as he wasn't a father he didn't seem to harp on that aspect.

This was just days after Eddie's arrest. Clarence had already started his own website, had created a sort of following. Some of his short stories—the ones he considered his best—he posted on the site for people to read. Again, any publicity was good publicity.

And then Elizabeth Piccioni and her son disappeared, and all eyes, for some reason, turned toward Clarence Applegate. It did not take him long to come up with the theory, no matter how outrageous it was. Clarence may not have been a very good writer, but he certainly knew the market, understood what sold, and commercial success—the very thing he craved—mostly hinged on the idea of sensationalism. That's what got people going, what made them start frothing at the mouth, and so he was the very first to put it out there on his website:

Elizabeth Piccioni was obviously her husband's partner in murder.

Todd shifted in his seat. "And people went with it, just like that?"

They were on the Pennsylvania Turnpike now, about two hours away from Harrisburg.

Elizabeth said, "What do you expect? Most people are sheep."

Whether or not Clarence Applegate actually believed his claim to be true, nobody could say for sure, but he suddenly made it a priority. He created another website, one called *Where In The World Is Elizabeth Piccioni,* and he offered a reward for any information leading to her capture. The police and FBI did not quite agree with the idea, though they did note they were very interested in getting in contact with Elizabeth. Was she a person of interest? They never said one way or another, but they did acknowledge that she was a witness.

Very quickly Clarence Applegate began to understand the media. He learned that the more outrageous he became, the more publicity was pushed his way. He began making more claims about Elizabeth. How she was really the brains behind the whole killing operation (that's what he called it, too: *the killing operation*). How if anything, Edward Piccioni was a helpless puppet in Elizabeth's diabolical game of murder (again, that's how he put it: *diabolical game of murder*). What's more, he claimed their newly born son was a demon seed, that Edward and Elizabeth's plan was to groom him into the family business to become the ultimate serial killer.

It was at that point the media began distancing themselves from Clarence Applegate. His fifteen minutes of fame was finished, as far as anyone was concerned. But he still had the book contract and he still had his websites and he still had his stories. And as the days turned into weeks and the weeks into months, people began to forget all about Elizabeth Piccioni.

But not Clarence.

He posted on his website how he was making it his mission to see that the evil bitch (again, his phrase) be brought to justice. He speculated on the different ways Elizabeth was raising her son to become another serial killer. He even played with the idea that Elizabeth fed her son human blood.

Elizabeth—at this point already living on the third floor of Riley's Pub—began seeing the awful things Clarence Applegate was posting about her and her son. Having just run away from a life where her husband had raped and murdered six women (if not more) to find that now she was being accused of not just participating but also being the brains behind the entire thing ... it was just way too much for her to handle.

Todd said, "So he shifted the entire focus off your husband and placed it on you."

"He didn't have much of a choice. The other book—one written by an actual true crime writer—was already given a release date. Clarence had barely written one hundred pages of his. He knew he had to stay with the idea he had proposed, about life through the eyes of a husband whose wife was murdered by a serial killer, but he was a lazy researcher, even lazier than the other guy. He didn't want to look into my husband's history. Besides, he figured the other book would show that stuff, so he wanted to do something different."

"Let me guess—he said you were the main cause."

"That's right. He even tried to take the nickname he had given Eddie and give it to me, tried calling me The Widower Maker. He speculated about what had driven me to want to kill. He did very little research into my own life. Mostly, he contacted people who had known me—close friends, past students—asking them for their opinion. Most of them told him he was crazy. Some though ... some actually went along with the idea."

"What about your family?"

"My mother was never mentioned. She had probably died by the time he started writing the book."

"What about your brother?"

"He was still over in Africa at the time. And I'm sure if Clarence had managed to track him down, Jim would have told him to go shove it up his ass."

"So this guy, he has this book published, and then what?"

"His overextended fifteen minutes of fame was over. It had taken him too long to write the book, and by the time he completed the thing nobody cared anymore. The publisher canceled the contract. Clarence's agent parted ways with him. Desperate, he published the book himself and sold copies off his website. He continued what he claimed was his rightful duty to bring the true Widower Maker to justice. He began offering a reward on his website to anyone with any information leading to my eventual capture and arrest. The amount started small, like one thousand dollars, and grew over time."

"How much?"

"A lot. Last I saw, it was over one hundred thousand dollars."

"*What*? How was he able to raise that much money?"

"By his followers, people who believed what he said about me. He accepted donations. All the money went to the reward."

There was a brief silence, and then Todd said, "How many followers does he have?"

"I don't know the exact number. But the reward"—she shook her head—"over the years it became less of a reward for my capture than it became something else."

"What's that?"

Elizabeth said, "The money became a bounty for my head."

31

It didn't hit Elizabeth until they had passed Carlisle that today was Saturday. She thought about what she and Matthew should be doing today. How on Saturdays they slept in until ten o'clock when she made pancakes or French toast or waffles (depending on what Matthew was in the mood for), with eggs and sausage. They would eat at the kitchen table and talk about their week at school and then they would shower and dress and go do some kind of activity. If there was something appropriate and interesting playing at the theater, they would go see a movie. If the weather was nice enough, they would play miniature golf. If the weather wasn't too nice, they might go to the bowling alley. Then it was back home for a nap, where she would let Matthew sleep an extra hour while she tried to get some chores done. Like cleaning the kitchen or bathroom, always alternating week by week, squirting Soft Scrub into a sponge and scrubbing down the floors and tub and sink. Then it was a late lunch, either grilled cheese and soup or hamburgers and macaroni and cheese, and afterward they would sit on the couch and Elizabeth would read aloud from a book they'd gotten from the library.

At least that was how their Saturdays had gone until recently, when Todd entered the picture, accompanying them to the movie theater or mini-golf or bowling. Elizabeth remembered one time at the mall, Matthew walking between them, grabbing hold of both of their hands like they were an actual family.

"Are you hungry?" Todd asked.

She shook her head. "Are you?"

"A little."

"Stop whenever you want."

"We're not that much farther though, right?"

A tightness formed in her chest at the knowledge that home was less than two hours away.

"No," she said softly, "we're not."

A little while later, having passed through Harrisburg, Elizabeth took a breath and shifted in her seat so her back was to the window.

Todd said, "What's wrong?"

"Nothing."

"Elizabeth."

Still keeping her back to the window, she said, "There's something coming up off the highway in the next minute or so I don't want to see."

Todd opened his mouth but quickly shut it. By this point he knew better than to ask questions. If Elizabeth wanted to tell him, she'd tell him.

Fifty-two seconds later—she was counting them off in her head—Todd said, "You mean that self-storage place?"

She couldn't help it, she glanced out her window and there it was, right off the highway, protected by a tall chain-link fence, a sprawling space of storage units. It looked as if in the past ten years they had expanded, and there was a new sign, brighter colors exclaiming *U-STORE-IT, WE-PROTECT-IT.*

It was there, right beside them for only a few moments, and then it was gone.

"More and more stuff is starting to remind me of Eddie. Like in the next couple miles, there will be an exit that would take you to a nice fancy restaurant. He took me there one year for our anniversary."

"So that self-storage place," Todd prompted.

"Eddie and I both graduated from Penn State, him one year before me. He wanted to stay close to me my last year and got an apartment near State College. He used up all his savings to stay there. When I graduated, I found a long-term substitute-teaching job in Harrisburg. Eddie still hadn't found a job yet, so we moved there. Problem was, we could only afford a very small apartment, just one bedroom, and our stuff ..."

"You guys kept it back at that place."

She nodded. "It was only for six months or so. By then I had found a teaching job in Lanton. Eddie applied to a bunch of places but couldn't seem to find any work. Finally a friend of his said he could get him a job working at the same pharmaceutical company, only it was down in Philadelphia."

"How far is that from Lanton?"

"About an hour and a half, two hours, depending on traffic."

Todd gave a short whistle. "Talk about a commute."

Elizabeth didn't know why but she smiled. "Yeah. And the crazy thing? He never complained about it. Not once."

She went quiet suddenly.

Todd said, "What wrong?"

But Elizabeth didn't answer. She'd spotted something

coming up on the side of the highway, what was no doubt a deer carcass.

"Elizabeth?"

She shook her head and closed her eyes so she wouldn't be forced to see the blood.

32

The closer they got to Lanton, the more her memory began to play tricks on her. In fields where there used to be just grass and trees were now endless developments of houses, and then she wondered if whether those developments had actually been there before she left. Strip malls hosted the same Radio Shack and Blockbuster and Chinese restaurant, though there were one or two stores that looked new and she couldn't tell which was which. The Toyota dealership was gone, replaced now by Honda. There was a new Best Buy, a new Olive Garden (the other one, from what she remembered, was on the other side of town), and at least two new McDonald's. There was so much more but she was seeing it all too fast and then wondering whether any of it was really new or just her imagination.

Though Todd maintained the speed limit it felt like they were moving at a crawl. Elizabeth found herself leaning forward in her seat, as if that might help make the Prius move more quickly.

There was only one person she could think to see—the only person who had the best shot of getting her in to see

Eddie—and she gave Todd directions to Foreman's. Like back in Indianapolis, she suddenly remembered the roads and streets and could picture them perfectly in her mind.

After ten minutes they came to Foreman's street. He lived in a development much like everyone else in Lanton. The houses all looking different but also looking the same.

Before Todd even had the hybrid parked in the driveway, Elizabeth had her seatbelt off.

"Stay here. I'll be right back."

Then she was outside, striding up the walkway to the porch, listening to the stillness of the neighborhood, breathing in the air, and she didn't know why but she thought there was a different texture to the oxygen here than there had been in Kansas. She hurried up the steps, came to the door, rang the doorbell once, waited a moment, then rang it again.

Elizabeth glanced back at the Prius in the driveway. She thought about the best way to introduce Todd, the delicate manner in which she would explain their present condition, and then the door opened and Elizabeth turned back, already smiling, already opening her mouth to say hello.

An older black woman stood in the doorway, squinting back at her through a pair of reading glasses. "Can I help you?"

Elizabeth opened her mouth, shut it, opened her mouth again and said, "I'm looking for Michael Foreman."

"I beg your pardon?"

Elizabeth thought fast, said, "We're from out of town," motioning at the Prius. "I used to work at Michael Foreman's law firm. We were friends. Last I knew, he still lived here."

The woman shook her head. "I'm sorry, but my husband and I moved in here about three, four years ago."

"Oh." Elizabeth glanced around the porch, at the pumpkins and the decorative wooden chair facing the street. "You wouldn't happen to know where he moved to, would you?"

"I do not." The woman gave her a particular look. "But if he's your friend, wouldn't he have told you his new address?"

"We've been out of contact for a while. My husband and I were just passing through, and I thought I'd surprise him. I'm sorry to have bothered you."

"No problem at all." The woman smiled. "You have a blessed day now."

When Elizabeth returned to the car, Todd said, "Wrong house?"

"Apparently he moved."

"Now what?"

"Now we try Sheila."

Sheila Rodgers had been her best friend. From day one when Elizabeth started at the middle school they had hit it off. They were not part of the same team—the seventh grade was split up into three teams—but since Sheila taught Computer Science and saw every class, she knew a great deal about all the students and teachers and other faculty and made it possible for Elizabeth to quickly learn the ins and outs.

Sheila was very web-savvy. She had created a website designed specifically for her students, so if they had any questions at home, they could log onto the website and receive almost any answer. Sometimes it amazed Elizabeth just how much Sheila knew. Elizabeth was no novice when it came to the Internet, but she was content with simply using email and occasional searches on Google. She had no interest in social interaction. So she was amazed by Sheila's knowledge of computers and the Internet. Once Sheila even showed her a tracking program on her school website, how every time a student visited the site she could tell whether or not that student was using dial-up or cable, the type of browser, sometimes even the location in the county where that student was right that moment.

Sheila had once told Elizabeth if she thought that was scary, some websites can even track the location of your street, what floor you're on, what room.

Elizabeth and Eddie had been regulars at the Rodgers', making almost monthly appearances at dinners and other social gatherings. Eddie had gotten along well with Sheila's husband, Bill, as well as their five-year-old twins, Caleb and Tyler. When Elizabeth eventually became pregnant, it was Sheila who helped her along every step of the way, telling her which foods to eat and which books to buy and, when Thomas was born, the secret mothering tricks that couldn't be found in any baby books.

When Todd pulled into the driveway fifteen minutes after leaving the house Michael Foreman once owned, Elizabeth was relieved to see the name RODGERS still labeled the mailbox. Like before, she threw off her seatbelt and had her door open before Todd even had a chance to stop the car. Moments later she was at the front door, ringing the doorbell, murmuring, "Come on, come on, come on," under her breath.

What she would say when Sheila answered the door, Elizabeth didn't quite know, but she imagined Sheila would do a double take. Sheila's own mind would insist that what she was seeing was not real, that it couldn't be real, that her old best friend Elizabeth was gone and would never come back. But that would only last a few seconds, enough for the mind to then acknowledge the fact that yes, Elizabeth was really here, and then Sheila would step forward and open her arms to embrace her.

The door opened, and there stood a little boy, almost ten years old, one of the twins Caleb or Tyler, and she smiled, felt her eyes starting to water, as she said, "Hi there, sweetie. Is your mommy home?"

A voice carried through the house, a woman's voice saying, "Tyler, who is it?" and then saying, "Caleb, put that down," and then the sound of footsteps approached and Elizabeth braced herself for seeing Sheila for the first time in five years.

Only the woman who appeared behind Tyler wasn't Sheila.

Sheila, from what Elizabeth remembered, had long dark hair and was well rounded, not fat exactly but not skinny either. This woman here was skinny but in a healthy way, a woman who probably did yoga or Pilates every day, with her blond hair pulled back into a ponytail.

"Can I help you?" this woman who wasn't Sheila asked.

"I'm"—Elizabeth cleared her throat—"I'm looking for Sheila."

Something in the woman's face changed. She leaned down and said into Tyler's ear, "Go back in and play with your brother, okay?" and when Tyler scampered away the woman crossed her arms and tilted her head at Elizabeth. "What's this about?"

"It's important. I'm an old friend of hers, and I really need to see her."

"She doesn't live here anymore."

Elizabeth frowned. "What about Bill?"

"Bill and that woman divorced years ago," the woman said, her tone almost venomous when she used the phrase *that woman*.

"Is Bill home? He might be able to answer my question."

"What question?"

"I'm looking for another friend of mine. His name is Michael Foreman. He—"

"How dare you," the woman said, her voice suddenly sharp. "Coming to our house, knocking on our door, asking for her and then him. Just who do you think you are?"

Elizabeth didn't know what to say. This entire conversation had taken a completely different direction in which she had imagined. She said, "Look, I don't know what your issue is, but I really need to speak to Sheila or Michael Foreman. Do you know how I can contact either of them?"

The woman continued to stand there, glaring back at her.

"What about Bill?" Elizabeth said, her patience starting to wane. "Let me speak to him if you don't think you're capable of helping me."

The woman's jaw tightened. "He's not home," she said through gritted teeth. Then, "Wait here," and she walked away, leaving the door open. She was gone for maybe a minute, while Elizabeth could hear the twins running around inside the house, shouting and laughing. Then the woman appeared with a Post-It in hand and held it out to Elizabeth. "That's her address, okay?"

Elizabeth took the Post-It and stared at the woman's loopy cursive script, and before she could say anything (even a half-hearted thank you), the woman had shut the door in her face.

33

The address the woman had given her took them to an apartment complex on the other side of Lanton, the side that they had entered nearly a half hour before. Elizabeth was immediately put in mind of Summer Ridge, her own apartment complex back in Kansas, cookie cutter buildings all huddled close together, the only thing distinguishing them the different colors—reds, blues, greens, yellows—of the doors and window frames.

Todd drove them through the sprawling serpentine of townhouses until they spotted 178. This time Elizabeth waited until they were parked before she unclipped her seatbelt. The entire drive, she had been replaying her conversation with the woman—the new Mrs. Rodgers, apparently—and none of it made sense. The last time Elizabeth had seen Sheila, her best friend had been happily married and very much in love with her husband.

She walked up to 178—this door was painted a faded red —and knocked. Like before, she glanced back at where Todd had parked the car, imagining all the different things that might happen when Sheila opened the door. And like before, when the door finally did open, Sheila was not the one standing there.

"Help you?"

A man stood in the doorway, big and bald and wearing only a towel wrapped around his waist. He had a tattoo of an eagle over his left bicep.

"I'm looking for Sheila," she said, then quickly added: "I'm an old friend."

The man stepped back and shouted, "Yo, Sheila, somebody's here to see you!"

"Be right there," a voice called back, and the man looked at Elizabeth just once and shrugged and walked away, leaving the door open.

Elizabeth didn't move. She just stood there, waiting, until forty seconds later a woman came down the steps, a big-breasted, heavily-makeup-faced woman wearing a bathrobe who looked nothing like her best friend.

This woman, this woman who could not be Sheila Rodgers, saying, "Hi, can I help—"

Their eyes locked then, Elizabeth's and Sheila's, because yes, of course this was Sheila, this was her old best friend, her dearest friend in the entire world, and so what if she was wearing way too much foundation, so what if the red of her lipstick was enough to make Elizabeth cringe? This was Sheila, Sheila Rodgers, and nothing—not the day-old perm, not the apparent work she'd had done on her breasts, not the smell of sex wafting off her body—changed that at all.

"Liz?" Sheila's tone was incredulous, just as it was to be expected, though somehow her voice managed to raise an octave on the end of that simple one-syllable word. "Is it—is it really you?"

Elizabeth said, "You need to get me in contact with Michael."

Something changed in Sheila's face, her nose crinkling just slightly, and she glanced back inside, then stepped out and shut the door behind her. "What are you talking about? What's wrong?"

"I'm in some trouble. That's all you need to know. And it's very important I speak with Michael."

"How's Thomas? Where have you *been*?"

"Sheila, please, I need to speak with Michael. Can you tell me where he lives?"

Sheila's face fell, and she studied Elizabeth for a few seconds. "What kind of trouble are you in? Legal trouble?"

"It's best if you don't know the details."

"Liz, you show up at my door after five years ..." She shook her head. "I'm trying to get my thoughts collected."

"When did you and Bill separate?" The question was out of her mouth before she could stop herself. "Sorry, I shouldn't have—"

"If you're in so much trouble," Sheila said, crossing her arms over her chest, "why don't you go to the police?"

The sudden hard tone wasn't one Elizabeth had expected, not from the woman who had once been her best friend and who had helped her escape her old life with the idea to start a new one. This hadn't turned out anything like she had imagined, and so she crossed her own arms over her own chest and glared back at Sheila.

"Do you or do you not know where Michael Foreman now lives?"

Sheila glared back at her for another second or two, before nodding slowly. "I do. And when I tell you, you're not going to believe it."

It was true: Elizabeth didn't believe it. None of it made sense. She felt like a storybook character, falling down a hole or walking through a wall or going through some kind of portal that brought her to a world that was similar but completely unlike the one she remembered.

When she returned to the car, Todd said, "What's wrong?"

She didn't answer.

"Elizabeth"—he reached over, placed a hand on her leg—"you're trembling."

"Drive," she said.

By now Todd had learned it best not to ask questions and shoved the Prius into gear. After a couple miles he asked where they were going and she started giving him directions. It felt strange, giving him directions like this, especially to this particular address. But then minutes later they arrived, and the house looked no different than the last time she had seen it.

"This one?" Todd asked, pulling into the driveway.

"Yes." Elizabeth couldn't take her gaze off the house. "I can't believe he's now living here."

"Why? Who lived here before?"

"I did."

34

The last time she had seen Michael Foreman was in the rearview mirror of the car he had purchased for her for five hundred dollars, a rundown Dodge Neon that was hardly a promise to take her halfway across the country. He had been forty-one then, already had a gut, was already losing his hair, and wore glasses only for reading.

The man that opened the door now looked not five years older but at least ten, his gut still there, his hair almost all gone, and the glasses perched on his nose the kind a person wears from the moment they wake up in the morning to the moment they lie down to sleep at night.

He didn't seem at all surprised to find Elizabeth standing on his doorstep. He simply glanced past her at the Prius in the driveway, tilted his gaze back at her, and said, "I can't believe you actually showed up."

This wasn't quite the greeting Elizabeth had expected. "Sheila called you?"

"An FBI agent. He called earlier this morning. He said there was a chance I might see you."

"Why?"

"He wouldn't say. But he left his number. He said it's important that you call him immediately."

Elizabeth didn't know how to react to this news, so she didn't react at all. She said, "I'm in a lot of trouble."

Foreman nodded. "I assumed as much."

"Can we come in?"

"Sure," he said. "But who's we?"

It was Foreman's idea to switch out his car in the garage with the Prius. That way if anybody passed by on the street (such as, say, the police or FBI) all they would see was Foreman's second-rate Mercedes in the driveway.

Once they were inside, Elizabeth made quick introductions. Foreman nodded and smiled and shook Todd's hand like it was just any other day. Then he turned to her, his face all at once serious.

"Where's Thomas?"

She handed him the BlackBerry and gave him a condensed version of the past two days. Foreman listened carefully, his gaze focused on the BlackBerry screen, and when she was done, he said the exact thing she knew he would say.

"You need to contact the FBI."

"I can't."

"Why not?"

"If I do that, Cain will kill Matthew."

Foreman frowned. "Who?"

"Thomas," she said. "His name is now Matthew."

"Why are you here?"

"I thought that would be obvious by now."

"Such as?"

"Such as you need to get me in contact with Mark Webster."

"I don't think I can do that."

"You're going to have to."

They were standing in the living room, which hadn't changed at all since the day Elizabeth walked away from her old life. The carpet, the couch, the armchairs, even the coffee table—they were the exact same.

Foreman said, "You're wondering why I'm living in your old house, aren't you?"

Elizabeth nodded.

"I figured as much. But it's not as weird as you might think it is. At least not yet. Let me show you the basement."

———

The last time Elizabeth went down into a basement she had found a half-naked man strapped to a chair, an explosive collar around his neck. She knew she would find neither of those things here, not in this basement, but still her mind played tricks on her, telling her that while she might not find Reginald Moore tied to a chair, she might find somebody else.

Foreman led the way. He seemed to have trouble walking down the steps and needed to grip both railings tightly. At the bottom he paused, took a breath, turned to her.

"As you can see, I did my best to keep them as organized as possible."

She had about ten more steps to go, her view of the basement itself blocked by the sloping ceiling. She had no idea what he was talking about but then she reached the bottom and as she stared around the basement her heart skipped.

Plastic storage containers, hundreds and hundreds of

storage containers, stacked up and labeled by a deftly skilled hand in black Sharpie marker. One said, *Books: nonfiction.* Another said, *E's dress shoes.* A third, *Kitchen utensils.*

She took in the entire basement—all that was here were those storage containers, nothing else—and then she glanced at Todd. She could tell at once he saw the distress in her face. He gave her a questioning look, and she shook her head once and turned to Foreman. The light wasn't bad but still he appeared to have aged an additional five years in the space it took him to walk from the first floor down here to the basement. His face was wrinkled, he had bags under his eyes, and his shoulders appeared more slouched than ever.

"You kept everything?"

He nodded. "I didn't have much choice."

"What does that mean?"

"Until the whole thing happened with Eddie, I never knew there were so many people interested in the belongings of serial killers."

"Death collectors," Elizabeth said.

He nodded again. "Weeks after you had left, when it was clear you wouldn't be coming back, some people started trying to break into the house. It was just some kids at first, some teenagers, but then the police caught actual adults. One guy had driven five states away just to see the house. He said he didn't want much, just a coffee mug would do."

Foreman paused, and in that pause the silence that embraced them was a scary thing. Down here in a basement she had once called her own, surrounded not just by the house she had once lived in but by everything that had once been hers and Eddie's—even Matthew's back when he was named Thomas—she almost preferred to be back in Reginald Moore's basement. At least that, in the most morbid way, made some kind of sense. This here now, all these things that she had managed to forget, waiting for her like one day she would return looking for an old hair brush, unsettled her.

"It was Eddie's idea I buy the house. He contacted me through Mark Webster. He said he would rather have somebody he knew, a friend, buy and move into this place than a complete stranger who would do God knows what with it."

Elizabeth had to look away from him. She didn't like the idea at all that Foreman was here because her husband had asked him to be. Just like in her previous life, where Eddie had manipulated her, here now Eddie had manipulated Foreman.

Todd said, "So you agreed, just like that?"

"Of course not. I had a place of my own, had just paid off the mortgage a few years before. I was happy. But then Sheila and I started seeing each other."

Elizabeth looked up sharply. "You and Sheila dated?"

He stared back at her for a very long time before answering. "Yes, we did."

A thousand more questions flooded Elizabeth's mind—Elizabeth now remembering the way the new Mrs. Rodgers had tightened her jaw at even the mention of Foreman or Sheila—but before she could ask anything else, Todd spoke.

"So how much did Eddie sell you the house for?"

"A dollar."

"A dollar," Elizabeth repeated flatly.

Foreman nodded. "For the house and for everything in it. He just made me promise that I wouldn't throw any of it out in case ... well, you know, in case you ever came back."

Elizabeth found herself with her arms crossed again. She didn't like it down here. She didn't like being back in this house at all. And now, with what Foreman had just told her, which was what Eddie had told him, that he should keep everything in case she ever returned ...

Shivering, Elizabeth said, "Let's go back upstairs. Being down here is really starting to give me the creeps."

35

Todd asked Foreman if he had a computer with a working Internet connection. When Elizabeth gave him a questioning look, he said, "Isn't it strange that the FBI is already involved? That probably means there's news of you. I just want to see how bad it is."

Foreman led him to the study at the end of the hall—what had once been Eddie's study—and then when Elizabeth said she wanted to get some fresh air, Foreman walked with her out to the back deck.

But the moment they were outside she remembered the deck they were now standing on, how it had been one of Eddie's few pet projects when they had first bought the house. How when it came to "man things"—hunting, sports, cars—he had very little interest, and would instead rather read a nonfiction book about one of the World Wars. But the idea of building a deck, one grand enough that it boasted a railing and even had slots where Elizabeth could put flowers, well, that was something he was determined to do. And he did do it, though it took nearly two years, and once it was done he insisted they sit out here late at night with all the lights off in the house and stare up at the sky and watch the stars, hoping to maybe spot one falling.

Despite the surprisingly warm temperature, Elizabeth crossed her arms and hugged her elbows.

"You need to call that FBI agent," Foreman said.

"I already told you that's not an option."

"How do you think this is going to turn out? Honestly, when you stop and really think about it, do you see this having a happy ending?"

"I have a plan."

"And what's that?"

"Like I told you, I need to get in contact with Mark Webster."

"And what is he going to do?"

"Hopefully get me in to see Eddie. When Eddie finds out what's happened, he'll tell me where to find his ..." But she shook her head, refusing to say the word.

"Do you actually believe that? Do you actually believe that your serial killer husband is going to give a shit about you?"

"Not me, no. But his son? I think so, yes."

Foreman shook his head. "You're wasting your time. Mark Webster won't help you."

"How do you know?"

"You were his key witness. The defense had nobody else to put up there to talk on Eddie's behalf."

"Even if I had stayed, I would have refused to speak on Eddie's behalf."

"Listen, the long and the short of it is Mark Webster was pretty ticked when you up and vanished. There he was, a young up and coming lawyer with a national case, and his only witness disappeared. He wasn't happy. I very highly doubt he will help you now."

Elizabeth's arms were still across her chest, and she hugged herself even more. In a soft voice she said, "Could you talk to him for me?"

"It won't work."

"Please."

Foreman sighed. "He's not even in the area anymore. Last I heard, a law firm up in Manhattan hired him."

Elizabeth didn't like where this conversation was headed. The entire ride here, she had had ideas, thoughts, theories on how this could all turn out. Everything that had seemed so simple just hours ago was now so very complex, and while Foreman was the one telling her the reality of the situation, she knew she had been fooling herself all along.

Staring past Foreman at the house next door, she said, "Do the Greers still live there?"

Foreman obviously knew what she meant, but he still turned to glance at the house anyway. "No, they moved out two years ago. A young couple lives there now, named Padron."

"What about the Rafalowskis?"

"They're still next door. In fact, they're probably home right now. We shouldn't be standing out here in case one of them sees you."

"Think they'd recognize me?"

"I can't imagine they wouldn't."

"So I haven't managed to change my appearance at all?"

Foreman hesitated a beat. "You look just like the Elizabeth Piccioni I knew."

Elizabeth was quiet for a moment. "What happened between you and Sheila?"

Something changed in Foreman's face. It was an almost imperceptible change, the sides of his mouth tensing for just an instant as he clenched his teeth, and then it was gone.

"Never mind," Elizabeth said. "It's none of my business."

Michael Foreman was a widower. His wife, Janice, had been a beautiful and petite woman who, from every picture Elizabeth had ever seen, looked like she didn't even know what a frown was. She had died of a sudden aneurism nearly a decade ago. Foreman was devastated. From what Elizabeth had heard he had spent days in his house crying before, one day, he went into work like nothing had happened. Ever since then he had not dated or even gone on any social outing with a person of the opposite sex, as if even the idea of dating (or being with someone who might consider it a date) would be a direct slap in the face of Janice's memory.

But now Foreman looked nervous. No, strike that; he looked *extremely* nervous, like a kid on his first date walking up the porch steps, almost ready to ring the doorbell, preparing in his mind what he would say and do even though he knew that when it eventually happened none of it would go according to plan.

He cleared his throat. "A lot changed after you left. Your disappearance, we knew it would be a big deal, but not as big as it became. The police and FBI came to me and Sheila and everyone else who was close to you, asking us if we had any idea where you had gone. They knew someone had helped you and they more or less threatened that if they found out it was us we'd go to jail. And then that Applegate guy came out with his theory on how you were actually in cahoots with Eddie on the murders, and ..."

"Did you believe him?"

"What? No, of course not. But like I said, the whole thing was a mess. And Sheila and I, the secret we had, it was growing so big inside us, like a balloon ready to pop. We couldn't just stop thinking about it. So we started meeting for coffee, speculating about where you had gone. Then ..."

He was that nervous boy again, standing at the door, having just rung the doorbell, his palms sweating and his knees wobbly.

Elizabeth said, "What happened?"

He took a breath. "We had an affair. It was brief, lasted only a couple of weeks. Her husband found out. As you can imagine, he was furious. Even so, it looked like he was going to forgive her until he found out she was pregnant."

Elizabeth closed her eyes. Didn't know what to say. Sheila had been her best friend and she had had no idea, no idea at all about any of this, and it now made more sense why Sheila acted the way she did with her earlier.

"Wait," she said. "Why would Bill not just assume it was his?"

"Because after the twins he'd gotten a vasectomy."

"Oh."

Foreman nodded again. "From what Sheila told me, they had a big fight. Bill wanted her to get an abortion. She refused. He said he wanted a divorce. She said that was fine with her, she was in love with me anyway."

"She really said that?"

"That's what she told me."

Elizabeth was still having a hard time wrapping her mind around the idea of Michael Foreman and Sheila Rodgers not just being a couple but being intimate. Sheila at least ten years younger than Foreman, both nice enough people but completely different personalities. Sheila more forward, more direct, and Foreman, well, he was patient, the kind of person to let the cards lay where they may, which was strange because he also happened to be a very successful lawyer.

"Sheila gave up custody of the kids. She moved out and came to live with me. We ..." He paused. "You know I haven't been with anyone since Janice's death. I had promised myself I never would. Yes, I know some people think that's foolish, but it was just something I had promised myself and something I intended to keep. But Sheila ... I was in love with her. There was something about her that I just couldn't get out of my head. So she came to live with me and for several months we were very happy, even when the divorce went through and was finalized. We were together, and she was pregnant, and then..."

A breeze picked up, rustling the few leaves still in trees, the oak in the backyard suddenly reminding Elizabeth about Eddie, how he had said it would someday make a great tree in which to put a tree house for their son, didn't she agree?

"And then?" Elizabeth prompted.

"Our baby died four months after being born. He was a boy. We named him Bruce, after my father. He died of SIDS."

Elizabeth's hand went to her mouth. "Oh my God."

Foreman shrugged, now staring out at the backyard. "Do you remember the Greenwood Cemetery, the one along the highway toward that Walmart? There's this section near the back, hidden by trees, they call it the Baby Lot. That's where we buried him."

Elizabeth reached out and touched his arm. "Michael, I am so sorry."

He waved her off. "It's not your fault."

No, she thought, maybe not, but in a way it was and she thought both Foreman and Sheila knew it.

Foreman wiped at his eyes. "Anyway, afterward, Sheila and I, went our separate ways. In fact, we haven't seen each other in over a year."

"She's changed a lot."

"Has she? She won't talk to me anymore."

"Is she still teaching?"

"As far as I know she's still at the middle school."

"What did Sheila think about living in this house?"

"She got used to it. It was your brother who thought it was weird."

Hearing mention of her brother made Elizabeth's body go tense. Besides her mother, Jim was the only family she had, and she had left him behind without even a goodbye.

"He came here?"

Foreman nodded. "He went through all the containers down in the basement piece by piece. He said he was just curious to see what was left of you."

"When did this happen?"

"About a year after you had left. He had just come back from Africa. Well, officially."

"Officially?"

"The Peace Corps had allowed him a week off after"— Foreman cleared his throat—"your mom died."

Elizabeth closed her eyes. She said softly, "When did she die?"

Foreman didn't answer.

She opened her eyes, turned to him. "When?"

"Less than four months after you left."

A tear fell down her face, followed by another, then another. Elizabeth went to wipe them away but stopped. If she owed her mother anything, it was to shed some tears.

All this time she knew her mother had died—she had to have, the cancer was just too bad—but she had never learned the exact date. She had forced herself not to look online every day, searching for her mother's obituary, for fear that her mother's death would bring her back home. Elizabeth just prayed that when her mother went it would be quickly and without much pain, and that, when she eventually saw her mother again in whatever afterlife there was, her mother would understand and forgive her for abandoning her like she did.

"Liz," Foreman said, touching her arm.

She pulled away, began wiping at her eyes. "Where is she buried?"

"She wasn't. Jim had her cremated."

"What? Why?"

"That's something you should ask him. In fact, he should know you're here."

"No."

"Liz."

"I said, no. He doesn't need to be involved in this."

Foreman said, "Your brother really needs to hear from you. For the first year or so he was going out of his mind with worry. I'm sure he still is worried. Just call him. Let him know you're okay."

"No."

"He doesn't live that far away, actually. He lives in Trenton, works in Manhattan."

"Doing what?"

"Some non-profit work, I forget for what organization. Look, if I called him now, he could be here in three hours. I know he'd really like to see you."

"I think we'll save the family reunion for another time. Right now I'm more concerned with saving my son's life. So what I would really like you to do—please—is get me in contact with Mark Webster."

Foreman took another deep breath, opened his mouth, but before he could speak the sliding door opened and Todd said, "Elizabeth, you need to see this."

The webpage Todd showed them was from CNN. It was only a couple paragraphs, but it included a picture of Elizabeth, though the picture used was one she barely recognized. It took her a few seconds before she realized it had been in the middle school yearbook, taken last year, Sarah Walter having been there long enough that the staff and students began to treat her like one of their own and so she was invited to sit in for a picture. It wasn't a very flattering picture, and for CNN's purposes, it didn't need to be. Not with those couple paragraphs explaining about Reginald Moore and his sudden and explosive (they actually used the word *explosive*) death and how Sarah Walter, a teacher's assistant at a local middle school, was believed to be involved. How police had traced a bomb threat at the local elementary school back to Sarah Walter's phone, and how she was now missing, as was her five-year-old son.

Foreman shook his head and whispered, "My God."

She turned to him. "You said that FBI agent had already called you, said I might show up, right?"

Staring at the screen, rereading the article, he nodded slowly.

"What else did he say?"

He blinked at her. "Nothing, really. He just gave me his number and asked me to have you call him if I spoke with you."

She frowned at Todd. "That doesn't sound right, does it?"

He only looked at her, helpless.

"I think the FBI is already one step ahead of the media. The media is placing me there at Reginald Moore's death, almost making it sound like I was responsible, but they don't know about what happened at Riley's Pub. Not yet."

Todd said, "We really need to get out of here."

Elizabeth nodded. She said to Foreman, "Where do you think we should go while we wait?"

He blinked at her again. "Wait for what?"

"For you to get me in contact with Mark Webster."

"Liz, I told you, there's no guarantee—"

"My face is now online in connection with a child molester being killed and a bomb threat and an abduction of my own son. Once someone in the media recognizes Sarah Walter as Elizabeth Piccioni, my face will be plastered everywhere. We don't have time to screw around. I'm not asking for your help anymore, Michael. I'm demanding it."

His gaze had gone back to the computer screen. He glanced at her, sighed, and nodded. "I can think of a place for you to stay while I get things sorted out."

"Perfect," Elizabeth said. "Let's go."

36

They ended up at a Holiday Inn Express two miles outside of Lanton, a slim and nondescript two-floor building that hosted maybe eighty rooms total. Judging by the vast emptiness of the parking lot, finding lodging—and being left alone—would not be a problem.

Elizabeth asked Foreman to pay for their room on the off chance the FBI was now looking for Todd, too. They ended up with room 42, located at the other end of the motel, past the lobby and the gift shop and just a few doors away from the vending and ice machines. The room could also be accessed from the outside, a door opening up to the parking lot like it was a patio, and as they entered Elizabeth felt a strange sense of relief to note that the room held two beds.

Todd walked the room, checking the bathroom and closet and flipping through the cable list propped up on the TV, while Foreman sank into one of the chairs by the window, seemed to deflate right before Elizabeth's eyes like he had been nothing this entire time but an elaborate circus balloon.

"How long?" she asked him, standing in the middle of the room, her arms once again crossed cupping her elbows.

Foreman frowned. "How long for what?"

"Before you can get me in contact with Mark Webster."

He sighed, which seemed to have the effect of filling his balloon-like body with air. Leaning forward, he said, "Trust me, Liz, he is not your best bet right now. Your best bet is taking this to the police. Or that FBI agent." He suddenly patted his chest, like there were invisible pockets there. "Shoot, I wrote down his name and number but must have left it at the house."

"I don't want to talk to the FBI. I want to talk to Mark Webster."

Foreman sighed again, this time releasing the sigh of a man who knows he has no choice in the matter. "I'll see what I can do."

Later, after Foreman had left, promising to call once he found something worthwhile to call her about, Todd said, "I don't know about you, but I could use a shower."

The truth was she could use a shower, too, the past twenty-four hours having drained her of something that could easily be restored by standing underneath the smooth and steady hiss of water.

Todd volunteered to wait but Elizabeth told him to go first. She claimed the bed by the outside door and clicked through the channels on the TV. She stayed primarily on the news channels, dreading to see her picture flash across the screen.

At some point the BlackBerry dinged. She glanced at the picture, at the time (**59:00:00**), and set it aside.

The bathroom door opened and Todd came out, dressed and drying his hair off with one of the towels.

"You look exhausted," he said.

"I'm fine."

"You only slept, what, three or four hours in the past two days?"

"I said I'm fine."

Todd sat down on the end of his bed facing the TV. "Anything worthwhile happen in the past ten minutes?"

Elizabeth swung her feet off the bed and stood up. She tossed the remote on Todd's bed and headed for the bathroom, saying, "If either Cain or Foreman calls, let me know immediately."

———

She hadn't thought it possible, but the shower felt amazing, and she let herself relax, if only for a few moments, let herself ignore everything else—Cain and what he had done and what he wanted and what he would do if he didn't get what he wanted—and she closed her eyes and became entranced by the soothing rhythm of the water.

Elizabeth took a much longer shower than was needed, almost falling asleep under the showerhead—she hadn't realized just how exhausted she really was until now—and then she turned the water off, stood still for a moment, just dripping, then reached for a towel as she stepped out of the tub.

The towel Todd had placed on the floor was wet, and as her foot came down on it the fabric somehow shifted, just a bit, hardly an inch, but it was enough to send her reeling. In the instant she fell—her arms pinwheeling, her eyes going wide—she understood that everything in her life had led up to this moment. That, in the next few seconds, she would knock her head in that special place that would cause all life to escape her body, as if it were trapped and had always been looking for a way out.

She couldn't remember later, but she may have cried out, may have even screamed, but as she fell back toward the tub her other foot found traction and she managed to stay balanced, just for a moment or so, before colliding with the back of the shower and then sliding down the tiles toward the tub itself. She bruised her ass, the back of her head, even her elbow, but it was nothing compared to what it might have been, and for an instant she considered herself lucky, fortunate, blessed, until behind the door Todd called her name, his voice nervous and hurried, and then the door opened and in he stepped, his face filled with concern until after a moment he saw she was okay and after another moment he saw the scars ravaging her body, the patchwork of a quilt that was her skin, and in that moment she had never felt more naked, more exposed, and she snapped, "Get out!" and that was just what he did, turning at once, closing the door behind him, the suddenness of his departure creating enough disturbance in the air that it formed a swirl of steam in its wake.

37

Foreman called just after ten o'clock that night.

Elizabeth was sitting on the bed, her back against the headboard. The TV was on but she wasn't watching it. She was lost in her thoughts, running through everything that had happened in the past two days, when the room phone went off and startled her.

Todd, sitting on his own bed, grabbed for the phone first. He answered it, listened a moment, then held it out to her.

"It's Michael."

She took the phone from him. "Mike, I hope you're calling with good news."

"That depends," he said, and with only those two words Elizabeth could tell just how exhausted Foreman was, and she knew he had been on the phone and computer ever since the moment he got home, doing whatever he could to find her the information she needed.

"You found him?"

"Yes and no."

Elizabeth said nothing, waiting, watching Todd who sat watching her. The TV was on and the light from the screen bounced around the room, illuminated almost faintly on the corner of his left eye.

"He lives in Queens, that's all I was able to get. His address is, as you would expect, unlisted, and every contact I have, and even their contacts, doesn't have a home address for him. But"—and here the exhaustion disappeared from Foreman's voice, replaced with a kind of renewed energy—"I know where you can find him tomorrow."

"Where?"

"The law firm he works for, the head partner is a staunch Catholic, and our Mark Webster will do whatever it takes to suck up to him. So every Sunday our man takes his wife and kids into Manhattan to have morning mass at Saint Patrick's Cathedral. Always the 10:15 mass, because that's the one with a choir. From what I hear, he never sits with his boss, but always a couple rows behind him. Just, you know, wanting to make sure his boss knows he's committed."

She was already picturing the high-vaulted ceiling, the meticulously crafted stone pillars, the wooden pews and the votive candles and the stained-glass windows. In high school she had taken a field trip to the city for a day, had gone to see a Broadway show—*Les Misérables*—and after the performance they had had two hours to kill before the large coach bus picked them up so different groups went off to different tourist attractions. Her group had gone to Saint Patrick's, had walked up the steps and entered the church, and though Elizabeth had never been very religious she had felt something stir inside of her, as if God or the Holy Spirit or whatever was there actually existed and wanted to get her attention.

"How do you know this for certain?"

Foreman said, "One of my contacts attends the same service. He always sees Webster. Says that he and his family are there every Sunday like clockwork. If you want to speak to him, that's going to be your only chance."

It wasn't quite the news she had wanted, but it would have to do. "Thank you," she said, "thank you so much," and she told him she'd call if she needed anything else and wished him a good night and then hung up the phone.

Todd sat on the edge of his bed, staring at her, expectant, and she told him exactly what Foreman had just told her. A frown creased his brow, and he looked away, stared at the television for a long moment before speaking.

"So then we're going to New York."

He said it not as a question but as a statement, and in those seven words—those seven very simple words—Elizabeth realized she loved him.

For a while neither one of them spoke. Todd had muted the TV when Foreman called so there was complete silence in the room. Earlier, after he had walked in on her and quickly shut the door, she had stayed in the bathroom for nearly an hour. She hadn't wanted to come out. But eventually she did, dressed once again in her clothes, as if they would somehow erase the image that had no doubt been seared into Todd's brain. He didn't bring it up, hardly even spoke, and she had climbed onto her bed, lay her head down on the pillow, closed her eyes and opened them four hours later.

"So," Todd said, his tone amicable enough, though she still couldn't find herself ready to speak.

The truth was, her mouth tasted awful. She couldn't remember the last time she had brushed her teeth. Yesterday morning, she guessed, and since then she hadn't had any gum, not even an Altoid or LifeSaver.

"I need to brush my teeth," she said. "I'm assuming you don't have a toothbrush on you."

"Sorry. I left them in my other pants." And he smiled,

wanting her to smile too, though she couldn't bring herself to, at least not yet.

"This place has a gift shop, doesn't it? They should have a toothbrush and some toothpaste. At the very least, some mouthwash or gum." She realized she was rambling and quickly stood up, dug into her pockets even though she knew they would be empty. "Do you have any cash?"

She decided not to wear shoes. Not for the quick jaunt down the hallway to the lobby, and besides, she had been wearing her shoes for the past twenty-four hours, even more than that, and sure they were sneakers but still, sometimes your feet just needed room to breathe, to stretch, to do whatever it was feet did when they weren't pressured into the restricting confines of footwear.

She padded down the hallway in her socks, the origami-like ball of Todd's cash clutched in her hand. In the lobby she expected to hear some kind of muzak but it was quiet, almost too quiet, and the gift shop was dark, the glass door closed.

A large woman with frizzy hair and a bad complexion sat behind the front desk. She had a book open in front of her, was staring contently at the page as her lips moved sound-lessly along with the rhythm of the story. Elizabeth stood there for nearly a minute before it was clear the woman wasn't going to look up, and only until Elizabeth cleared her throat did the woman give her any kind of attention.

"The gift shop's closed," Elizabeth said.

The woman just stared at her.

"I need to buy something."

"Sorry, but the gift shop closed at nine," the woman said, though she didn't sound sorry at all.

"I just want a toothbrush, some toothpaste."

The woman shrugged, offered up another insincere apology.

"Can't you open it up? It won't take more than a few minutes."

"I'm not allowed to leave the desk."

"But it will only be a minute. Besides, you'd only be going *right there*." And she gestured at the gift shop, maybe twenty feet away, as if the woman might be confused to which closed gift shop they were talking about.

"Again," the woman said, "I'm sorry, but I'm not allowed to leave the desk."

That origami-like ball of cash had become smothered in her grip. Elizabeth could feel her fingernails biting into her palms. This wasn't right. This wasn't fair. All she wanted was a toothbrush, some toothpaste. Even some goddamn gum would do the trick. Anything to rid her mouth of this awful taste. She didn't even care what kind of toothbrush it was, it could be one of those cheap ones they always give you on your way out of the dentist's office, just as long as she could brush her teeth, scrub the back of her tongue, do whatever it took to make her mouth feel at least halfway clean and fresh.

The woman said, "Maybe the Hess."

"Excuse me?"

"It's a gas station. Down the road, about a mile or so. They should have some toothbrushes there."

"You don't know?"

The woman shrugged again. "Everybody who comes here already has a toothbrush. Either that or they get here before the gift shop closes."

Elizabeth turned away without saying a word. Went directly down the hallway. She didn't stomp off—she wouldn't give the woman the satisfaction of seeing that—

and walked as calmly as she could. At least, that was what it should have looked from behind, while anybody viewing her from the front would see her teeth clenched so tight they threatened to crack.

It didn't help matters any that when she came to the room she realized she had forgotten the key. Not that it was a big deal—she could knock and Todd would open the door—but it was the helplessness she felt in that instant that was too much for her. Suddenly, her throat was dry. She needed a drink. Water, soda, beer if this place had it, which she seriously doubted it did. The vending machines were right around the corner. Even from where she stood she could hear them humming, as if each machine was trying to out-hum the next.

The alcove housed a Pepsi machine, a Coke machine, a candy and snack vending machine, and ice machine. She stared at the snacks—the line of Payday bars standing upright in their twirling fence caught her eye—but she didn't want to chance putting in one of her way-too-crumpled dollar bills. The night she was having, the machine would keep rejecting it, no matter how many times she smoothed the bill out, and she would do something rash, there was no doubting that, and the last thing they needed right now—the last thing Matthew needed—was the cops being called because she had broken the machine by shattering the glass with her sock-protected foot.

It didn't cross her mind when she inserted one of the bills into the Coke machine that the same thing might happen. But it didn't, and then she punched the button for a Diet Coke and listened to the grinding of gears behind the machine, the drop of her can of soda. She bent and plucked it from the bottom, wiped her shirt on the top, gave it a quick tap-tap-tap with her index finger. The carbonated hissing when she opened the can was the sweetest sound she had heard all day, and then she had it to her lips, was drinking it nonstop, almost the entire thing, and as she did she started to turn away and there stood Clarence Applegate, only a few feet behind her, glowering at her as he kept the barrel of his handgun trained right on her stomach.

38

"Careful now. Don't speak. Don't even move."

The years had not been kind to Clarence Applegate. While Foreman and Sheila had gone through the normal changes that signaled the downslope of adulthood— slower and heavier for Foreman, overcompensating for Sheila—the changes in Clarence were almost obscene. Elizabeth remembered seeing pictures of him, watching interviews he'd done on TV, and he had appeared handsome enough, despite an obvious overbite. He had had good height, a decent body build, a full head of hair. But this man standing before her now, leaning against the side of the alcove with the gun tucked in to conceal it from anybody passing by, was disproportioned in all the wrong ways.

"The can of soda, put it down on the floor. Slowly."

As she bent her knees, began to lower in a slow crouch, she was amazed by how thin he had become, either by lack of proper diet or the overuse of drugs, she couldn't tell which. His eyes were hollowed and bloodshot, like he had gone weeks without sleep, and he looked pale, so pale in fact it almost seemed like he had hid himself in a cave for the past five years.

"That's it, just set it down there. Good. Now stand back up, slowly."

His jeans were a deep dark blue, looking like they had just been bought from the store, and he had on a hooded pullover windbreaker. A pair of tan work boots on his feet, a green worn baseball cap on his head, the number 8 centered in the middle, signifying some race car driver, and when he reached out with his free hand—his left hand—to hold up a finger, she noticed his fingernails had been chewed to the quick and that on his thin pale finger he still wore his wedding ring.

"You do what I say and there won't be any trouble, okay?"

The gun was a Sig Sauer P250—she could read the engraving on the slide—and it trembled slightly in his hand, the barrel now pointed right at her chest.

Elizabeth said, "I don't have what you want yet."

"Shut up."

"I need more time."

"Shut your goddamn mouth or else I'll shut it for you."

His glare burned into her, livid with hate, and at once Elizabeth felt he was overplaying himself. *Shut your goddamn mouth or else I'll shut it for you*—that was a line from a movie, not from real life.

He took a step back, quickly glanced both ways up and down the hallway, returned his glare. "Now we're going to go to your room."

"No."

The barrel was suddenly in front of her face, Clarence much quicker than he looked, the perfect circle of darkness not even trembling in front of her eyes.

"Rule number one," Clarence breathed between his teeth, "you never say no to me."

Again, a line out of a movie, and she considered her options, just what might happen if she kicked him in the shins, knocked the gun out of her face, how many seconds she might have before he brought the gun back up and pulled the trigger. Her main priority was Matthew, not herself, but how could she protect him if she was dead? She couldn't, and so she nodded, keeping her gaze level with Clarence's glare.

He had her go first, standing just a few feet behind her. She went directly to the room but then just stood there, staring at the door.

"What are you doing?" he whispered. "Open it."

"I don't have a key."

"Bullshit."

"It's true."

She could almost make out his reflection in the tiny circle of the peephole, looking up and down the hallway.

"Fine then," he said, "knock. But don't force me to shoot you."

Todd didn't answer the door right away. She had to knock twice, and when still nothing happened she wondered if maybe he had been alerted to Clarence's presence here, was right now debating on how to handle the situation. But then she heard the doorknob turn and the door opened and there he stood, Todd, the man who minutes ago she realized she loved, smiling, saying, "Where have you—" before his eyes shifted past her to Clarence and the smile faded.

"Inside," Clarence breathed, and all Elizabeth could think about was Matthew, her son, her only reason for being, strapped to a bed somewhere, an explosive collar around his neck.

She started inside, slowly, sensing Clarence directly behind her. As she walked she began to lean forward until she suddenly stopped and snapped her head back. She could feel the cartilage in Clarence's nose breaking just as he cried out and pulled the trigger. She had no time to worry about whether she had just been shot and spun around, jabbing him in the throat with her fist.

Clarence's eyes bulged. His free hand, which had been holding his nose, now went to his throat. Blood was pouring down his face. He still had hold of the gun and was waving it around wildly, shouting something unintelligible.

Before she knew it Todd had stepped in front of her, creating a shield with his body, shoving Clarence back out into the hallway and slamming the door shut. But he wasn't fast enough. Clarence managed to fire off three more rounds and one of them struck Todd in the leg. He cried out but still managed to close the door and lock it.

Immediately Clarence began kicking at the door. He even fired off two more rounds at the lock. Todd stumbled back, holding his leg now covered in blood.

For an instant Elizabeth was paralyzed. One part wanted to go to Todd and comfort him, another part wanted to race to the phone and dial 911. A third part wanted to open the door and confront Clarence Applegate, take the gun away from him and demand he tell her where her son was located.

But then she realized Todd was already moving across the room, grabbing the BlackBerry off the bed, turning to her and saying, his voice hoarse, "Let's go."

Behind her came the sound of Clarence's heavy boot against the door.

"But—" she began.

"Now!" Todd shouted, his face starting to pale, opening the door leading out to the parking lot.

Elizabeth hesitated for only a second. Then she hurried through the door into the night, grabbing the car keys Todd extended, and ran directly for the Prius. She was inside and had the engine going a moment later. She shoved it in gear and lurched forward and almost hit Todd as he quickly limped toward her before swerving out of his way and stopping for only a few seconds, enough for him to open the door and climb in, and then he was shouting, "Go, go, go, go!" and she pressed her foot to the floor, not even pausing at the exit as she fishtailed out of the parking lot and onto the highway.

39

For the first mile or so neither of them spoke. Todd wasn't wearing his seatbelt and sat at an awkward angle, his butt pointed toward the door, his shoulder pushed into the seat, watching the road behind them as he gripped onto his leg, grimacing.

Then, abruptly, Elizabeth jerked the wheel and slammed on the brakes, the Prius skidding to a halt on the side of the road.

Todd, wide-eyed, stared at her. "What are you doing?"

"We have to go back."

"What? Why?"

"That's *him*. We need to go back, catch him, call the police."

"*Catch him?* Elizabeth, this isn't a game of tag. That guy just shot me."

She looked at him for the first time, really looked at him, and said, "Elevate your leg."

"What?"

"Put it up on the dash. Lie back down in your seat. You

need to elevate the wound above your heart to control the bleeding."

"How do you know that?"

She turned toward the backseat, searching for something to use as a tourniquet.

Todd said, "What are you looking for?"

"Give me your shirt."

"My shirt?"

"Goddamn it, Todd, hurry."

He started undoing his shirt, fumbling with the buttons. Elizabeth told him not to worry about it and yanked it open, sending several buttons flying around the car. Todd struggled out of the shirt, and she took it and wrapped it around his leg, pulling it as tight as she could.

"We can't stay here," she said. "The police will be responding any minute."

"But isn't that what we want?"

She thought about it for a moment. "No."

"What do you mean, *no*?"

"By now Clarence will be long gone. Our main priority is to save Matthew."

"You mean *your* main priority. Jesus Christ, Elizabeth, I just got shot."

She found a rip in the fabric of his slacks where the bullet had entered. She tore it open enough to inspect the wound.

"It doesn't look too bad."

"Are you kidding?"

"The bullet obviously didn't shatter any bones and it's definitely not lodged in there. You were basically just grazed."

Todd sucked air in through his teeth. "That's comforting. How do you know all of this stuff anyway?"

An eighteen-wheeler roared past them, rocking the hybrid, and Elizabeth placed the car back in gear.

"What are you doing?"

"I told you. We can't stay here."

"You're actually going back?"

"No. Clarence is long gone by now."

"What about my leg?"

"We'll take care of it."

She pulled back onto the highway and they drove for less than a minute before two cop cars whipped past them in the oncoming lane.

Todd said, "How did he find us anyway?"

And that was the question, wasn't it? How *did* Clarence find them? How was he able to sneak up on her like that, without even making a sound, sneak up on her like they were old friends and he wanted to spook her for fun?

"Foreman," she said.

"What? You think he tipped him off?"

She shook her head again. "No, we have to call him. The police will find the room is registered under his name. They'll go looking for him. Here, give me the phone."

Todd offered up the BlackBerry and she grabbed it, pressed the button for the stored numbers—Foreman's was the only one listed—but then paused. Her left hand on the steering wheel, her right hand holding the phone, her gaze shifted past the phone's glowing screen to the glowing navigation screen on the dashboard.

"GPS," she whispered.

Todd still hadn't moved from his position, his leg elevated on the dash, his hands holding the makeshift tourniquet in place. "Huh?"

"He's tracking us by GPS."

"How do you know?"

"This phone—it's GPS enabled. He can track us wherever we go as long as it's turned on."

"So let's get rid of it."

"We can't. We need it in case he calls."

"Turn it off, then. If he calls, he can leave a voicemail."

Todd's words dripped of sarcasm, but she knew he had a point. And thinking this now, she wondered why Clarence hadn't called yet.

Foreman picked up after three rings, his voice hesitant and sleepy. "Hello?"

"Mike, it's me. There's been an incident."

She quickly filled him in on the events, and when she was done, Foreman said, "Oh my God. Is Todd all right?"

She glanced over at him. "He is for now. Listen, since you paid for the room, the police will come for you."

Foreman didn't answer.

"Are you there?"

"Yes," he said, sounding more exhausted then ever. "I ... I can go for a long drive, I suppose. Disappear for a little."

"I'm sorry I dragged you into this."

"No, no. Don't be silly."

"Mike—"

"Where will you go now?"

"New York, I guess."

"If you're going that way, maybe your brother can help you."

"Mike—"

"At least call him."

"When this is all done and over with, sure, I'll call him."

"He might be able to help."

Elizabeth didn't want to get into this with him. She said, "I have to go. Keep your phone on you. We'll call when we hear anything."

She disconnected, not wanting to continue the conversation. She didn't want to think of her brother, not now, not with everything that had just happened. She only wanted to—

The BlackBerry rang in her hand. Without thinking she placed it to her ear and said, "Mike, please, it's best if you don't..."

She understood quickly that it wasn't Foreman on the other line. There was a different quality to the background noise, a vacuous silence that seemed infinite.

"Hello?"

More silence.

She swallowed. "Clarence, I—"

"No more games," said the dark robotic voice.

There was another moment of that deep silence, and then the phone went dead in her ear.

40

Just before Allentown, they managed to find a vacant gas station bathroom. It was an old Sunoco, already closed for the night, the time now nearly three o'clock in the morning. Elizabeth parked the Prius around back. It was dark and secluded enough from the sporadic traffic on the highway that nobody would see them. Elizabeth told Todd to wait there and went up to the door at the back of the gas station. It was locked just like she thought it would be, a simple clasp held in place by a padlock, and she used the claw of the hammer she'd purchased earlier at Walmart to tear the clasp off the door.

Surprisingly the bathroom was not as disgusting as she had feared it would be. The floor, the toilet, the sink, even the mirror—they all looked as if they were cleaned regularly, the only sign of disarray the single light bulb in the ceiling flickering every couple of seconds.

She helped Todd out of the car, giving him support as he limped inside, then went back to the hybrid for the rest of the supplies she'd picked up at the store. Four bottles of hydrogen peroxide, five packages of sterilized gauze, and two elastic bandages. It was probably more than she needed but she didn't want to take any chances.

The first thing they did was get him settled on the floor. He had kept pressure on the wound for the past two hours, enough to make sure it had clotted properly, and there had been no more bleeding. But still they had to get him out of his pants, and once they managed to lower him to the ground so his back was against the wall, Elizabeth used scissors to carefully cut his pants off.

Then she opened one of the hydrogen peroxide bottles and said, "This is going to sting," and poured half of it on the wound.

Todd gritted his teeth, squeezed his eyes shut, but managed not to cry out. He produced a low moaning sound and squeezed his fists tightly together.

It didn't take long to clean and bandage the wound. Like Elizabeth told him earlier, it was only a graze.

"You're lucky," she said.

"Yeah." He was quiet for a moment, the light bulb above them flickering. "To be honest, I'm starting to regret bringing you those flowers."

She looked up at him sharply, not sure what to say. But then she saw him grinning, and she found herself grinning too.

"Thank you," she said.

"For what?"

"For everything. For putting yourself between me and Clarence. That was very brave of you."

He shrugged. "That's just what us guys are supposed to do, right?"

"I'm sorry this happened."

"It's not your fault."

"Yes, it is."

"It was me who was in the wrong place at the wrong time."

"It was a sweet gesture, bringing me those flowers."

"Yeah, and now look what it got me."

"I said I was sorry."

"I know. And I said it was my fault."

"But it's not."

"It is. It's my fault because ..."

She was cleaning up the bloody gauze, putting them in the trashcan, and turned to him. She opened her mouth to ask what he meant to say when she saw the look in his eyes, the sudden solemnity, and knew immediately what he was going to say.

"Because," he said, "I'm in love with you."

Elizabeth didn't say anything.

He shifted his eyes away, suddenly looking embarrassed. "I know we haven't been together that long, at least for people our age, but I ... I love you. I've felt it for a while now. And even after everything that's happened these past two days, even after learning about your hidden past, those feelings haven't gone away."

Elizabeth was moving before she knew it, walking toward Todd, lowering herself down onto the tiled floor beside him. She opened her mouth, shut it, opened her mouth again, trying to find the right words, the right thing to say, but before she could say anything Todd leaned forward and kissed her. It was a simple but meaningful kiss, and when he leaned back to look at her she leaned forward and kissed him. This time it was more passionate, their tongues darting between each other's lips, and she placed her hands on his chest, on his arms, on the back of his neck, moving them around his body. In the back of her mind she knew this was wrong, that she shouldn't be doing this while Matthew was still abducted. But so much had happened not only over the past two days but the past five years, all the secrets she had kept, all the lies she had told, all the times she had kissed Todd and wanted to go further but never had, and now here he was, the man who had taken a bullet for her, and she wanted him more than she had ever wanted anyone else, and their kissing became even more passionate, even more frantic, his hands on her now, moving up her arms, over her chest, and it wasn't until one of those hands slipped underneath her shirt and felt her skin, the scars, did she stop kissing him and immediately pull away.

They stared at each other then, neither one of them saying a word, while that light bulb flickered above, momentarily bathing them in complete darkness.

41

At nine o'clock that Sunday morning, Elizabeth and Todd took the Holland Tunnel into Manhattan.

The sky was dark and filled with rain. It had been raining for the past two hours and had only gotten worse. They had decided to bypass the turnpike—fearing too many state police—and had instead gone up toward Allentown and taken I-78 east.

Despite his injury, Todd drove. He said as long as he didn't put too much pressure on his right leg, it didn't hurt. He wore the new slacks and sweatshirt Elizabeth had purchased when she bought the rest of her supplies at Walmart. Elizabeth herself was dressed in new clothes: jeans and a hooded sweatshirt and raincoat and a Yankee's baseball cap. She had also bought a cheap purse. Inside the purse was one of two throwaway phones. Todd had the other phone.

———

"It's not what you think."

"What don't I think?"

"The scars."

Todd hadn't moved from his place on the bathroom floor. She could see his erection pushing against his boxer shorts and averted her eyes.

"I don't care about the scars."

"That doesn't matter. I do."

———

They exited the tunnel and followed the traffic toward Sixth Avenue. They made a left and headed uptown, the rain seeming like it was falling even harder, the tires of the cars around them hissing like snakes.

———

"You're thinking Eddie gave them to me."

"No, I'm not."

"I can see it in your eyes."

"Elizabeth—"

"I did this to myself."

Todd was quiet for a long moment. Finally he asked, "Why?"

"As punishment."

"Punishment for what?"

"For wanting to kill my son."

———

They came to a red light and stopped, watching the people with umbrellas moving from one sidewalk corner to another.

Todd whispered, "What if this doesn't work?"

Elizabeth stared out her window at a homeless man

standing against a building, a Styrofoam cup in his hands. "It has to."

"You ... you wanted to kill Matthew?"

Elizabeth ignored the question. She turned away and kept cleaning up the rest of the discarded supplies.

"Elizabeth," Todd said, attempting now to stand. "Why did you want to kill Matthew?"

She paused, staring down at the bloody gauze in the trashcan. Eventually she looked up at Todd, tears in her eyes.

"I thought he had it in him, whatever it was that made Eddie a killer. I thought ... I thought Eddie had somehow passed that evil onto our child. And I couldn't in all good conscience let him grow into a monster. But just ... I couldn't do it. Every time I considered doing it, I took one look at my son and realized he was no monster. I realized he was never going to be a monster. And so I ... I started cutting myself, every time I had those thoughts. It eventually came to the point I started having those thoughts just so I would have an excuse to cut myself."

Todd stood leaning against the wall, putting all his weight on his left leg. He watched her without a word.

"So it's not what you think. Eddie had nothing to do with it. Eddie never laid a finger on me. He was never abusive. In fact, I never thought he would be capable of it. When I was with him ... I felt safe."

They passed Radio City Music Hall, went up another block, made a right onto East 52nd, then made another right onto

Fifth Avenue. The light had just turned red and here Elizabeth got out, the rain tapping at the brim of her baseball cap. She watched the church as she crossed East 51st, walking to the statue of Atlas with the world on his shoulders. She waited there against the corner of the Banana Republic, directly across from the church, watching the people walk by, most of them with umbrellas, and she cursed herself for forgetting to purchase an umbrella of her own.

Her gaze was so focused on the church that, five minutes later, she didn't see the man before it was too late. He had come up and grabbed her arm and squeezed it and said her name. She started and stared, wide-eyed, thinking this was it, Clarence was through playing games and was finally here to kill her. Only it wasn't Clarence, was instead the furthest thing from that psychopath.

Jim, her brother, said, "What the hell do you think you're doing?"

42

The last time she had seen her brother was when she had driven him to the airport. He had been living down in Maryland then, just outside of Baltimore, and while he could have easily taken the bus or a cab to BWI, she had insisted on taking a day off from school to drive him. He had entered the Peace Corps, a last-ditch effort to do something meaningful with his life, already now past thirty with no real job or relationship, and he had decided he wanted to get into non-profit work and thought the Peace Corps would look great on his resume. And besides, he would get to travel, or at least he would be put up somewhere out of the country for two years, even if it was in some small African village whose name she would always have trouble remembering.

She had become pregnant six months before, and she had begged Jim not to go, at least not until the baby was born. He had said sorry but he had already committed, and besides, he would email and call as much as he could, which he did, off and on, until the day she disappeared.

The car ride to the airport had been a quiet one, the only noise between them the radio playing at some monotonic level. It wasn't until they had actually arrived and Elizabeth insisted she park and wait with him in the terminal did he become animated, telling her she didn't have to do that, he appreciated the ride and everything, but to pay for parking, especially at these rates, was ridiculous. She wouldn't hear it, though, and found parking and went in with him but of course she couldn't wait in the terminal, not without buying a plane ticket herself, the rules and security having become much stricter since that infamous day in September.

She had stood there then, smiling and trying not to cry. He was her brother, her big brother, who she had shared everything with since they were kids, and she was going to miss him more than she had thought she would.

He set his bag aside (he'd already checked his suitcase) and pulled her into an embrace. "You take care of that little bun in the oven, okay?"

She nodded her head into his shoulder, holding back her tears.

"And Mom," he said. "I'll call her when I can, but you take care of her too."

Their mother was a sore subject between them, a woman barely even into her fifties who was dying more every day from the cancer inside her.

"What about Eddie?" she asked, gently pushing away from him. "He'll want to hear from you."

Her husband was on another one of his business trips, currently somewhere in the Midwest.

"I'll give him a call while I'm waiting in the terminal." Jim smiled. "I'll call collect from one of the payphones. Eddie will accept the charges."

She smiled but said nothing. She didn't want to tell him just how worried she was about him, how she feared for his safety. She had been reading articles about the gangs in

Africa, about the wars, the violence, the awful things that happened to the women and children and even some of the men, and she didn't want to think that her big brother might get stuck in the middle of it.

The terminal was filling up, people passing them on either side, and Jim said he had to go. He hugged her again, kissed her cheek, told her he loved her and that he would email as much as possible and call when he could. Then he grabbed his bag and walked away from her, making it the very last time she would ever see him.

Until now.

Jim wore slacks and a dark blue rain slicker, and he looked good, a little more tan than she remembered, and he had begun to lose some of his hair in front, but he had it cut short enough that it came across well, not at all hurting his features. He stood right beside her, holding an umbrella above their heads as he continued to grip her arm.

He said, "Well?"

"Well what?"

"Just what the hell do you think you're doing?"

"What," she said, "is that how you say hello these days?"

"You need to go to the police."

"How did you find me?"

"Foreman called. He told me everything. Christ, Liz, this guy *attacked* you?"

Her body went rigid, instantly going into defense mode. "He abducted my son. He has a bomb strapped around my son's neck."

Something flickered in Jim's eyes, the anger fading away. "Even if you get this guy what he wants, do you really think he'll let your son go? He's going to kill you and your son and probably that guy that's with you—Foreman told me his name but I forget it now."

"Todd."

"What?"

"The guy that's with me, his name is Todd. He's"—she hesitated—"my boyfriend."

The rain tapped an inconsistent beat on the umbrella above their heads.

Elizabeth asked, "What are you doing here anyway? And how did you even *find* me?"

"Foreman told me where you were going. I've been waiting out here for over an hour, ready to talk some sense into you."

She stared across the street, past the traffic, at the front doors of the church. Foreman. Goddamned Foreman. When she saw him next she was going to give him a piece of her mind. He was just trying to be helpful, sure, okay, she could see that, and yeah, she had brought a lot of trouble his way recently, but why bring Jim into this mess too?

"Hey." Jim had let go of her arm but now touched it again. "You really need to stop this and go to the police. They can help."

"No."

"Liz—"

In her purse, one of the phones rang. Immediately she thought it was Todd, calling to check in on her status, but when she opened the purse and looked at the two phones, she realized it wasn't Todd who was calling, but Clarence.

43

"Where are you?"

She stared at the church across the street, not seeing the traffic or the people moving past her.

"Elizabeth, I asked you a question."

Jim lightly touched her arm. She blinked and saw him standing in front of her, the pole of the umbrella against his shoulder, his face filled with worry as he mouthed, *Is that him?*

Elizabeth turned away from her brother, mumbled into the mouthpiece, "I'm here."

"Yes, Elizabeth, I know you're there. Obviously you're there, as you are now speaking to me. That, however, wasn't my question."

Despite the heavy rain the city breathed life around her: that ubiquitous stench of garbage and exhaust, the distant sound of sirens, every other car or taxi passing by on Fifth Avenue honking its horn like it were some kind of game.

"I'm in New York City," she said, because she knew he already knew her location. He could track her with the cell phone; this whole thing was just to get under her skin, so why lie?

"And what, pray tell, are you doing in New York City?"

"I'm trying to get you what you want."

"I certainly hope so. Because you know what will happen if you don't."

She closed her eyes—she couldn't help herself. "Yes."

"Good. Just keep that in mind. Oh, and Elizabeth? Say hello to your brother for me."

———

When she hit the END button, Jim said, "Was that him? What did he say?"

She threw the BlackBerry into her bag, pulled out the throwaway already preloaded with Todd's number. "He's here."

"What?"

Flipping open the phone, dialing the resend number. "He's close by somewhere, watching us. He knows you're with me."

She caught only a glimpse of Jim's face—his sudden ashen face—before she turned away and held the throwaway to her ear.

Todd answered after the second ring. "Elizabeth?"

"Where are you?"

"On Central Park West. I just passed the Dakota. Why? What's wrong?"

"He's here."

There was a pause. "Who's there? Clarence?"

"He just called. He's somewhere close. I need you to stay nearby in case something happens."

"I'm heading back in that direction now. Do you want me to park and meet you?"

She turned and noticed Jim watching her again. The worry had left his face now, knowing that she wasn't talking to their antagonist this time but instead to the man she had just recently referred to as her boyfriend. Suddenly she had a flash of being back in high school, the dark look of disapproval on her brother's face when she was talking to a boy he didn't know anything about and had yet to approve of.

"I should be fine. I'll call you when I'm done."

"Are you sure?"

"Yes."

There was another pause, this one lengthier, and then Todd said, "I love you."

She hesitated then closed the phone and placed it back in her bag.

"That was what's-his-name, right?"

"Todd."

"Yeah." Jim nodded slowly. "You trust him?"

She snapped her bag shut. "Believe it or not, I don't need your approval on who I can and cannot date."

"That's not what I meant. I just—"

"Jim, not right now."

He held up his free hand, shook his head, took a step back. Just like they were teenagers again.

She glanced across the street at the church.

Jim said, "Who are you waiting for anyway?"

"Mark Webster."

He snapped his fingers. "That's right—the lawyer. How do you know he's in there?"

"I don't."

"Do you even know what he looks like?"

She remembered the day she first met Mark Webster, the

young brazen lawyer coming to her house and sitting in her living room and talking to her like they were old friends.

"I'm sure he hasn't changed much in five years."

"I wouldn't be so sure about that. Working in Manhattan does something to your genes. Scientists still haven't figured out what it is yet." He reached into his pocket, pulled out an iPhone. "What law firm does he work for?"

She didn't answer him at first, only smirked.

"What?"

"I never thought I'd see the day you had a cell phone. You used to be one of those doom and gloom people, always certain they would bring brain cancer."

"That's still inconclusive. Besides, after living in pretty much squalor for two years, you begin to miss all kinds of technology. So having a super smartphone in my pocket, yeah, I'm okay with that now." He looked at her again. "The law firm name?"

She gave it to him and he typed it in and moments later he had brought up the law firm's website, then the page that gave brief bios of all its lawyers, including pictures.

"Here he is," Jim said, handing her the phone, and the face that stared back at her was one she wasn't entirely surprised to see. Yes, it was Mark Webster, but the Mark Webster she remembered—the arrogant little shit lawyer—had fallen away like a cocoon and the man she saw now was somehow more handsome, with stronger, sharper features, darker hair, a better complexion. It wasn't the genes that were affected so much working in Manhattan, she thought, but rather the work of a skilled personal trainer.

"So again," Jim said, "how do you know he's in there?"

"He has to be."

"Maybe he went to an earlier service."

"No."

"Maybe one of his kids is sick and he stayed home with them."

"*No.*"

She realized she was shaking and handed back the phone.

"Liz, you have to be realistic here. This is not going to have a happy ending. I know all about Clarence Applegate. After all the shit he wrote about you, how could I not know about him? The guy is a psycho. He's not going to let you or your son live even if you don't go to the police. I mean, seriously, aren't you worried about your son?"

"Of course I am. But it's not just about him anymore."

"What does that mean?"

"Those trophies that Clarence wants—the fingers and the wedding rings. They need to be found."

For the first time she could remember, Jim looked at a complete loss. "Why?"

"What Eddie did to those women was vile and disgusting and evil. But when I saw Clarence last night, saw that he was still wearing his wedding ring, it reminded me about those women's husbands, and their families, and everything they left behind. And until those fingers and rings are found, those women's spirits will never be able to rest in peace."

She expected some kind of response from her brother, some kind of rebuttal, but he didn't say anything, not at first. He just stared back at her for a long moment while around them the city still continued to breathe its strange sense of life and the rain soaked the street and sidewalk and dripped off the umbrella.

Finally he said, "So now what do we do?"

"We wait."

They didn't wait long. A half hour passed before the service ended and the doors opened and people began exiting the church. Mark Webster wouldn't be one of the first—he would want to lag behind, share small talk, make sure his boss saw him—but when he did exit it would be through the main entrance, down the steps. Five minutes passed, ten minutes, and then there he was, Mark Webster and his wife and their two children, all wearing their Sunday best, looking like the perfect American family as they huddled under a pair of large black umbrellas and descended the steps one unhurried step at a time.

44

They watched Mark Webster and his family walk to the end of the block, then wait at the corner for the light and cross over Fifth Avenue toward their side.

Jim said, "How much do you want to bet they're headed to the subway station at Rockefeller?"

Elizabeth stood silent beside him, the rain beating at the umbrella. She watched as the family headed down East 50th Street, disappearing from their sight, and then said, "Let's go."

She led the way, not quite sure yet how she was going to do this. What she would say, what she would do—these were all things she had been worrying about since the moment they entered her mind, and she had always assumed that when the time came everything would fall into place. It hadn't, though. No, if anything she was at an even greater loss for words or actions, and as she rounded the corner and spotted Mark Webster and his family farther down the block, she hurried her pace.

"Elizabeth," Jim said behind her, but she ignored him and continued on, crossing over the street to Mark

Webster's side, the rain assaulting her now, her hurried pace matching three strides for every one stride the Webster family took.

Then, before she realized it, she was right behind them, the only thing separating her and the family a thin sheet of rain, and before she could second-guess herself any further, she called out Mark Webster's name.

As one unit the family paused, and Mark Webster shifted so he could glance back at her.

Elizabeth said, "Could I have a moment of your time please?"

"Mark," the man's wife said, annoyed, and Mark Webster sighed, said, "Listen, if this is about the Rodriguez case, a statement was already issued Friday afternoon. And come on, this is Sunday. I'm with my family."

"This isn't about the Rodriguez case," Elizabeth said. Jim had caught up and now stood behind her. "This is about Edward Piccioni."

Mark Webster's eyes narrowed slightly at the name, and he stared at her with a renewed kind of interest.

"Mark," his wife said again, the children standing between them—a boy and a girl, completely adorable just as they were expected to be—looking up at their father as if seeking some kind of wisdom.

He shifted his gaze away from Elizabeth to his wife. "Head inside. I'll meet you there in a minute."

"Mark," she said again, now glaring at him, and he said forcefully, "Julia, it's okay. Head inside and I'll meet you. I won't be more than a minute."

Julia Webster—a beautiful blonde in her thirties with piercing green eyes—glared back at Elizabeth for a second before she said something to her children and ushered them ahead, around the corner into the courtyard of Rockefeller

Plaza. The moment they were gone, Mark Webster cleared his throat.

"From what I read in the news," he said, "the police are looking for you."

"I'm being setup."

"Is that right?"

"A man abducted my son. If I don't do as he says and get him what he wants before a certain time, he's going to kill him."

Mark Webster didn't seem impressed by this news. He glanced past her and nodded at Jim. "Who's that?"

"My brother."

"So this is like a family event, huh?"

"This is a serious matter."

"I'm sure it is."

"The man doing this is Clarence Applegate."

Mark Webster nodded slowly, this news not seeming to impress him either. "I'm familiar with the name."

"He wants my husband's trophies."

"That's nice." The man stood stock-still, holding his umbrella up straight, the space between them less than ten feet. "Why are you bothering me with this information?"

For an instant Elizabeth didn't know what to say. She'd thought her reason for coming to him would be obvious, and she realized after a moment that maybe it was. Mark Webster had been an asshole five years ago, and it looked like he was an asshole now. Just a bigger, more experienced, and better paid one.

"I need you to get me in so I can speak to my husband."

Mark Webster shook his head. "I'm afraid that's not going to happen."

"Without speaking to my husband, I won't be able to get Clarence what he wants."

With a bored expression Mark Webster held his umbrella with his right hand, jerked the wrist of his left hand so he flashed an expensive Rolex. He glanced at it and said, "I've given you more than your minute. Now if you'll excuse me, I'll be on my way."

He turned and started down the sidewalk.

Elizabeth glanced at Jim. Jim glanced at her. She opened her mouth but no words came out. Her entire body shook. Her blood boiled. Before she knew it she was moving, hurrying down the block, coming around the corner into the plaza and catching up with Mark Webster.

"You have to help me," she said, stepping in front of him.

"I don't have to do anything."

"He's going to kill my son."

"I don't give a shit."

"How can you say that?"

"I tried to help you five years ago, but you wouldn't let me. Instead you disappeared. You ruined my case."

"Eddie was going to jail whether I stayed or not."

"Perhaps. But I needed you as a character witness."

"I wasn't going to step foot inside a courtroom. Not for him."

Mark Webster said, "My family is waiting for me inside. I'm going to go meet them, and when I see the next police officer I'm going to tell him that Elizabeth Piccioni is out here. So if I were you, I would get the fuck out of my face."

He went to step around her and she moved to block his way again. Beyond him she could see Jim standing a couple feet back, just watching her, a look of complete helplessness on his face.

"Just call and put me on the list," she said. "Please, I'm begging you."

The corners of Mark Webster's mouth twitched. "Begging

me? That's rich. I'd have you get down on your knees and beg, but something tells me you're just so desperate enough you'd actually do it. I'm sorry, but none of this is my concern. If I were you, I'd go to the FBI."

He went to step around her again and this time Elizabeth didn't move. She stared past him at Jim who stared back at her, and then she noticed movement beyond her brother—something more than the passing traffic and the other people in the plaza—and there was Clarence Applegate, bundled up in a trench coat, coming around the corner and reaching into his pocket, his hand shifting just enough for her to see the flash of gunmetal in the rain.

45

Later, she would review the events in her mind, thinking of all
the different possible ways she could have reacted so that
what happened did not have to happen. In the end she knew
it was trivial, though, because in that moment with the rain
falling around them in the courtyard, she acted on pure
instinct.

Seeing Clarence Applegate appear out of nowhere wasn't
what put her into action. She was already feeling defeated,
Mark Webster having stepped around her, heading toward
his wife and children inside, and in that instant she understood this was over. Then she looked at her brother, and
beyond her brother she saw Clarence, and as Clarence headed
toward them, coming quickly, he reached into his pocket and
began to pull out a gun—not the same gun he had used last
night to threaten her and to shoot Todd in the leg with, but
no doubt just as dangerous.

And Elizabeth had no choice but to do the only thing she
could do.

Shouting her brother's name, she stepped forward,
pushed him aside, and in the same moment reached with her

other hand inside her jacket, pulling out the gun she had tucked in the waistband of her pants. She raised this gun at the same moment Clarence Applegate raised his gun out of his trench coat pocket.

They stared at each other, less than thirty yards apart, the rain tapping at her baseball cap and dripping off the brim.

Clarence had his teeth clenched. His face was red. He wore no hat and his hair was soaked and he looked so harmless, so pathetic, nothing like the monster he had proven himself to be. But she could see the hate in his eyes, the pure and intense hate, and she said the only word she could think to say.

"Don't."

Clarence fired first.

Elizabeth closed her eyes and pulled the trigger, once, twice, three times, and then there was silence except for the rain and she opened her eyes again and saw Clarence was moving away from her, holding his left arm, the gun he'd just fired several times abandoned on the ground.

She stood frozen for a moment, completely stunned, certain that she had been shot but just not certain what part of her body had taken a bullet. Hadn't she read somewhere that the first thing you felt was numbness? Or did you feel instant pain? She didn't feel anything—no pain, no numbness, nothing—and before she could even begin to check herself Jim called her name.

Spinning around, the last thing she expected to see was the blood on her brother's hands. It wasn't his blood, though. He was on his knees, holding Mark Webster, who had been shot in the chest.

Instinct took over again and she flicked the safety back on the gun, returned it to the snug comfort of her waistband as she hurried forward and crouched down beside Jim and Mark Webster.

"What happened?"

"What do you think happened?" Jim said. "He was fucking shot!"

The chest wound was worse than it had first appeared. Mark Webster had been shot two times, once in what looked like the heart, once in his stomach. It was his stomach that was pumping out most of the blood.

She glanced up past Mark Webster—who was already gone, his face completely pale in the rain—and saw the trio of faces staring at them through one of the doors. Other faces were staring at them, too, even people who had been caught in the rain when the gunfire started had begun to stand back up, confident now that the shooting was over. But the faces she saw now were those of Mark Webster's wife and children. Julia Webster screaming, tears in her eyes, hysterical, while the twins—the boy and the girl—simply stared back at Elizabeth.

"We have to get out of here."

Jim was still cradling Mark Webster, visibly shaken. "What?"

"The police will be here in seconds. We need to move."

"We can't leave now. This man just died."

"My son—"

"*Elizabeth*," Jim said, staring at her hard, but then, suddenly, the hardness faded and he nodded. "You're right." He gently placed Mark Webster's body on the ground, stood up, pointed toward where Clarence had gone. "I'll go that way. You go that way. Hopefully at least one of us makes it."

He started around her and she reached out and grabbed his arm and said his name.

"I'll get in contact with you if I can," he said. "And if I don't, good luck."

Then he was running, faster than she thought possible, around the corner and gone.

She realized that from the moment Clarence first appeared not even two minutes had passed. She glanced once again at the window. Julia Webster was gone but the children were still there. Staring out through the glass, both of their eyes vacant and listless. Elizabeth wanted to go to them, take them into her arms, tell them how very sorry she was. But she couldn't do any of that, because she had her own child to worry about right now.

Elizabeth ran.

46

Again, instinct took over. Elizabeth didn't think about running; she just ran, as fast as she could, and when she came around the corner of the building and almost collided with the two cops coming her way—a black and white combo, both bundled up in rain slickers—her mind didn't even light on the fact she had a weapon concealed on her body.

"*Oh my God, help!*" she screamed, one hand to her mouth, the other jabbing a finger at the courtyard. "*They shot him!*"

The two cops already had their hands on the butts of their guns, and now they drew them, stepping around her. She turned, walking backward, watching them disappear around the corner of the building, and then she spun around, walking forward again, picking up her pace.

The rain was still coming down hard, the drops drumming her hat, which reminded her that she would have to lose this hat, as it was one of the easiest ways to identify her. She doubted Julia Webster would know her, not until she calmed down and reviewed the brief conversation Elizabeth had had with Mark Webster in her presence, and for the time being the only form of ID Julia might be able to provide the police was the simple fact Elizabeth had been wearing a baseball cap.

She had just crossed underneath the NBC Studios marquee when she heard the shouting behind her.

Elizabeth paused briefly and glanced back over her shoulder and there were the two cops again, their weapons in hand. They weren't running exactly but they weren't walking either. She could hear one of their voices through the rain, telling her to stop.

She turned back around and kept walking, a little faster now, playing it off like the cops weren't talking to her. But they were—it was obvious—and after a few seconds she picked up the pace until she found herself sprinting, now both cops shouting at her as they gave chase.

As she reached the intersection the light had just turned, the traffic stopped, and she sprinted across Sixth Avenue. Weaving through the scattered crowd of people, almost tripping over the sidewalk curb on the other side of the street, her hand slipped into her bag and brought out the throwaway. She flipped it open and called the only stored number and waited three rings before Todd picked up.

"Is everything okay?"

"Where are you?"

"I'm circling around the church. I just turned onto Fifth Avenue. What's wrong?"

She risked a glance behind her and saw the cops through the crowd, having just crossed the street. They were at least fifty yards away.

"Clarence showed up."

"What?"

"He killed Mark Webster."

"*What?* My God, where are you? It sounds like you're running."

"I just passed over Sixth Avenue. Todd, the cops are chasing me."

There was a silence.

"*Todd!*"

"Where are you now?"

"I don't know."

"Are you at an intersection?"

"Not yet."

"When you get there, tell me the street."

She was there fifteen seconds later, breathing heavy now, the rain pounding away. "West Forty-Ninth and Seventh."

Todd was quiet for a moment before saying, "Go left."

She wasn't as fortunate at this traffic light, the cars coming down 49th having the green, but she darted in front of a taxi anyway, its driver slamming on the brakes and leaning on the horn. Then she was up on the sidewalk again and sprinting, even harder now, dodging in and out of the people hurrying through the rain. She could hear sirens rising in the distance.

The phone still to her ear, she heard Todd ask, "Where are you now?"

"Almost to the end of the block."

"Keep going."

"Where are you?"

"I'm coming."

Despite the rain she could tell where she was headed—she had been to the city enough times to recognize famous locations—and she asked, "Why are you leading me toward Times Square?"

"Just keep going."

"There's going to be a hundred cops there."

"Just keep going."

"Todd."

"Where are you now?"

"I just crossed over Forty-Seventh."

"Keep going."

She refused to look behind her, for fear that the cops would be even closer. She also understood it was a possibility that they had given up pursuit. If that were the case, they would have called in her description to other cops in the area if they hadn't done so already. And here she was now, almost to Times Square, which would be swarming with police.

She kept the phone to her ear as she ran and she could hear Todd talking to himself, saying, "Come on, come on, come on," under his breath.

Elizabeth said, "Where are you?"

"Where are you?"

"Next block up."

"Good. Keep going."

There was a massive group of people waiting outside Planet Hollywood, forcing her to slow down and thread her way through the throng. "Excuse me," she said loudly, but it did no good, hardly anyone moving out of her way, and before she knew it she was pushing and shoving until she had broken through to the other side.

"Are you at the next block yet?" Todd asked.

"Almost."

"Turn left."

She did so seconds later, this time risking another glance. The cops were still there, also slowed down by the massive group, only the people there were being much more cour-teous because of their uniforms and badges.

"I see you," Todd said into her ear, and she glanced up the street, at the taxis and cars waiting for the traffic light to turn green. She spotted the Prius a second later and immediately ran to it, opening the door and throwing her hat in the back and sliding in and slamming the door and reaching out and grabbing Todd's neck and pulling him forward.

"What—" he began but then their lips were together, nothing too passionate, just a quick deep kiss shared by a new couple waiting for traffic to move again—which apparently it had begun to do, the taxi behind them beeping twice.

They broke apart, Todd moving them forward, and Elizabeth looked out the window and saw the cops had already passed them. That was the reason for the kiss, after all, to make sure her face wasn't the first thing the cops saw when they turned the corner. But now they were behind her, slowing their hurried pace because they had obviously lost her.

"Now what?" Todd asked, his fingers white around the steering wheel.

"Drive." Elizabeth leaned her head back against the headrest, trying to slow her breathing, her heart. "Just drive."

47

It rained intermittently on the drive back. Todd did not turn on the radio and neither of them spoke, so the only sound was the squeak of the windshield wipers and the constant rush of their wet tires on the highway.

After the first hour, Elizabeth said, "Thank you."

"For what?"

"For saving my ass."

"What happened back there?"

She filled him in on everything that had happened. From the moment she had stepped out of the Prius on Fifth Avenue to the moment she scrambled back into it.

Todd was silent for a long time before slowly shaking his head. "Jesus Christ." Then, "So you don't know what happened to your brother?"

She shook her head. "It doesn't make sense."

"What doesn't?"

"Mark Webster was the key to getting me in to see my husband. Clarence had to have known that. So why kill him?"

She used the throwaway to call Foreman's cell. It went straight to voicemail. She started to leave a message but then stopped. What she worried about was saying something on the message, something that would somehow incriminate Foreman somewhere down the line.

For the next hour she tried calling his cell. It kept going to voicemail until they were less than an hour away from Lanton and he picked up.

"I saw the news," he said. "Are you okay?"

She gave him the rushed version of events, then asked about Jim.

"I haven't heard from him yet."

"Have you tried calling him?"

"Yes. Repeatedly. It keeps going to voicemail."

Elizabeth closed her eyes. Too many people had died because of her. She didn't want to think she had somehow gotten her brother killed, too.

Foreman said, "It's getting too dangerous for me right now in Lanton. As you had figured, the police have connected me to the shooting at the motel and they're trying to get in touch with me."

"Meaning?"

"Meaning I'll meet you somewhere outside the county." He was quiet for a moment, then said, "And I know exactly where."

The Green Meadows Motel was a narrow two-story structure squatting in front of a copse of trees a half mile from the turnpike. It was fifteen miles outside of Lanton, and despite the few cars in the parking lot and the shoddy exterior, the rooms were refreshingly clean and neat. Foreman—who had been waiting in his car until they arrived—gave Todd enough cash to score them a room with two double beds (Foreman paranoid that the desk clerk might somehow recognize him and call the police), and then they were in their room located on the second floor.

Foreman went directly to the sliding door that led out onto a narrow balcony, peeked out through the curtains, then turned to face Elizabeth. "You're running out of time."

She sat on one of the beds, staring down at her hands. Todd was in the bathroom.

"I'm well aware of that fact," she said.

"I stopped by my place before coming here. I drove by three times to make sure nobody was watching it. I needed some spare clothes and ..." He paused long enough to dig into the front pocket of his slacks and withdraw a business card. He handed it to Elizabeth. "This was taped to my front door."

The card was simple but direct. What gave it credibility was the familiar seal of the Federal Bureau of Investigations. Anybody could have a card like this made up, of course, but the name printed on it—David Bradford—was very much real. He was the lead agent who had come that day five years ago to arrest her husband. On the back, written in black ink:

Elizabeth, I must speak with you __immediately__.

"Cain—I mean Clarence—said no police or FBI."

Foreman said, "At this point I don't think you have a choice. How exactly do you expect to see Edward? Just drive up to the prison and knock on the gate?"

The toilet in the bathroom flushed and water began running from the sink. Moments later the door opened and Todd emerged, drying his hands on a towel. He sensed the tension at once and frowned at them. "What's up?"

Elizabeth showed him the card. "He wants me to call that FBI agent."

"Maybe you should."

"Absolutely not."

Todd tossed the towel back in the bathroom. "At this point"—he raised his hands in the air—"time's running out."

She forced herself to take a deep breath. "We've already discussed this."

"And people ..." Todd shook his head. "People are getting killed."

Elizabeth had jumped to her feet before she even knew it, her eyes brimming. "Don't you think I know that? Don't you think every second that goes by I'm not reminded of the simple fact that people are dead now because of me?"

Her voice had risen much higher than she intended. She could see it in both of the men's faces, their hope that nobody outside the room had heard her.

Foreman said, "When was the last time you had any sleep?"

"I'm fine."

"I'm serious, Liz. Without any rest, your judgment becomes impaired."

"I said I'm fine."

"Did you get any rest on the drive back?"

"No," Todd said. "She didn't. She hasn't slept in over twenty-four hours."

Great, now they were both ganging up on her. This was the last thing she needed, but it was true. She was exhausted.

"I don't know about either of you," Foreman said, "but I'm starving. How about I go out and get us something to eat? Liz, you can lie down in the meantime."

She opened her mouth to protest but Todd spoke first.

"That sounds great. I'll walk you out."

They left, the both of them, faster than she had thought possible ... though the more she thought about it, the more she wondered if maybe they were moving at a normal speed and her mind—her very tired mind—had made it seem like they were moving in fast forward. She shook her head, rubbed at her eyes, found herself yawning.

When Todd returned to the room, he said, "Seriously, you should lie down. I'll wake you when he gets back with the food."

"I'm not tired."

"Elizabeth."

"I'm not."

But she was, and she couldn't keep fooling herself otherwise. Another yawn came, this one longer.

Todd said, "Isn't it strange?"

"What?"

"He hasn't called. He did right after what happened at the motel last night, but not after this."

This was something that had been troubling her, too. But she had kept receiving the pictures of Matthew, right on time, as if nothing had changed.

She whispered, "Maybe he is already dead."

"Who?"

"Matthew. Maybe Van was right. Maybe Clarence took all of those pictures at once and then killed him. God, I should have asked him again for proof of life. No, I should have *demanded* it."

"Stop."

"But it might be true. He might be dead."

"He's not. You can't think that way. He's still alive, and we're going to get him back."

Elizabeth liked the way he used the first person plural as if it were so commonplace he hadn't even thought to do it.

She said, "I think ... I think I should lie down for a little."

"Good."

"Just for a little."

"Sure. Like I said, I'll wake you when Michael gets back."

She went back to the bed she had earlier claimed and lay down on top of the comforter. She placed her head on the pillow but immediately said, "If Clarence calls—"

"Yes, I'll wake you. Now just rest."

She didn't want to rest. Not until she got Matthew back. Not until she knew for certain he was still alive.

Elizabeth closed her eyes, and was asleep within seconds.

She had no dreams. The last thing she remembered was glancing at the alarm clock on the bedside table before closing her eyes. It had been almost four o'clock. Now she opened her eyes to see the time was now ten o'clock, which couldn't be right at all, because she shouldn't have been asleep that long.

A hand touched her arm. She jerked and twisted her head to find Jim standing beside the bed.

"Two family reunions in one day," he said, smiling. "What are the odds?"

48

Despite being chased by the police through the rain, Elizabeth had managed to leave the city in pretty good time. Jim, however, did not.

The reason being, he told her as they stood out on the narrow balcony overlooking the front parking lot and highway beyond, he hadn't thought once to jump into a cab. Instead he had run to the closest subway station, like he and it were two magnetic ends, and it wasn't until he had gotten onto the train (after waiting almost four mind-numbing minutes for it to arrive) did he realize it was headed uptown.

He hadn't dared get off, though. Because after the second stop a transit cop got onto his car. The cop tried to act inconspicuous, but Jim knew what he was doing. Trying to scan the faces of all the passengers for a likely match to the shooting. Jim had kept his head tilted down, staring at the screen of his iPhone. There was no Internet connection, but he opened an ebook he had been sloughing through for the past couple weeks on the train to and from work, staring at the words without really reading them. As the train barreled through the tunnel the cop made his way through the car. He had paused momentarily in front of Jim, though Jim suspected it was because a cluster of people was blocking the way. Then the cop managed to squeeze through them and went through the door to the next car.

Jim didn't move from his seat for at least another fifteen minutes, doing nothing more than staring at the screen of his phone.

Eventually, when he felt brave enough, he got off at the next stop. He was almost in the Bronx now. He didn't think he had ever been to the Bronx. He waited for the next train headed downtown and hopped on.

He switched only one more train before coming into Penn Station. There he was on familiar ground again, though the place was swarming with police ... or maybe not, though in his mind there seemed to be almost one hundred cops walking around, if not more. He made his way to the New Jersey Transit terminal, got on his train, and rode that all the way to Trenton.

"I was so paranoid, I thought the police would be waiting at my car when I got there."

It had begun to rain again. Jim was smoking—a vice of his since high school—and despite herself, Elizabeth had already bummed a cigarette off him.

"Where is your car anyway?"

"Hmm?"

"Your car. I don't see it."

Jim shrugged, gave her a sheepish grin. "It's parked in the back. What can I say, I'm still pretty paranoid. The whole drive here, I expected to get pulled over any second."

Another silence passed. Elizabeth found herself tightly gripping the cold metal of the balcony railing.

"Thank you," she said softly.

"For what?"

"For trying to help me."

"What do you expect? You're my little sister."

"But you didn't need to involve yourself."

Jim didn't answer and just stared out at the rain.

Elizabeth said, "It doesn't make sense."

"What doesn't?"

"Why Clarence would kill Mark Webster. And *how* he did it. I've been thinking about this ever since it happened. I was the one right there in front of him. He had the gun aimed at me—or at least that's what it felt like—but somehow Mark was the one who got shot."

"You can't blame yourself."

"Are you kidding? If it weren't for me that man would still be alive. His wife wouldn't be husbandless. His children wouldn't be fatherless."

"Liz, stop."

"Do you think I'm a coward?"

"What?"

"For running away like I did, back when Eddie was taken in."

"You ... you didn't have a choice."

"Yes I did. I could have stayed."

"You did what you thought was best for your son."

"You think *this* was the best thing for him?" She shook her head. "I've never forgiven myself for leaving Mom like I did."

She thought about the last time she had spoken to her mother, after the FBI had taken Eddie away. The caller ID showed it was her mother calling but Elizabeth had refused to answer the phone. Finally, after her mother had tried calling at least a dozen times, Elizabeth answered, and the first thing her mother said was, "It's not your fault, dear," and Elizabeth had broken down into tears.

"What did you do with her ashes?" she asked suddenly.

Jim hesitated. "Why?"

"I'm curious."

"They're still at my apartment. I never knew what to do with them, so they just stayed in that box in my closet."

Elizabeth closed her eyes. She didn't want to think that her mother's eternal resting place was in a condominium closet somewhere in Trenton. Then again, what say did she really have in the matter?

Jim went to light himself another cigarette but stopped, staring at her.

"What?"

"This isn't going to end well. You need to go to the police."

"I know what I'm doing."

"I think you *think* you know what you're doing. But let's be honest here."

"If you came all this way to lecture me, you can get back in your car and go home. I told you, I know what I'm doing."

Jim continued staring at her for another couple of seconds. "Okay, then. So what's your plan?"

"I need to see Eddie."

"Right. But what's your plan to get in there? Now that Mark Webster is"—he hesitated again—"dead, you don't have many options left."

"Maybe we can call the prison."

"And what—ask to be put through directly with Eddie? It's a maximum security prison, not a hotel."

"There has to be *some* way of getting in touch with him."

She was biting her lip now, tears threatening. Jim saw it and sighed.

"Does this place have Internet?"

"I don't know. I would think so."

"What about a computer to use? I don't remember seeing one in the lobby."

Elizabeth shrugged.

Jim stared out at the parking lot for a moment, thinking something over, then reached into the pocket of his slacks. He frowned, checked the other pocket.

"What is it?"

"My phone's not on me."

"Is it in your jacket?"

His rain slicker was hanging off one of the doorknobs inside.

"Maybe," he said. "But I might have left it in the car. I'd used the car adapter on the drive down to keep the battery full."

They went into the room. Todd was sitting on one of the beds, his back again the headboard, flipping from one news station to the next.

Todd said, "Everything okay?"

Jim ignored him as he began searching the pockets of his jacket. After a few seconds he glanced up at Elizabeth and shook his head.

"Want me to come with you?" she asked.

Todd said, "What's going on?"

Jim ignored him again. "If you want, sure, but I'll only be a minute."

Todd swung his feet off the bed. "Goddamn it," he said, "what's happening? Is everything all right?"

"Settle down, buddy," Jim said, holding a hand out to him. "No need to curse around my sister."

Elizabeth found this whole scene suddenly disturbing. Two grown men facing off against each other, one her brother, the other her lover ... or would-be lover. Jim had always done the big brother thing and scrutinized the men she dated. He had only approved of Eddie, and that was because he and Eddie had been roommates and friends. Now these two barely knew each other, and it didn't help that tensions were high because of everything else.

"He's looking for his cell phone," she told Todd calmingly.

"What does he need his cell phone for?"

Jim said, "Because not all of us can sit around and watch TV. Some of us actually need to try to help my sister out."

Todd's face went instantly red. He took a step forward, his mouth opening, and Elizabeth hurried between them.

"Let's not do this now, okay?"

Todd kept his glare on Jim. Jim kept his glare on Todd.

On the bedside table, the BlackBerry dinged.

Elizabeth closed her eyes, released a slow breath.

"Is that another one?" Jim asked.

She nodded slowly.

"Can I ... see it?"

Elizabeth said, "Just go get your phone."

She kept her eyes closed until Jim left and only then did she look at the BlackBerry on the bedside table, its notification light blinking an ominous red.

49

Todd said, "I don't like him."

Elizabeth turned to face him. He stood with his shoulders squared, his face set.

"I mean"—Todd held up his hands, shaking his head— "what was his deal anyway? All I wanted to know was what you guys were talking about."

Before she could respond—and what she would say, she didn't even know—one of the phones rang. She immediately headed for the BlackBerry before realizing the ringing phone was the throwaway in her bag.

"Congratulations," Foreman said dryly when she answered. "You've made the news two days in a row."

"What are you talking about?"

"Somebody recognized Sarah Walter as you. Now your face is all over the news. Turn on HNL."

She turned to the TV, which happened to already be on CNN. She grabbed the remote and asked Foreman what channel number and when he told her she punched it in. She expected it to be some quick segment, her face only flashed on the screen for a few seconds, but it was worse. Here now was Nancy Grace talking to two analysts about the recent events regarding Elizabeth Piccioni. She saw it had been a good excuse to bring Eddie back into the limelight, talking about Elizabeth's disappearance and sudden reappearance and the related deaths.

"The main question on everybody's minds, of course," Nancy said to the camera, speaking to her analysts, "is not only why has Elizabeth Piccioni resurfaced after five years, but why is she leaving a trail of bodies in her wake?"

"That's not all, Nancy," said one of the analysts. "My question is, where is Clarence Applegate? His Twitter account hasn't been active for over two days now, and he hasn't been replying to emails."

"That's an excellent point, Henry," Nancy said. "Our people have tried getting in contact with him all day." She looked into the camera. "Clarence, if you're out there, give us a call!"

Elizabeth was standing only a few feet away from the television.

In her ear, Foreman cleared his throat. "This is becoming much too big for you to handle."

She stepped forward and punched the power button with more force than was necessary. The TV went dark, the room silent.

In her ear, Foreman cleared his throat again. "Liz, I think—"

"I'll call you back."

She snapped the phone shut. Stood there a moment, staring into space, before she realized Todd was watching her.

"I ... need to use the restroom," she said, and turned away. Her legs were shaking. She shut the bathroom door behind her and turned on the lights and fan. She placed the throwaway on the counter and gripped the edges, leaning forward and staring at her reflection. She moved her tongue between her teeth and bit down hard. She tasted blood. It was okay, though, because the pain was there, the only thing keeping her at that moment from screaming.

Five minutes later, she emerged from the bathroom. Todd was sitting on the bed again. The TV was off. The room was eerily silent, the only sound that of the rain outside.

Todd was watching her. She had washed her face, making sure to clean up any blood that might have trickled out of her mouth. She stared at Todd, not sure what to say. This entire thing had been snowballing from the start, and it needed to stop. Once Jim returned, they would all sit down and talk about their options. They would discuss—

The BlackBerry rang.

Todd jumped, startled, and turned toward the phone. He went to reach for it but Elizabeth said, "Don't," and hurried across the room, picked up the phone, and placed it to her ear.

"How did it feel?" Clarence Applegate's dark robotic voice asked.

She purposely kept her back to Todd. "How did what feel?"

"The first time you killed someone."

"I've never killed anyone."

"We both know that's a lie. Why do you keep denying the truth to yourself?"

"Because what you believe is true is not really true."

"I can see why you like it. The killing. There's a power to it that's ... preternatural. It's like a piece of yourself has been missing since you were born, and then, once you make that first kill, that piece is put in place. You become whole."

Behind her the bedsprings sighed as Todd rose to his feet.

Clarence said, "I want my trophies."

"I'm working on it."

"You're not working fast enough."

"I tracked down my husband's lawyer, the only person who could get me in to see him so I can get you what you want. But then you had to come and kill him. Why? Why do that?"

"He's not the only one."

"What?"

"I've purposely placed somebody in your path to guide you to what you need. I'm trying to make this simple for you. You're the one making it difficult."

She frowned, not at all sure what he meant by this. She thought about everyone she had come in contact with in the past three days. Half of them, she acknowledged with rising trepidation, were dead.

"Do you think it could be a disease?" the dark robotic voice asked. "Murder, I mean. That it's something you can catch? Something you can pass on? Because I ... I'm starting to like it. I think I'm starting to like it too much. I didn't mean to be as brutal as I was, but there was something about being in that moment, watching him die, that was quite satisfying. Still, I fear I may have gone too far."

She turned then, staring back at Todd. He saw the alarm on her face and opened his mouth but said nothing, just watched her.

"Clarence," she said, trying everything she could to keep her voice steady, "what have you done?"

"I don't remember the very last thing I said to my wife. I remember we were on the phone. We normally ended our conversations by telling each other we loved one another, but that day we had been having a fight. I don't think I told her I loved her. I don't think she told me the same."

The dark robotic voice had taken on a thoughtful tone.

"That's always haunted me, you know. That not being able to remember. It's important to remember the very last words we say to a loved one. So I ask you now, Elizabeth. Think carefully. What were the very last words you said to your brother?"

The rain hadn't let up at all in the fifteen or twenty minutes since she had last been outside. If anything, it had increased. She had left the motel room in a blur, racing down the corridor, down the stairs, and then to the exit door, that she hadn't even bothered to grab her jacket. She just ran without thinking, straight outside, went directly to Jim's car. It was easy to find his car, because it was the only one parked in the back. A wall of trees was clustered behind the motel, giving excellent cover to anybody wishing to stay concealed from the highway.

Despite the rain and the half-darkness—the only security light hung over the exit door, and even that didn't give off much light—she could see the pebbles of glass scattered on the asphalt. Enough light from the dim security lamp hit them just right that they twinkled like stars. Those were from the driver's-side window, which Clarence must have shot out first. It didn't look like Jim even had a chance to do anything. He had been seated, having rushed out into the rain, into his car in search of his phone. He had shut the door, turned away, turned on the dome light which still on, making it possible for her to see that Clarence really had lost all control.

How many times he had shot Jim (with a suppressor, he *must* have used a suppressor or else they would have heard the shots), it was impossible to say, but her brother had been shot at least twice in the face, twice in the chest, maybe more elsewhere. She even saw Clarence in her mind, standing just outside the car, having tapped the window with the barrel of his gun to get Jim's attention, and then firing ... and firing ... and firing.

And Jim having nowhere to go, stuck in his seat like a prisoner, his body jerking violently with every bullet that entered it.

———

Later, she would wonder how she had been so calm, turning back to Todd who had followed her outside, who just stood there in the doorway, his face ashen. How she had gone up to him and told him they needed to leave, leave right this instant. How they had then walked around the motel to the front parking lot, not running but not taking their time either, just walking with a clear destination in mind. How they got into the Prius and Todd started it up and drove them out of the parking lot. How once they were at least a mile from the motel, with no cars behind them, did she dig into her pocket for the business card Foreman had given her, the card the FBI agent had taped to his front door. Later, she would understand that she had been so calm because she had had no other choice, none whatsoever. Not if she wanted to get through this. Not if she wanted to save her son.

Having found the business card, she took out the throw-away phone, opened it, and began to dial.

PART III
WHAT DENNY THE DRAGON KNOWS

50

Despite last night's heavy rain, some drops of blood spotted the back parking lot of the Green Meadows Motel. There were only a few, barely even noticeable unless you were looking for them. The pebbles of safety glass were easier to find. Not all of them had been swept up by Clarence, who had also presumably moved Jim's car along with Jim himself. In the early morning light, the pebbles sparkled like diamonds.

Special Agent David Bradford crouched over the area with the spots of blood and pebbles of glass. He had positioned himself so the sun could shine just right and not have any chance of getting his shadow in the way. Standing a few feet away was Special Agent Julia Hogan, who in her smart dark pantsuit also stood back enough so the sun's rays wouldn't be distracted.

"What are you thinking?" Julia Hogan asked.

He stayed crouched for another few seconds, staring down at the spots of blood and pebbles of glass, before standing back up. He was in his late forties and one of his knees popped with the effort.

"I'm thinking," David Bradford said, "that those spots

there on the asphalt *could* be blood. And those pebbles of glass there, they *could* have come from a shattered car window. And that the supposed victim, James McEvoy, *could* have been killed here last night."

"That sounds like a lot of coulds," Julia Hogan said.

David Bradford nodded, still staring down at the ground. "Yes, there is definitely a pattern forming. Of course, without the actual body, or even the car that was supposedly here, it's impossible to make a solid conclusion. There are no security cameras back here. In fact, there are no security cameras out front either."

"So again, what are you thinking?"

"That depends."

"It does?"

"Yes. It depends all on whether or not I want to believe a woman who disappeared five years ago only to reemerge and become the focal point of a series of unexplained murders. A woman who, in my opinion at least, is not trustworthy at all." He paused, tilting his head up so his gaze was even with hers. "What do you think about that, Elizabeth?"

She had stood in the same spot for the last ten minutes, not moving, just standing enough distance away that she didn't feel too close to the FBI agents, but not too far away either. Last night she had told Special Agent David Bradford to meet her here at seven o'clock and had disconnected and turned off the phone before he could say anything else or even call back, and a half hour ago Todd had dropped her off a half mile away and she had walked here with only the BlackBerry Clarence had given her.

She explained everything, or at least almost everything, leaving out one or two details about her time at Van's place, but besides that she had come clean with these two because right now she didn't know what other choice she had. And, surprisingly, the two of them had listened to her, Special Agents David Bradford and Julia Hogan, the woman somewhere in her thirties, with a pretty face and short black hair, the man looking exhausted, like he hadn't slept in days.

Now she held up the BlackBerry and said, "The pictures of my son are on here, all of them."

"Why didn't your boyfriend come with you?"

"In case this doesn't work out well."

"Meaning?"

"I want him to have the least amount of involvement in this as possible on the chance we eventually face charges."

David Bradford glanced at Julia Hogan. "That's probably for the best."

Elizabeth said, "What's for the best?"

"Doesn't it seem odd to you, Elizabeth?"

"What does?"

"Clarence Applegate—if he really is the person behind all of this—hasn't seemed to care much about his killings so far. First he killed that child molester back in Kansas, then your friends in Indianapolis, then that lawyer in the middle of Rockefeller fucking Plaza. And then he comes here to kill your brother but he cleans up the scene and takes away the body. Why?"

Elizabeth stared down at the spots of blood on the asphalt. "I don't know. To push me over the edge, I guess."

"And why do you think he'd want to push you over the edge?"

"He hates me. He wants to see me suffer."

"Do you think your son is still alive?"

She didn't answer, still staring at those spots of blood.

"Elizabeth."

She blinked and looked up at David Bradford as the agent

reached into his pocket and pulled out his phone. It was a BlackBerry, the same model as hers.

"Look familiar?"

She started shaking her head slowly. "I don't ... I don't understand."

"Then understand this. I've been trying to contact you for the past two days. Even last night when you called me, I tried to tell you something, but you wouldn't listen."

Her gaze narrowed, she looked at Julia Hogan, then back to David Bradford. "What are you saying?"

"This past weekend was supposed to be my weekend with my son. We were going to a ballgame. That night we ordered pizza. Even now I believe the guy who delivered it is the one who's doing this—and truthfully it may have been Clarence, because he had a hat on and I wasn't even paying attention—but the next thing I knew I woke up in the morning to a terrible headache and my son had been abducted."

With frustration he shook the BlackBerry like a maraca.

"This was beside me, with a photo on it of my son strapped to a bed in his underwear and a gag in his mouth. Just like you I receive a new photograph of him every hour to let me know he's still alive. And the only way I can get him back is to help you. That's what the messages sent to me say. That's why I needed to find you. I want to get my son back, and the only way I can do that is by helping you. And I know exactly how we're going to do it."

51

The very last place Elizabeth expected to find herself that Monday morning was a changing room in the women's department of Sears. Earlier Julia Hogan had asked her size and then picked out a pantsuit and a blouse, and now here Elizabeth stood in the new clothes, staring at herself in the mirror.

There was a knock at the door. Julia Hogan asked, "How's it going in there?"

Elizabeth kept staring at herself. "Fine."

"I've brought you two pairs of shoes. You said you were a size seven, right?"

When she emerged from the changing room a few minutes later, dressed once again in her dirty jeans and shirt, David Bradford was pacing around one of the displays for winter wear, his own cell phone to his ear. Julia Hogan took the clothes and shoes from her and asked if they fit okay. Elizabeth only nodded.

While Julia was paying, David quit his call and walked toward them. He looked even more exhausted, which now made sense to Elizabeth, who figured he, like her, hadn't slept much in the past two days.

As the cashier swiped Julia's credit card, Julia turned to David and asked, "Well?"

"It's a go."

"Just like that?"

"I spoke directly to the warden. I'd met him a couple times before. He knew I'd been transferred out of the division but didn't seem to care. He promised me at least a half hour."

"When?"

"At noon."

Julia glanced at her watch. "That's in three hours."

David nodded. "And it's a two hour drive, so we need to get going."

The cashier bagged up the clothes and handed them to Julia with a plastic smile. She then turned the plastic smile on Elizabeth and asked, "How are you today, dear?"

There are over twenty state correctional institutions in Pennsylvania. Edward Piccioni had ended up in the largest maximum-security prison in the state, located in Graterford, about thirty miles northwest of Philadelphia. There he had been for at least the past four years, calling whatever tiny cell he'd been forced into his own, and it was this prison that Special Agent David Bradford planned on taking her into today.

His plan was crazy, of course. Completely off-the-wall nuts. Even he had to know that was the case, but that didn't seem to slow him.

After Sears they made a quick stop at Walmart (Elizabeth in the back of the car, David Bradford up front, neither one of them speaking while Julia Hogan ran inside), and then they stopped at a motel, a very rundown and inexpensive motel, and got a room.

The room had the two things they needed: a bathroom sink and a chair.

Julia folded one of the towels and placed it on the edge of the sink. Elizabeth sat in the chair and tipped her head back so her neck rested comfortably on the towel. Julia began running the water.

"Tell me if it gets too hot," she said, starting to open the package of L'Oréal Paris she pulled out of the Walmart bag.

For the first couple minutes Elizabeth didn't speak. She kept her eyes closed and let Julia do her thing. With each snip of the scissors, Elizabeth felt herself tense. Julia's hair wasn't that short—only a few inches shorter than Elizabeth's—but still it pained her to know she would be losing all of it.

"Do you really think this is going to work?"

The bathroom door was closed and it was just the two of them.

Julia Hogan didn't answer for the longest time, working the dye into Elizabeth's hair. Finally she said, "It has to."

Elizabeth remembered saying something very similar not too long ago. Right before somebody got killed.

"It's a crazy idea."

Julia said nothing.

"He could lose his job. You could lose yours."

Julia was quiet for another couple of moments. "We're both aware of the risk."

"I understand why he's going to this length—it is his son, after all—but why you?"

Julia kept working her gloved hands through Elizabeth's hair, not saying anything.

"I don't remember you being one of the agents who came to arrest my husband."

Still nothing.

Elizabeth said, "Are you two sleeping together?"

The water falling on Elizabeth's head suddenly became scalding. Elizabeth flinched and cried out. The door opened and David Bradford poked his head in, asking what was wrong.

"Nothing," Julia Hogan said, turning the hot water down.

David Bradford glanced at his watch. "We need to leave soon," he said, and closed the door.

"Bitch," Elizabeth murmured.

Still working the dye into her hair, Julia Hogan leaned forward to whisper into her ear. "That man out there is a good man. He got screwed over because you ran away and disappeared."

"How did I—"

"His superiors didn't look kindly on the fact he lost the suspect's wife. Especially after Clarence Applegate came out with the idea you were part of the killings. Dave was made out to look like a clown, and because of that so did the Bureau. And as you can probably guess, the Bureau doesn't like being made to look like clowns, so he was transferred across the country, put on desk duty until the day he retires."

"That still doesn't answer the question of where you fit into all of this."

The water stopped. Julia Hogan leaned away from her and said, "You can open your eyes now."

Elizabeth opened her eyes right as Julia threw a towel at her face.

"Not bad," David Bradford said.

"You really think she'll pass?"

"They're just going to glance at our IDs, not study them. She'll do fine."

Elizabeth stood in the pantsuits and blouse and shoes newly purchased from Sears, her hair now short and almost black. Julia Hogan came to stand beside her. Both women looked into the body-length mirror. Despite the fact Elizabeth was three inches taller than Julia, they could have passed for twins.

"Okay," David Bradford said, but before he could say anything else, his BlackBerry beeped again. Something twitched in his face. His jaw tightened. It was clear he intended to keep it in his pocket, but Elizabeth turned and extended her hand.

"May I see him?"

Julia Hogan said, "Of course he won't let you—" but David Bradford shook his head and waved her off.

"No, it's fine. Here."

He brought the BlackBerry out of his pocket and handed it to her. She stared down at the screen. She saw that this was just one of over fifty pictures sent to this phone over the course of two and a half days. Just like with her, a new picture every hour.

Elizabeth stared at this new picture for several long seconds. A boy just a few years older than Matthew, naked except for his underwear, his arms and legs tied to each side of the bed. A gag in his mouth. An explosive collar around his neck. The camera was positioned just off to the side, facing the bed. A TV was beside it. She could see the light reflecting off the boy's eyes, which had lost some of its life and taken on a defeated, vacuous quality.

She felt completely hollow as she handed back the phone. "I'm so sorry."

David Bradford slipped the phone back into his pocket without looking at it. "Yeah," he said. "You should be."

52

They'd been driving for nearly an hour in silence, the two FBI agents in the front, Elizabeth in the back, when she cleared her throat and asked, "Agent Bradford, do you think I'm an idiot?"

This entire time he had not once glanced at her. Now his eyes shifted just slightly to meet hers in the rearview mirror before focusing back on the highway.

"Is this a trick question?"

"I consider myself bright, or at least I like to consider myself bright, and here I was with a man for nearly seven years who was apparently raping and murdering women. And I had no idea. Not one iota of a clue. Almost every day I saw that man, almost every night we slept in the same bed, and not once did I wonder if he was possibly a serial killer. So again I ask you, do you think I'm an idiot?"

For a long time David Bradford didn't answer her. He just sat behind the wheel, his focus on the highway. Beside him, in the passenger seat, Julia Hogan tilted her head slightly and watched him from the corner of her eye. Another couple of seconds and Elizabeth figured the silent treatment would continue, but then he spoke.

"There are always warning signs."

"Really? Well, when I got married I apparently was never given that memo."

"Nearly every serial killer in the United States shares the same fundamental characteristics. The majority are single white males. They often—"

"My husband wasn't a single white male. Obviously."

"That's why I specified the sentence first with the *majority*. So again, the *majority* are—"

"Yes, yes, yes. I've read all the books, too. I know all about the general characteristics about the bed-wetting and fire starting and abusive family members. And personally, I don't believe it."

"So what—you think it's nature over nurture? That these people are born this way?"

"Not entirely, no. But I also think every person who has wet the bed and started fires and tortured animals and come from families who have criminal or alcoholic histories don't turn out to be serial killers either. Some of them are able to control those urges."

"Yes, but they still have the urges."

Elizabeth bit her tongue. She hated that he had managed to pounce on that last point so quickly.

David Bradford said, "Let's take a look at your husband's past, shall we? He grew up without a family. He went from one foster care home to another. And believe it or not, Elizabeth, those foster care homes are not a bundle of hugs and sunshine. After he was arrested we went into his foster care file. Did you know when he was eight he set a cat on fire?"

Elizabeth sighed. "Believe it or not, Agent Bradford, I did know that. Eddie told me the story once while we were dating. He felt terrible about it. But it wasn't just him. One of the boys at the home—the woman's own son—was the one who did it. Eddie was there and tried to save the cat. In the end, the son told his mother it was Eddie and so he was sent away."

"And you believed him?"

"At the time, I had no reason not to."

Plus, she remembered the sincerity and regret in her husband's voice when he was telling her what happened. There had been no hint of pleasure in the story. The episode had haunted him all those years, and he had felt by telling her he might be somehow absolved from that horrific event.

Or at least that's what he had told her, now that she thought about it. He had *told* her he might be somehow absolved from that horrific event, but maybe it had just been a story. One of many.

"He refused to speak to us, you know," Bradford said. "Which, honestly, was rare. Most of the times these guys want to talk about their victims once they're caught. They know they're fucked anyway—forensic evidence never lies—and so they want to brag about how they had managed to last so long. But your husband, he wouldn't tell us anything. He'd just sit there and stare down at the table. No matter what we did or said he refused to say a word. Which always bugged me, too, because I'd always wanted an explanation on why he had started cutting off the ring fingers."

He paused, catching a warning glance from Julia Hogan, but seemed to dismiss her.

"Your husband's MO was pretty basic. He picked up young married women. These women were obviously not happy with their marriages, because it appears they went willingly enough. And from what I understand about Edward Piccioni, he was a likable guy. Had charisma and class. So talking these women into bed wouldn't have been a problem for him. But once he had them in bed, that's when he went to work. He'd strangle them while he fucked them—sorry if that's too crude for you," he said, his eyes shifting up momentarily to meet hers in the rearview mirror, "but that's what happened—and then after they were dead he'd fuck them again. A couple of times."

"No," Julia Hogan said, the sudden sound of her voice in the car making Elizabeth jump. Obviously she knew the woman had been there the entire time, but while David Bradford spoke all she had been concentrating on were his words and thinking about the man she had known, all the moments alone she had spent with him, every single time they had told each other I love you.

David Bradford said, "What no?"

"That's wrong. He didn't start playing with the bodies until at least the third victim. Before that there was no extra tearing around the vaginal area. After the third victim, all the bodies showed the same post-mortem penetration."

Elizabeth closed her eyes and took a deep breath. She kept her eyes closed for a long time, then opened them and stared out her window. It didn't help relieve the nausea.

"Plus," David Bradford said, "when we put the stats into the ViCAP system, we came up with two likely hits. Women who had been strangled during sex. Their bodies were hidden away just like the rest. Speaking of which, Elizabeth"—eyeing her again in the rearview mirror—"your husband sure did know how to cover his tracks. Just like yourself. You had mentioned you ended up in Kansas. Where exactly?"

"Oakville."

"Is that right?" David Bradford gave Julia Hogan a curious glance.

Elizabeth said, "What is it?"

Bradford glanced at Julia again. Julia shrugged.

"What is it?" Elizabeth repeated.

"We actually got a hit three years ago about you being in Oakville. We sent some agents there but it was just for a day. You know, more important things in the world than to chase what was no doubt a wild goose."

"What do you mean you got a hit?"

"It probably doesn't surprise you to learn we have people monitoring the Internet twenty-four seven. One of the places we monitor is Clarence Applegate's message board, as he's generated quite a following of wackos. One day an anonymous user posted that you were located in Oakville, Kansas. Clarence asked how this user knew that information. There was never any reply."

The initial nausea had changed into a different kind. She wondered just who would have done that. Nobody had known that she ended up in Oakville.

"What you said before," Elizabeth murmured, "about my husband covering his tracks. What does that mean?"

"It means he knew how to clean up his murder scene. He knew how to hide the bodies, too. Wrapped them up not in garbage bags but clear wrap, so tight that nothing could get in. Then he'd bury them, almost always in the same kind of place."

Elizabeth knew pretty much all of this already from what she had read online and in *Never Coming Home: The Edward Piccioni Murders*. There had been a full chapter that detailed how her husband cleaned up his crime scenes and how he hid the bodies. All of them buried in the strips of land between major highways, all of them overrun with trees. Motorists drove past the burial spots for weeks, sometimes months, before the bodies were eventually found.

"But those first two victims," David Bradford said, "their

ring fingers were still intact. So were the rings. At that point he hadn't started collecting his trophies."

"Or evolving," Elizabeth murmured.

"What was that?"

"Evolving," she said. "Isn't that how you FBI people put it?"

The glance that met hers in the rearview mirror this time was more of a glare than anything else.

Elizabeth said, "If my husband refused to speak to you before, what makes you think he'll speak to us now?"

"Because of you. Because of your son."

"You don't know that," she said, and immediately wondered why she said it herself, as she hoped it wasn't the case.

David Bradford snorted air through his nose and shook his head. "You just don't get it, do you?"

"What?"

"Despite whether or not your husband was natured or nurtured, the psychological proof is evident. We may never have had a chance to actually talk to him—from what I hear he still never speaks—but the evidence alone proves what he was working up to."

Elizabeth still wasn't seeing it. "What are you talking about?"

"His trophies," David Bradford said. "The ring fingers he cut off. Why do you suppose he was doing that? My God, Elizabeth, you asked me whether or not you're an idiot, and the plain and simple truth is yes, you are. Don't you get it? Every time he murdered, it wasn't one of those women he thought he was killing. In his dark and demented mind, he was killing you."

53

A couple miles just outside the Graterford Prison was predictably a strip mall, and just as predictably that strip mall had a Starbucks. This was where David Bradford parked the car, a few spaces from the entrance.

In the front passenger seat, Julia Hogan had been playing with her sidearm for the past several minutes. Only *playing* wasn't the right word for it. She was handling the piece like a pro, ejecting the magazine and taking out each individual bullet. These she gathered first into her lap, then into her palm which she used to transport them to the safety of the glove box. By the time Bradford parked, she was finished and turned to pass the gun, along with the belt holster, back to Elizabeth.

Bradford was faster than Elizabeth had at first taken him. He managed to turn and grip Julia's wrist in the space of only a second.

"What do you think you're doing?"

"Relax," Julia said. "It's not loaded."

"I don't care. She doesn't need a gun."

"Yes, she does. She'll need to check it in once you two arrive. Without one it might raise suspicions."

Bradford maintained his grip around Julia's wrist for another couple of seconds, and then let go. It was clear he wasn't happy about the situation but knew it wasn't worth fighting.

Elizabeth took the proffered (and unloaded) weapon and, without thinking, said, "Thank you."

Julia looked like she might just say *You're welcome* but caught herself and turned back around. She opened her door and stepped out.

Elizabeth got out, too. She took a moment to stretch her legs and clip the holstered gun onto her belt. "What are you going to do?"

"Get something to drink. Maybe a latte. You know, try to relax."

Julia Hogan even attempted a smile, but her eyes carried a worry that couldn't be hidden.

Elizabeth slid into the front passenger seat. Julia shut the door and walked around the front of the car to David Bradford's side. He rolled down his window.

"Good luck," Julia said. She went to step away but Bradford reached out and grabbed her arm and pulled her down to kiss her deeply on the lips.

Leaning back, Bradford said, "We'll be back soon."

The entire drive there she had been feeling nervous—or something close to nervous—but now in the front passenger seat, the prison less than a mile away, she had begun to shake. Her breathing increased. She tried to hide both things but David Bradford caught them.

"What's wrong?"

"Nothing."

"Don't screw this up."

"I won't."

But then when they came around a bend in the road and the prison appeared she wondered if that was true. More importantly, though, she wondered if she would even be able to go through with this. Five years ago she had decided to take her son and leave her old life behind. Leave Eddie behind. She had never wanted to see him or even think of him again. He was a monster. He had destroyed their lives. He could rot in a metal box for all she cared. Or no. She had wished worse for him. Some kind of torture. Maybe starvation. Something medieval, definitely.

And now ... now she was coming to see him.

As they approached the prison gates, Bradford said, "You need to relax."

"I'm trying."

"Try harder."

But it wasn't that easy. Not for her. And it didn't make sense, because after everything she had been through from the very start of this, when she received that first phone call, she had managed to fight through all her worries and doubts and fears. But this was different, and she knew it.

"I think I might throw up," she whispered. The temperature in the car had suddenly risen. Her forehead had begun to perspire.

They were on the drive leading into the prison. The walls were only yards away. David Bradford was already going at a slow speed, and now stopped.

"What are you doing?"

"Turning back around."

"Why?"

"Because you're going to fuck this up."

In the back of her throat she could taste bile rising but managed to fight it back down.

"No, I won't," she managed.

He stared at her, studying her face. After a moment, he smiled. "Who am I kidding? At this point, we're both fucked." He pressed his foot back down on the gas and drove them through the gates.

———

The warden's name was Henry Banks. He was a short man with gray hair and thin glasses. He met them right after they'd shown their IDs and checked in their weapons and walked through the metal detectors. He stood with his penny loafers pointing straight out and his hands clasped in front of him.

"Special Agent David Bradford," he said with a nod and held out his hand. "It's been a while."

"Yes it has." Bradford gestured to Elizabeth. "This is Special Agent Julia Hogan."

"Pleasure," Henry Banks said, shaking her hand, too. "Are you with ViCAP?"

She hesitated, not knowing what to say, but it didn't matter. Bradford answered for her.

"She's not."

Henry took his hand back from her and returned to the hands-clasped-in-front-of-him pose. He said to Bradford, "And from what I understand, neither are you. So what exactly are you two doing here?"

Elizabeth's heart sank. She tasted that bile again in the back of her throat. Everything so far had not been going smoothly, but it had been progressing, and here they were so close to getting what they had come for. Except for this man. This man asking a very simple and direct question.

"Why the third degree?" Bradford asked kindly.

"Because while I may be the warden of this facility, I am still a state employee and I always need to watch my step. The way the economy is, I can't afford to lose my pension."

"Nobody ever said you would."

"That's beside the point."

"Then what is the point?"

"You were kicked out of ViCAP five years ago. From what I heard, you were reassigned to be some desk jockey in Oregon. And that, as I'm sure you know, is not close to this prison at all."

Despite the sudden tension, Bradford managed to keep the kind tone in his voice. "Call my SAC. He'll confirm the reason for my visit."

"Maybe I already did contact him."

"No you didn't, or we wouldn't be having this conversation." Bradford sighed and gave Elizabeth an irritated glance. "Listen," he said to the warden, "haven't you been watching the news? Elizabeth Piccioni has resurfaced. She's a person of interest in a number of strange murders that have occurred over the past forty-eight hours."

"So what"—Henry Banks grinned—"you think The Monk will give you an idea where she is?"

"Is that what they're calling him now?" Elizabeth asked before she could stop herself.

Henry Banks didn't seem to notice her sudden break of reticence. "The man has apparently taken a vow of silence. Been that way since he came here. Nobody's heard him speak, though occasionally we'll get some nut job claiming they heard him whispering something." He shook his head. "Cries for attention on their part is what it is."

Bradford gestured to Elizabeth again. "Agent Hogan is simply my driver today. After Elizabeth Piccioni's sudden reappearance, I was requested to come here and try to speak to Edward." He frowned. "I'm surprised you weren't contacted by one of the SACs."

"And what—keep me in the loop?" The warden gave a dry laugh. "Hardly. Listen, like I told you on the phone I can give you a half hour with The Monk, no problem there. But you're wasting your time. The man won't speak for anybody."

Bradford shrugged. "Then what's the harm in at least trying? If anything, I can bounce some new jokes off him. See if he cracks a smile."

The warden escorted them personally to the interview room. The room in question was equipped with video and audio recording devices. Bradford requested they be kept off.

"You know," he said, smiling, "in case I decide to do something foolish."

Then they were in the room, which contained just a table and three chairs. Two of the chairs were positioned on the far side of the table facing the door. These were the ones David Bradford and Elizabeth took. They sat there, neither one of them speaking (Elizabeth had begun to shake again), until a few minutes passed and the door opened and Elizabeth saw her husband for the first time in five years.

54

Two guards escorted him into the room. His arms and legs were shackled. He had on the typical prison jumpsuit. He looked surprisingly good for having been in prison for five years. His features had become more pronounced. It was clear he had been working out and eating less.

One guard pulled out the chair facing Elizabeth and Bradford; the other guard shoved him down onto the chair. Then they backed away and left the room, closing the door behind them.

"Hello, Eddie," Bradford said. "How's it hanging?"

Eddie didn't say anything. He just sat on the chair and stared at the FBI agent who had come five years before to arrest him. It wasn't a glare, either—Elizabeth had assumed that was all he would give them at first—but a look of complete indifference. He was here, Bradford was there, and still the world turned. It was the nature of things. No sense being angry about it.

"Or should I say, hello there, Monk. Would you prefer that instead?"

The kind and good-natured tone in David Bradford's voice

was starting to peak. Elizabeth thought she heard a tremor in it. In the next couple of seconds, if her husband kept sitting there with his cold indifferent stare and said nothing, Bradford might lose it.

"Eddie," she said softly.

This entire time he hadn't once glanced at her. She knew this because the entire time she had been watching his eyes. Now those eyes—light brown eyes, speckled with some green, eyes she used to love staring into—shifted briefly to hers, then shifted back to continue the indifferent stare with Bradford ... and then shifted back to hers again.

His eyes narrowed slightly. His lips parted. It looked like he was going to speak but then stopped. Cleared his throat. Tried again. Still nothing.

"Do you need some water?" Bradford asked. "Maybe a beer?"

Eddie ignored him. Still staring at Elizabeth, he finally managed, "Liz?"

Her throat tightened. Her body refused to move. Finally she managed to nod, just slightly, and whispered, "Yes."

"You don't need to whisper," David Bradford said.

That indifferent stare quickly turned into a glare, directed straight at the FBI agent. His face suffusing with color, Eddie said to her, "What are you *doing* here?"

"Trying to save your son," David Bradford said coolly, knowing a verbal push was exactly what Elizabeth needed to continue. "And in the process, trying to save mine, too." He glanced at her and nodded. "Tell him."

Eddie's gaze now stayed glued on hers. His voice remained flat. "What's happened to Thomas?"

Now it was Elizabeth who had no voice. Her first instinct was to correct him, explain that their son's name wasn't Thomas anymore but Matthew. But that, she feared, would cause too much confusion. What she needed to do now was stick to the basics.

"He doesn't have much time. Clarence abducted him. He's strapped a bomb around his neck, a whole thing of C-4."

Eddie looked like he had just been slapped. "A bomb around his neck? Clarence—" He paused. "Clarence who?"

"Clarence Applegate."

He frowned again. "Clarence Applegate is doing this?"

"He's already killed a number of people. God, Eddie, he killed Jim last night."

"*Jim?*" The frown deepened. "No, that can't be right. That can't—" His eyes shifted to Bradford again, and he stopped talking. Was quiet for a couple of long seconds, and then said again in his flat voice, "So let me guess—the person doing this wants the fingers."

"Yes," Elizabeth said, nodding, feeling like they were finally making progress. "Yes, that's exactly right. Clarence calls them your trophies. He says ..."

But Eddie was no longer paying her any attention. His focus was back on David Bradford, just as it had been when he first entered the room. And the indifferent stare had been replaced again by the glare.

"I'm sorry, Liz, but I can't help you."

"*What?* But you have to!"

"He brought you here?" Eddie said, lifting his chin at David Bradford.

"Yes. His son has been abducted, too."

"And you know this for a fact?"

Beside her Bradford shifted in his chair. He leaned forward. Elizabeth reached out and placed a hand on his arm to keep him seated.

"I saw a picture," she said.

"I've seen a lot of pictures. None of them ever proved anything."

Beneath her hand she could feel Bradford's entire body trembling. She squeezed down on his arm to keep him in place, but he shrugged her off and shot to his feet, knocking the chair to the ground.

"You son of a bitch! How fucking selfish are you? You're not going to help us because my son's life is also in danger? You're a real piece of shit, you know that?"

He came around the table, and Elizabeth was sure he was going to deck Eddie, but Bradford kept walking toward the door.

She rose to her feet. "Where are you going?"

"Leaving," Bradford said simply.

"But you can't!" She turned to Eddie who hadn't moved in his seat, still facing forward. "Please, Eddie. *Please* tell us."

At the door, David Bradford shook his head with disgust. He raised a fist to knock on the door but paused when Eddie spoke.

"Do you remember when I proposed to you?" He was still facing forward, not looking at her. "We were down at the Inner Harbor, right next to the water. On the drive back we were both hungry and stopped at that Denny's. Do you remember?"

She just stared down at him.

"And they had one of those crane games in the lobby. Two chances to win for a buck. So we put in a buck, and do you remember what we won?"

"Of course," she whispered. "A dragon."

"Yes." His mouth twitched in what may have been a smile. "We called him Denny the Dragon. We decided to keep him for when we had a child. It would be the baby's first stuffed animal."

At the door, David Bradford said, "Fuck this bullshit. Elizabeth, come on."

Eddie turned his face to look up at her. In his eyes was more sadness than she ever thought she'd see in a man convicted of six murders. "Right now he's the answer you're looking for. He knows."

"He knows what?"

Eddie just nodded. "He knows."

55

"What was that?" Bradford said, driving them through the prison gate. "Just what the *fuck* was that?"

"I don't know," Elizabeth said quietly. She was slumped in the passenger seat, staring out through the windshield.

"You don't *know*, or you don't want to *say*?"

She looked at him sharply. "Are you crazy? You actually think I'm hiding something from you?"

"Hmm, well let's see. You were the one who went into hiding five years ago when your husband was arrested. Doesn't quite make you the most reliable person in the world, does it? So come on, spill. Denny the Dragon. Just what the fuck does that have to do with anything?"

"I don't know," she repeated, though she wondered if that was true. She remembered the stuffed animal—a purple plush thing with black marble eyes and a large nose and a pair of green wings sprouting from its back—but she had trouble actually placing what may have happened to it.

"A sociopath," David Bradford murmured. "Your husband is truly a grade-A sociopath."

They didn't speak the rest of the way to the strip mall.

When Bradford pulled up in front of the Starbucks (he didn't bother parking in a space), he turned in his seat to glare at her.

"Get the fuck in the back."

Before she could move, though, the back door opened and Julia Hogan slid into the seat. "How'd it go?" she asked.

"Sit up front with me," Bradford said.

Julia ignored him. "How did it *go*?"

Bradford gritted his teeth. Sensing that neither woman was going to do as he had instructed, he shoved the car in gear and got them moving forward. Without being told to Elizabeth unclipped the gun from her belt and handed it back to Julia.

Julia sensed the tension at once. She took the gun and sat back in her seat with a sigh. "How bad was it?"

"Bad enough." Bradford glanced at Elizabeth. "Do you want to tell her or should I?"

Elizabeth just shook her head and stared out her window. Bradford cleared his throat and ran through the entire thing.

"What Denny the Dragon knows," Julia Hogan said in a quiet, musing tone. Despite the fact her back was to the woman, Elizabeth knew Julia was speaking to her. "What do you think it means?"

"I don't know."

Bradford snorted. He said to the rearview mirror, "Do you believe that shit? I think she's lying."

"I am not! Why would you say that?"

"Oh, I don't know. Why do geese fly south during the winter? It's just their nature."

Elizabeth looked back at Julia for support, but Julia was staring out her window. She turned to Bradford and said, as slowly and calmly as she could, "I am not lying to you."

"Whatever."

Bradford dug into his pocket for his cell phone and the BlackBerry. He hadn't turned either of them on since they left the prison and had to wait about a minute for both to power up. Immediately the BlackBerry dinged, signaling there was a new message. He ignored it and, using his own cell phone, started dialing a number.

"What are you doing?"

"I'm tired of playing games. I'm doing what I should have done in the first place."

"But you can't. What about your son?"

He gave her a look that was all at once somber. "Most likely my son is already dead, just like yours."

"You don't know that."

He nodded slowly. "I do."

But before he could finish dialing, the BlackBerry rang. He set his own cell phone down, picked up the BlackBerry, frowned at the screen. Hesitantly, he answered it. Listened for a couple of seconds, then glanced at her.

"It's for you."

And handed her the phone.

"So," the dark robotic voice said, "how was the family reunion? Was it everything you dreamed it would be?"

They were on the four-lane highway now, headed toward Reading. Bradford was doing easily ten miles per hour over the limit.

"What do you want?" She didn't bother asking Clarence how he knew they had already visited the prison.

"What I want is to talk to you. I called your phone but it went straight to voicemail. What's wrong—has the battery gone dead?"

She dug in her pocket, pulled out the BlackBerry, and turned it on. "There, it's on."

"That doesn't matter now. I'm already talking to you."

"What do you want?"

"You know exactly what I want. Now the question is, can you get it for me?"

She closed her eyes and was silent for a moment. In that moment the BlackBerry had powered up completely and, like with Bradford's phone, she heard that familiar ding. She whispered, "Yes."

"Good. *Very* good. When?"

"Soon."

The dark robotic voice's tone quickly soured. "When exactly is *soon*?"

Elizabeth didn't answer. She wasn't sure what to say. The truth was she had no idea how to get Clarence the trophies. If Eddie had tried to give her a hint—and why he just couldn't come out with whatever it was he wanted to say, she still didn't know—then he had failed, because yes, she remembered Denny the Dragon, but where was it now?

"Elizabeth?"

"I'm working on it."

"That doesn't answer my question."

"Soon."

"Again, I ask you when exactly is soon?"

Again, Elizabeth didn't answer. Bullshitting a man this insane was not a good idea, and yet she was trying the best she could, and she knew she was being sloppy.

"Okay," Clarence said. "Let me ask you this then instead. Has Special Agent Bradford done what was needed of him?"

She risked a glance at the man behind the steering wheel. He quickly glanced back at her, mouthing, *What?*

Shaking her head at Bradford, she said into the phone, "I'm not sure what you mean."

"What I mean is has Special Agent Bradford done what I instructed him to do? He got you in to see your husband, and your husband told you where you can find what I want. Correct?"

She was staring forward at the highway in front of her. She could feel Bradford watching her—could even sense Julia Hogan watching at her—but she forced herself to not acknowledge either of them.

"That's correct."

"Good. Then get rid of him."

"What?"

"Get rid of him. Do you need me to spell it out for you?"

"But what about his son?" she asked, and the car swerved suddenly as David Bradford's grip on the steering wheel twitched.

"His son will be fine. Believe it or not, I do consider myself a man of my word. And my word is that his son will remain safe. Of course, they won't be reunited just yet—not until you get me those trophies—so that last part is up to you. Are we on the same page?"

"Yes."

"Good. Now make it happen. As evidenced by the last picture that was sent to you, you have fourteen hours left or else I kill your boy."

He clicked off.

Elizabeth kept the BlackBerry to her ear for several more seconds. Then she blinked, turned in her seat, and extended the phone to Bradford.

He snatched it at once. "What was that about?"

"You need to let me out."

"Say that again?"

"Clarence says your part in this is through."

"What about my son?"

"He said your son will be safe as long as I can still get him the trophies. But you need to let me out."

Bradford's fingers were white around the steering wheel. He glanced up at the rearview mirror to see Julia's reaction to all of this. He seemed to think about it for another couple of seconds, and then shook his head.

"No." The car's engine gave a meaty roar as Bradford pressed his foot down on the gas. "No, that is not going to happen."

"Please," she said. "Be reasonable."

"Reasonable?" He laughed. "*You* are asking *me* to be reasonable? Are you fucking insane?"

"David," Julia Hogan said quietly in the back.

Bradford shook his head again. "No. What we're going to do now is call the Bureau. That's the smart thing to do. It's the *only* thing to do."

The car's needle was up to eighty now, the car swerving from lane to lane.

Elizabeth leaned back in her seat. She stared out her window. She closed her eyes, took a deep breath, and retched.

Bradford said, "What is it?"

Her eyes still closed, she retched again, holding her stomach. "Remember ... how I felt ... before we went ... into the prison?"

"Yeah, so?"

"I think ... I'm going to ... throw up."

56

David Bradford moved over into the right lane and slowed the car until they came to a stop. Elizabeth threw off her seatbelt and opened her door and nearly fell onto the ground, dry heaving, crawling away from the car up the grassy embankment.

This patch of highway was moderately busy, traffic streaming past in both lanes. Still she could hear Bradford's door opening and closing (he'd left the keys in the ignition, the car *ding ding ding dinging* while the door was open), the crunch of gravel as he came around the front of the car. Bradford saying, "Elizabeth, what's wrong?" and then saying, "If this is a ruse to keep me from calling the Bureau, you're wasting your time."

She stayed where she was on the ground, on her hands and knees, continuing to dry heave. She could hear the car's door opening and closing again, only this time it was the back door, Julia Hogan asking, "Is she okay?"

"She's fine." Bradford directly behind her now, only a few feet away, the sun positioned just right that she could see the top of his shadow next to her. Then, talking into his phone,

"Yes, this is Special Agent David Bradford. I need to speak to the Special Agent in Charge immediately."

Elizabeth dry heaved again. She stared down at the grass, stared at the top of David Bradford's shadow. Only a few feet behind her.

"Agent Bradford?" she said weakly.

The shadow grew just slightly, the man advancing a few steps. "What is it?"

"I'm"—another dry heave—"sorry."

The shadow grew even more. "For what?"

Instantly she was on her feet, spinning around and driving her fist into David Bradford's solar plexus. He let out an *oomph* and doubled over, the BlackBerry falling from his hand, and she managed to grab it with one hand before it hit the ground and turned into him, reaching for the gun holstered to his belt. She unsnapped it and pulled out the gun just as Julia Hogan shouted at her.

"Freeze!" Julia Hogan was slowly advancing up the embankment, her own gun aimed straight at Elizabeth's head. "Drop the weapon!"

David Bradford groaned and was standing up straight when Elizabeth stepped behind him and pressed the gun into his side.

"I don't want to shoot you," she whispered into his ear.

"What the fuck are you doing?" he said.

Julia Hogan shouted, "Put down the weapon now!"

"Stop right there," Elizabeth said to Julia. "You're not going to shoot me."

"I wouldn't be so sure about that."

Elizabeth whispered into David Bradford's ear, "Move toward the car."

He began moving toward the car, Elizabeth behind him. "You're fucking nuts. What do you think you're going to do?"

"I told you what Clarence told me."

"So you do know where the trophies are?"

"Not exactly. But I have an idea."

They stopped at the hood of the car. Elizabeth's gaze hadn't left Julia Hogan this entire time.

Julia Hogan said, "Let him go."

"You're not going to shoot me."

"I'm going to count to three."

"You won't do it."

"One."

David Bradford said, "Just give this up. It's not going to work."

"Two."

"The gun isn't even loaded," Elizabeth said, staring straight back at Julia Hogan, and immediately understanding crossed the woman's face. Her gaze shifted from Elizabeth to the car. "That's right. They're still in the glove box. You—"

Julia made a break for it, running straight for the car, assuming Elizabeth wouldn't fire. She was wrong.

Elizabeth held out the gun and fired into the grass just feet away from the female agent. Julia Hogan went motionless at once, her face suddenly pale.

"Jesus Christ," David Bradford shouted.

Elizabeth pushed him away toward Julia. She walked backward, around the hood, to the driver's-side door.

"I didn't want it to be this way."

"Yeah?" Bradford said. "What way did you want it to be?"

She balanced the gun on the roof, aimed at the two of them. She set Bradford's BlackBerry beside it, reached into her pocket and pulled out her own. She dialed the number to Todd's throwaway. It rang three times before he picked up, and she spoke into it quietly, the rush of traffic behind her hiding her words from the two FBI agents only yards away. When she was done, she disconnected the call, slipped it back into her pocket, and skimmed Bradford's BlackBerry over the roof to him.

"If I come up with anything, I'll give you a call."

"Wonderful," Bradford said dryly. He held up the phone. "You know I'm just going to call the state police once you leave. They'll pull you over within minutes."

"No you won't. Because deep down inside, you know your son is still alive. And the only way to get him back is through me."

"They're going to pull you over and arrest your ass and then both of our sons will die."

"Well, then," she said, opening the door, "I better drive really fast, huh?"

And then she was inside, the engine started, her foot on the gas, whipping out onto the highway and leaving the two FBI agents behind.

She didn't have to drive far. She had told Todd where they were most likely going to end up. That it would be a good idea to try to find a midway point between Lanton and Graterford if for some reason she needed to contact him. This happened to be Reading. So after she had called, he started down the highway toward her, and they met halfway in Douglassville at a Wawa Food Market.

Elizabeth parked the car around back and slipped into the Prius.

Todd did a double take. "*Elizabeth?*"

"Come on"—she was leaning forward in her seat, staring out at the road, watching for cops—"let's go."

"What happened to your clothes? What happened to your *hair*?"

"Just drive, Todd."

He silently put the car in gear and got them back out on the road. Elizabeth used the BlackBerry to try Foreman for what felt like the twentieth time and then disconnected the call.

"Shit."

"What's wrong?"

"I can't get hold of Foreman."

"What do you mean?"

"He's not answering his phone. It keeps going straight to voicemail."

"How did things go at the prison? Did you get in? What happened to that FBI agent?"

They were all fair questions, each and every one of them, but Elizabeth didn't answer. Instead she stared out through the window, thinking about Eddie and Matthew and how both of them, in different ways, were sentenced to death.

"Elizabeth?" Todd touched her arm. "What's wrong?"

She looked at him, tears threatening, and whispered, "Everything."

57

By the time they reached Lanton, two hours had passed, and by the time they reached Foreman's house (what had once been Elizabeth's house), another half hour had passed. Todd drove no more than five miles over the posted speed limit, wanting to ensure they didn't get stopped for speeding. Elizabeth tried calling Foreman every ten minutes, always getting his voicemail. She left a number of messages, each one more frantic than the last, but still he never returned her call.

Which meant he had done just like he said and went into hiding. Or the police had picked him up and he was behind bars right now, or in an interview room, being sweated by detectives. There was a chance David Bradford and Julia Hogan had gotten the word out on her, and as Foreman had obviously been her contact, they would have this place watched.

Todd dropped her off two blocks from the house. As she walked down the sidewalk, she was aware that most of the people in these houses were the same people who had lived here five years before. Not that she would have recognized many of them or even known their names except for a select few, but they had been here, eating and sleeping and fucking less than a quarter mile away from her, and she wondered how what had happened that Saturday afternoon five years ago had changed their lives. After all, it wasn't an every day occurrence for the FBI to suddenly show up and arrest someone for being a serial killer. Not on this block. Not in this town. So sure, some would have remembered the incident well, recalling it months if not years later, always a good anecdote at a dinner party or picnic ("Hey, did you know I used to live a block away from a serial killer?"), but by now, how many would remember?

Five years ago she had kept a spare key in a magnetic box behind the shrubs just beside the front door, and here it thankfully still was, albeit covered in cobwebs. She let herself in the front door, looking back over her shoulder just once to make sure the street was deserted. Once inside she pulled the BlackBerry from her pocket and dialed Todd to let him know she was in. Then she slipped the phone back into her pocket and called Foreman's name.

No answer.

Despite the urge to hurry downstairs and start rummaging through the plastic containers, she went into the garage and watched through the window for the Prius. When it appeared, she hit the button and listened to the screeching noise as the garage door slowly rose. Once Todd pulled in (the other space empty, Foreman clearly gone), she hit the button again and the door began to lower.

Inside the house, Todd said, "Where to first?"

"The basement."

Foreman—God bless him—had been kind enough to label the contents of each container. So it made their job easier, bypassing the containers filled with kitchen utensil and appliances, containers filled with bathroom towels and dishcloths and oven mitts. They pushed all these aside until they got to the ones labeled with anything related to baby—toys, diapers, blankets—and these Elizabeth opened by herself, digging through each, shoving the contents away in disgust when they didn't reveal what she wanted.

At some point Todd had stopped searching through the containers and stood watching her. It pissed her off and it made her work even more furiously, one time even punting an empty container across the room like a football. This was when Todd finally spoke.

"Stop."

But she didn't stop, going to the next container despite the fact she had already gone through all the baby ones, this container full of DVDs and CDs, movies and music she and Eddie had once shared together, had laughed at and cried to together, and the thought of it all made her sick. The lid off, she hefted the plastic container (it weighed about fifty pounds) and then upturned it, the jewel cases and plastic cases avalanching across the floor.

"Elizabeth, stop!"

She shot Todd a glare, menace in her eyes, and said, "Why the fuck aren't you doing something?"

"What else is there to do? We've looked through all these containers. It's not here."

"That can't be," she said, though she knew it was true, she could see it with her own eyes, the fact that every container worth opening had been opened. She began to shake her head, whispering, "No, it has to be here, it has to," and before she knew it she had kicked another empty container across the room. It sailed for a couple of feet and hit the wall with a dull thud.

"Maybe ..." Todd cleared this throat. "Maybe we should search the rest of the house."

She collapsed to the floor, first to her knees, then over onto her side. Her body shook but there were no tears in her eyes.

Todd stood motionless for several seconds before turning and disappearing upstairs.

In her pocket the BlackBerry dinged. She went to reach for it, pull it out, see what new picture Clarence had sent her, but her hand froze. She couldn't move it. She couldn't do anything. All she could do was lay there on the floor, shaking.

Above her she heard frantic footsteps and Todd's voice calling her name. Then the basement door opened and he said, his voice hoarse, "Elizabeth, you need to see this."

Foreman lay motionless on the queen size bed in the master bedroom. He looked peaceful enough, despite the wire wrapped tightly around his neck. It had cut deep into his skin, causing him to bleed, and for however long he had lain there, the pillow and the rest of the bed had been absorbing the blood. His face pale, his eyes shut, and his hands clasped on his chest, like he was prepped and ready for the coffin.

Elizabeth stood just beside the bed, staring down at him. Downstairs, she had cried without any tears, but here, in the place she had once slept with her husband, she had tears but did not cry.

"This is my fault," she whispered. "All of this, it's my fault."

"Don't say that."

"But it's true."

"Elizabeth, you can't blame—"

"First Van and Harlan, then Mark Webster, then Jim, and

now … now Michael." She shook her head as if to clear it. "And Reginald Moore. I can't forget him. He was the first."

Todd came up behind her and placed a hand on her shoulder. She instantly turned and held onto him, burying her face into his chest.

"This is all my fault," she repeated.

He stroked her hair, telling her to hush. Then he asked, "What should we do now?"

She didn't answer for the longest time. She kept thinking about Matthew and that explosive collar around his neck and those bright red digits counting down. She kept thinking about David Bradford's son, the explosive collar around his neck, too. She kept thinking about what Van had said, what Bradford himself had said, and how they were all probably right—Matthew was already dead.

"I don't know," she murmured, stepping away from him. They stared at each other for a long moment. Then her gaze shifted past Todd. Something must have changed in her face, some kind of tell, because Todd immediately stepped back and glanced in that direction.

"What is it?"

She walked past him toward the oak chest. At the pictures on top. Only six in all: one of Foreman's first wife, one of Sheila, one of Foreman and Sheila together taken at some beach during sunset. The other three were of a baby. One showed their son as a newborn, the kind where his eyes were barely open. The other showed Sheila and Foreman holding the baby together. The last showed the baby in his crib, asleep, curdled up next to a plush purple dragon.

It was a man who answered the phone. The first thing he said was, "Listen here, asshole, how many times do you have to be told not to call here anymore?"

For an instant Elizabeth didn't know what to say. She had known Foreman still had feelings for Sheila after all these years but couldn't imagine his infatuation had gotten this bad. Just how far it had gone, she had no clue, but here was a man—no doubt Baldy from two days ago—sounding like he was ready to come over here and kick some ass.

She glanced at the alarm clock on the bedside table, doing everything she could not to look at Foreman. It was almost five o'clock. How it had gotten this late so quickly, she didn't know, but time was running out.

"This isn't Michael. This is Elizabeth Piccioni. I need to speak with Sheila."

Despite the fact the man didn't say another word, she could tell he had instantly deflated. There was the sound of the phone changing hands, a quick whisper, and then Sheila was on the line.

"Elizabeth? What are you doing calling from Michael's?"

"Sheila, I need to ask you something very important, and I need you to think about the answer."

There was a slight hesitation. "What is it?"

"Your ... son?" Her throat had suddenly gone dry.

"What about him?"

"Did he have a purple dragon?"

"Yes ..." Sheila sounding suddenly guarded. "What about it? Michael was the one who gave it to him. He called it ... Dennis, I think. Yes. Dennis the Dragon."

Elizabeth couldn't help but smile at that. As far as she knew, Foreman hadn't even known what she and Eddie had named the stuffed animal. But it had been among the others left behind—she hadn't wanted to take a thing from their old life except what was needed, just the necessities—and she imagined him wanting to do something to please not just the newborn baby but Sheila, the love of his life. Maybe he had been on some kind of deadline, rushed, and hadn't had time to pick out a toy at the store. Maybe he had felt picking one of the toys in the basement would hold some kind of sentimental value. Whatever the case, in the end he had taken the dragon, given it to Sheila and the baby, and even named it.

"What happened to it?"

"What?"

"Denny the Dragon. I mean, Dennis the Dragon. What happened to it?"

Sheila released an agitated breath. "Why don't you ask Michael? You're right there in his house, aren't you?"

"Because Michael's dead," Elizabeth said, saying the words before she could stop herself, and the sudden silence on the other end of the line confirmed that it was the last thing Sheila had expected to hear.

"What ... what did you say?"

"Sheila, I don't have time for this. What happened to the stuffed animal?"

There was dead silence on the line again, and Elizabeth was sure Sheila had hung up.

"Please, Sheila, I need to know. It's important."

"Is he really dead?"

"Yes."

"How?"

"Sheila, the dragon. What happened to it? Did you ... throw it away?"

Another silence, this one lengthier, and Elizabeth wanted to scream.

"No," Sheila said finally. "We didn't throw it away." She sniffled. "It was our baby's favorite stuffed animal. He loved it. Whenever we took it away from him, he would cry, so we always kept it with him. So ... so when he died, we did what we knew he wanted."

Elizabeth closed her eyes. "What did you know he wanted?"

"To be buried with it," Sheila said, crying openly now. "It's with our baby, God bless him, and will be until the day Jesus comes down and takes his body to heaven."

58

"We can't do this."

"Elizabeth ..."

"We can't, Todd. It's wrong."

"What about Matthew, then? What about that FBI agent's son?"

"I don't care. This ... this is going too far. We just can't."

They waited until the sun had started to make its decent, until it was dark enough with the overcast sky, to enter the cemetery. Weaving through the motionless grave markers along the narrow drive, deeper and deeper into the grounds, they came to the spot in the back corner, mostly obscured by trees, known locally as the Baby Lot. Here Todd parked the Prius and got out. He went to the back and pulled out the shovel they had found in Foreman's garage. He paused to look at Elizabeth still sitting in the passenger seat, then continued forward, carrying the shovel in one hand, a flashlight in the other hand, the dull beam of light illuminating each chiseled name until finally he found the one he was looking for and clicked the light off.

———

"We've come this far already," Todd said. "It's insane to stop now."

They were still in the master bedroom. Foreman was still on the bed. Elizabeth sat on the floor, her back against the wall, her knees pulled up to her chest. Her vision was blurry. Todd hadn't moved from the doorway this entire time, but now he began to slowly make his way toward her.

"Are you listening to me? I don't want to do this either, but after everything that's happened, after everybody that's died, we just can't give up now."

She stared down at the carpet, refusing to meet his eyes.

Todd came to stand before her, bending down, placing a hand on her knee. "Elizabeth?"

Her gaze shifted up to meet his, and she shook her head firmly. "Absolutely not."

———

She didn't move for the next several minutes. She watched the dark silhouette that was Todd working. Her mind raced, thinking about everything that had happened since Friday afternoon. She thought about Matthew and she thought about Van and she thought about David Bradford and she thought about her husband, and the BlackBerry dinged and she withdrew it from her pocket and opened the picture and saw her son there, the bright red digits reading **07:00:00**. Seven hours left and here she was, sitting in the car while Todd worked. She started to dial a number, hesitated, then decided no, it was too soon. So she undid her safety belt, opened the door, and stepped outside.

———

Todd stared at her for a long time, then nodded and stood back up. "So then what do you want to do? You want to call the police? You want to call that FBI agent and his girlfriend? You think any of them are really going to help us?"

He waited for her to say something, and when she didn't he muttered, "Screw it," and turned away and started toward the phone on the bedside table, the one she had just used not five minutes before to speak to Sheila. The keypad was on the handset itself, and when he dialed the first number she spoke.

"Don't."

He paused, staring back at her.

She said, "The police will just make it worse."

"How can they possibly make it any worse than it already is?"

Elizabeth didn't answer. Todd kept his stare level with hers, waiting, and when it was clear she wasn't going to speak, he dialed the second number.

"Don't," she said again, pushing herself off the floor and onto her feet. She kept her back against the wall, leaning into it. "Just hang up the phone for a second. Let me think."

Todd stood motionless for a long moment, then placed the phone back in the cradle so gently it didn't make a sound.

———

Todd paused only briefly to regard her as she approached. She came to stand by the pile of dirt that was growing with every shovelful. There was no telling the exact length and width of the coffin below them, so Todd was digging a wide enough hole to hopefully accommodate. Above her the sky was thick with clouds, hiding the moon and stars and, if he was up there, God himself. Stop, she said after a moment, her voice cutting like a scalpel through the darkness. Todd didn't stop. Take a break, she told him, I'll dig for a little. He continued with one more shovelful before stepping out of the hole and handing her the shovel. It felt extremely heavy in her hands. She stared down into the hole for another half minute, then stepped in and started working.

"If we do this," Elizabeth said, "we need to be respectful of the body."

"Of course."

"We can't just tear it up and take what we want. We're not grave robbers."

"Nobody's saying we are."

"It's just—"

She felt it then in her stomach, working its way up her throat, the taste suddenly vile and disgusting. She hurried out of the bedroom and made it to the bathroom in time, throwing the toilet seat up and vomiting straight into the bowl. She was aware that in a normal instance her hair would be in the way and that she would have to hold it back, and here she tried doing that out of instinct but of course there was no reason to, not with her hair cut short just today, and the irony of it all (and was that even the right word for it?) made her want to laugh. And kneeling there at the porcelain throne, something she hadn't done since college, Elizabeth did begin to laugh. She couldn't help it. Then when Todd came into the bathroom, asking her what was so funny, she threw up a little more and began to laugh even harder.

———————

They worked for over an hour in silence, one only pausing to switch off with the other. Their eyes had adjusted enough that they didn't need the flashlight anymore to see.

It was Todd who made contact with the coffin, the wedding of the shovel tip and the casket lid making a dull and hollow thud. They worked even faster then, Elizabeth digging with her hands, which seemed incredible because they were already working as hard and as fast as they could. They weren't even going to try to pull the casket out of the ground, and so Todd positioned his feet on either side and bent down and undid the clasps while Elizabeth shined the flashlight. Todd paused only once before opening the lid, and he turned his face quickly away, his eyes squeezed tight and his nose wrinkled. Elizabeth smelled it, too, that awful odor of decay, and had she not already thrown up everything in her stomach, she may have just gone for a second round.

"Give me the flashlight," Todd said, and when he had it he bent again and aimed the beam into the casket.

Elizabeth looked away. She didn't want to see the nearly four-year-old remains of a child. Nobody did.

"Here," Todd said, and when she looked again he was holding it out to her, Denny the Dragon, that mythical purple stuffed animal that had once been trapped in the confines of an arcade crane game to then eventually become trapped in the confines of a child's casket.

She took it from him, hesitantly, forcing herself to forget that it had just been with a decaying child.

Todd climbed out of the hole. "Well?"

She stared down at the dragon in the dark. Because of the flashlight, her eyes needed time to adjust again. She felt around the animal, first its feet, then its wings, then its nose ... before she remembered something.

Right now he's the answer you're looking for, Eddie had said to her before she left the interview room. *He knows.*

"He knows," she whispered.

Todd came to stand beside her, holding the flashlight. "He knows what?"

"Not *he* knows," she said, reaching out to direct the flashlight to shine on the dragon's face. "*His* nose."

She grabbed the tip of its nose and began to pull. It was surprisingly easy. Of course it was. After all, not too many years ago, it had been removed for a reason and then either glued or stitched back in place.

"Holy shit," Todd murmured, as she extracted a key from the stuffing filling the nose. It was a small key, with the number 49 written on the side in black marker. "Do you know what it goes to? I mean, do you know what it unlocks?"

Staring down at the key in her hand, turning it around and around with her fingers, she nodded. "Yes."

"Great." He used the flashlight beam to glance at his watch. "Then let's go. We don't have much time."

"No," Elizabeth said, her voice forceful. She slipped the key into her pocket and gave him a hard stare. "Not yet. Not until we fill in the hole."

59

There was a gate blocking the entrance to the U-Store-It, We-Protect-It facility just off the highway. This was a standard gate, and to open it one needed to use the standard ten-digit panel beside the gate. You could reach out the driver's-side window and punch in the numbers.

When Todd pulled up to the gate, he said, "Please tell me you know what the code is."

Elizabeth hadn't remembered there being a gate here before. Or maybe that was wrong; maybe she did remember there was a gate and forced herself to forget. All that was written on the key was the number 49, and from the look of the panel hanging just outside of Todd's window, four digits were required.

"Elizabeth?"

She closed her eyes, took a breath. "Try zero three two one."

Todd lowered his window and stuck out his hand. His fingers punched the numbers. Nothing happened.

"Any other guesses?"

Her eyes shifted to the dashboard clock. It was just after

eleven. The last picture she received informed her she now had four hours left. She'd hoped the numbers she'd given him would work—it was her and Eddie's wedding anniversary, the first day of spring—and now she was at a loss.

Until she thought again about Matthew and said, "Try zero six zero five."

Todd punched in those numbers. This time, the chain-link gate in front of them began to roll back. Powering back up his window, Todd said, "How did you know that?"

"It's a date. June fifth. Matthew's birthday."

Todd drove them through the gate.

The storage facility was broken up into six long cinderblock buildings. Of course, they weren't buildings at all, just rooms ranging from small to moderate to large. Elizabeth couldn't remember how big the facility had been years ago, but it appeared as if they had expanded. Each section was clearly marked, each door's number visible. They found 49 two rows back, halfway down.

When they pulled up to the door—it was a moderate-sized unit, the door the kind you had to lift up—Todd turned off the Prius.

"Ready?" he said.

She wasn't. Ever since they entered the facility her body had begun to tremble. For the last three days they had been working toward something, and that something was right here beyond this door. Or so she hoped.

Elizabeth remembered coming here with Eddie once. They had just gotten married. They were still in that phase of their marriage where they liked to take risks, even if it was something done in public. One evening they had come to pick up a few things and Eddie had closed the door and taken her in his arms and kissed her hard. They had ended up making love in the storage unit, nothing at all romantic, both of them on their feet while he took her from behind, but the thrill of it all—the fact that this wasn't a safe place, like their apartment—was the fun part. And now that she thought about it, strangely enough it had been the only time Eddie had been spontaneous like that, almost reckless, knowing that on the off chance they were caught they might get arrested. Maybe that was the only time she had been spontaneous and reckless, too.

Beyond that storage door were, supposedly, her husband's trophies. The pieces of flesh and bone he had cut off each of his victims. Saving them for only God knows what. Saving them for his own perverse pleasure.

And now here she was, the serial killer's wife, ready to enter this storage unit and retrieve the things that had forced her to come here in the first place.

"Yes," Elizabeth whispered finally. "I'm ready."

Outside the hybrid, the world was quiet except for the rush of traffic on the highway just beyond the facility. Nobody else appeared to be here. They were alone.

They stood in front of the door, neither saying a word. Todd looked at her. She looked back at him. He nodded, and she reached into her pocket and extracted the key. It was such an innocuous thing, so simple and insignificant, yet right now it carried a mighty power. Once, long ago, she had had a key just like it (so had Eddie), and that was how she had recognized this one so easily.

"Wait," she said, looking up from the key and staring at the black 49 painted on the door.

Todd shifted impatiently beside her. "What?"

"It's been five years. Who's been paying for this place? I mean, without monthly payments they would have taken this place away. Maybe they already did. Maybe when we open this door—*if* the key even works—all we'll find is a slew of cardboard boxes holding books or some college kid's furniture."

Todd gestured at the key. "Guess there's only one way to find out."

After another moment's hesitation, Elizabeth crouched down and inserted the key into the lock. She was certain nothing would happen when she turned it, but it turned easily. She heard it click and then heard the melancholy groan of metal as the springs holding the door down sighed. She stood back up, bringing the door with her, the wheels along the metal rails screaming out in the dark. Then she stepped inside, reaching out to the left where she remembered the light switch was, and flicked it on.

60

Storage unit 49 was completely empty except for a metal box on the ground in the very center of the ten-by-twelve foot space. It may once have been shiny, but over the years dust had accumulated and covered the lid of the box with a nice, even layer.

Elizabeth began walking without even realizing it. She went straight to the box. She only stopped when she was standing directly over it. She thought about the fingers in the box, at least four if not more, and the ghosts of Eddie's victims waiting here in this cold and dark place, just waiting until someone like her came along to find the fingers. Were they watching her now? She lifted her gaze and looked in the corners, but all she could see was more dust.

"Elizabeth? Are you okay?"

The question was absurd but one that needed asked. After all, she had suddenly become a statue, just standing here inches away from the thing she had been searching for these past three days.

She did not crouch like she had when she went to unlock and open the storage unit door. Instead she got down onto her knees, feeling the cold cement through the fabric of her jeans. She placed a finger on top of the box and drew it across from one end to the other, revealing the shiny surface below in one long line and creating a dollop of dust on the tip of her finger. She held the finger to her lips and blew it away, then reached back down to the box, finding the clasps on the front. She unclasped both, paused, and then opened the lid.

For a long moment she did not move. She did not breathe. She did not do anything but stare down at what was inside.

Behind her, there was slow and hesitant footsteps, and Todd's voice saying her name in a near-whisper.

She felt her eyes beginning to brim and blinked rapidly but still one tear managed to roll down her cheek. She could not tell how far away Todd was, just how many feet, but she sensed him behind her, coming closer. She flipped the lid shut, took the box in her hands, and rose to her feet.

Todd stood less than a yard away from her. "Is that"—he swallowed—"it?"

She only nodded. Her mouth had suddenly gone dry and she could not speak.

"Good," Todd said unsteadily. "So ... now what?"

She swallowed, found her throat wasn't so dry anymore, and said, "Do you want to see?"

"Huh?"

"What's inside." She held up the box. "Do you want to see?"

He shook his head. "God, no. Why would I?"

"I want you to. You've come this far with me, you might as well see what's in here."

He hesitated. "Elizabeth—"

"Please. I want you to."

He started toward her then, staring not at her face anymore but at the box. She had been holding it with both hands but now held it just with her left, balancing it right on the palm of her hand. As he was a step away, reaching for the box, she reached behind her with her right hand, grabbed David Bradford's Glock that she had hidden in the back of her pants, and brought it back out swinging, connecting the weapon with the side of Todd's face.

He went down with a startled cry, and she stepped forward and kneed him in chest. That sent him to the ground on his side. He groaned, tried to get back up, but she had the Glock trained on his face, the barrel's sight on that spot just between his eyes.

"I never told you she was his girlfriend," she said. With the box now tucked under her left arm, holding the gun on Todd with her right hand, she stepped back toward the open door.

"What"—Todd spat blood onto the cement—"what are you talking about?"

"Special Agent Julia Hogan. I never told you she was his girlfriend."

Todd pushed slowly off his knee and stood up. "Elizabeth," he said, holding his hands out to his sides, taking a step forward.

"Stop right there or I'll shoot you."

He stopped.

She said, "Everyone that's seen you has died. First Van and Harlan, then my brother, then Foreman."

"I'm not the bad guy here. I didn't kill anyone. It was Clarence who did it. You know that. *Clarence* is the one."

She took another step back, keeping the gun aimed. "Your main mistake? You were just too perfect. No man in his right mind would have stayed with me through all of this."

"I didn't have a choice. You said Cain told you to kill me.

You talked him out of it, remember? The only way I was going to live was to come with you."

She hesitated, thinking about it, remembering being back in the parking lot of Summer Ridge, swapping out her license plate with that pickup truck's, and then there Todd was behind her, a bouquet of tulips in hand. He'd brought them to cheer her up, he later said, but right then, right when they'd been in the parking lot, Cain had called, a nice convenient coincidence.

Elizabeth stopped walking backward and thumbed the hammer back on the Glock. "Who is he?"

"Who?"

"Your partner."

This entire time Todd's expression had been a mixture of confusion and fear and pain. Now something in it changed, something almost imperceptible at first, until she could see the corners of his mouth curling into a grin. He began to lower his hands, bit by bit, and shrugged.

"Why don't you turn around and ask him yourself?"

Something round and cold touched the base of her neck just then, and a ghost said, "Put down the gun, sis, or else I'll blow your fucking head off."

61

For a man who was supposed to be dead, Jim looked good. He wore boots and blue jeans and a black long sleeve T-shirt. His hair appeared to have a certain texture, like he had recently taken a shower.

She took all of that in for an instant before her gaze shifted to what was really important: Matthew. Her son, dressed only in his underwear, that explosive collar around his neck, a piece of tape over his mouth. He was staring back at her, his eyes large and red from crying. He even tried screaming through the tape, pulling away from Jim, but Jim kept his grip on Matthew's arm.

"Idiot," Jim said to Todd. "How could you fuck that up?"

Todd walked forward, shrugging. He scooped the Glock up off the ground where she had placed it and grabbed the metal box from her hands and opened it. "Doesn't matter now. We have what we need."

"It's all there?"

"Look for yourself."

Jim glanced in the box and nodded his appreciation and then threw Matthew at her like he was nothing more than a piece of trash. Matthew came at her fast, tripping over his feet, and he almost fell to the floor before Elizabeth grabbed him.

"Enjoy the family reunion while it lasts," Jim said. "Because it's not going to last long."

"What are you going to do to us?"

"Lock you in here. Drive away. Then in about five minutes"—he reached into his pocket, withdrew a cell phone —"I'm going to dial this and ... well, ka-boom."

She was crouched in the middle of the storage unit, her son in her arms. After three days of being without him, she couldn't let him go. Not now. Not after everything she had been through.

"Don't do this," she whispered.

"Sorry. This is how it has to be."

The men started to leave the unit but stopped when she shouted, "Wait!"

They both looked at her.

"At least tell me why. I deserve that much."

Jim seemed to consider this, then said, "What do you want to know?"

"Just why."

"That's not an easy question to answer."

"But I don't get it."

"What's that?"

"I thought serial killers were supposed to work alone. But ... what—it was you, Todd, and Eddie?"

"For starters," Todd said, "my name isn't Todd. It's Frank."

"That's right," Jim said. "And *serial killers*"—he shook his head—"is such a nasty phrase. It has poor connotations."

Elizabeth asked, "What connotation do you expect it to have?"

"She does have a point," Todd (or Frank) said.

"Shut up." Jim cleared his throat. "Listen, Liz, here we have one of those situations in which I'm conflicted. On the one hand, you are my sister and that boy there is my nephew. On the other hand, you both have served your purpose and we no longer need you."

Elizabeth held Matthew even closer, her hand over his heart. "Let me guess. Eddie hid those trophies from you as some kind of insurance in case you ever tried to backstab him."

Frank grinned, nodding. "Not a bad theory."

"Not bad at all," Jim agreed. "But it's wrong. For starters, Eddie never killed anyone. Not that he wasn't culpable. He knew what was going on but he was, in many ways, powerless to stop it. You see, these quote-unquote trophies were something he had come up with. And it wasn't for any nefarious reason like the ones speculated in the news."

"Then what reason was it?"

Jim opened his mouth but Frank held up a finger and said, "Maybe you should go back to the beginning."

Jim thought it over for a moment. "Might as well. Won't take long anyway. Look now, Liz, here's the deal."

It happened, Jim said, on Spring Break. Back right before Jim and Eddie graduated, when Elizabeth was still a sophomore. They'd gone down to Cancun for five days. Eddie and Elizabeth had been dating for only six months then. Eddie had asked Elizabeth if it was okay for him to go. He and Jim had been planning it since the year before. Elizabeth said it was fine, she trusted him, though she really didn't. This, she decided, was the way to see just how much he cared for her. As petty as it sounded, if he was miserable down there without her, then that was a good thing. If he had the time of his life, that was a completely different thing.

"I met this girl down there the night before we left. She had come with some friends from school—they were from California, I forget which college—and her friends had ditched her that night. The girl was a real freak, loved to drink and party, and her friends had decided they wanted to take it easy the night before they left as they'd been partying hard all week. So I met her at this club and ended up leaving with her. We were going to go back to my hotel room but ended up taking a detour on the way. We ended up in this woodsy part off the main road, and this girl, I'm telling you, she was a nasty freak. Wanted to do all sorts of things. She didn't even want me to use a condom but I insisted, because, you know, a freak like this who knew what kind of diseases she might have. And so we're going at it and she tells me to squeeze her neck, squeeze it hard. Like I said, she was a freak, but I thought what the hell and went along with it. And ... it's hard to explain, exactly, but the sex all of a sudden got better. I don't know what it was, but squeezing her neck like that, choking her, made me feel so much stronger. I didn't even notice when she started fighting me. I just kept going, squeezing harder, until, well, there was no more reason to squeeze."

He'd checked for a pulse but there was none. He considered doing CPR but didn't know the right way to go about it, despite the fact he had taken a health course that semester. He covered the body up the best he could and left. He found Eddie in their hotel room reading a book. He told Eddie that something terrible had happened, that he needed his help.

"I took Eddie back out there, for some reason expecting that girl to be gone. Like she'd just been faking it for me or something, and then when I left she got up and walked away. Or that I'd hallucinated the whole thing. But she was still there. Eddie told me we had to call the police. I told him he was crazy. I said I could get arrested for this. Eddie said it was an accident, but he said it like it was a question, you know, sort of testing me. I could tell he wanted to run. His eyes were all wide. He was as freaked out as me. I told him we just couldn't do that. He wanted to know why not. I told him because of you."

Elizabeth frowned. "Because of me?"

"I told him you were suicidal. That you hadn't said anything to him about it because you didn't want to scare him off. But that if something happened to me, happened to the both of us, you'd try to kill yourself. I told him you'd already attempted it before. I told him you had tried taking a whole bottle of Valium when you were in high school because some guy didn't ask you to prom."

"I never did that," she said, this shocking her more than anything else, remembering now how gentle Eddie had been with her when he returned from Cancun, how he had asked her repeatedly about her feelings.

Jim grinned. "Of course I know that. But Eddie didn't. And he fell for it, hook, line, and sinker."

With the threat of Elizabeth possibly doing herself harm, Eddie agreed to help Jim. Eddie retrieved a shovel, and they took the girl deeper into the woods and buried her. Eddie told him they had to get rid of their shoes and clothes and anything else associated with what happened, as the authorities might be able to track them down with any slight thing.

"Your husband really was a bright guy," Jim said. "I guess it helped that he had taken some of those forensic courses the year before. Eddie, he was obsessed with that kind of stuff."

Elizabeth said nothing. She thought about the times when Eddie was home at night and they'd watch TV. How he would dissect everything wrong with shows like *CSI* and *Law & Order*. Typical Hollywood BS, he'd call it.

"So then we left, both of us more nervous than shit, but nothing happened. I mean, the girl's body was eventually found. There was an investigation and all that, but no cops ever came knocking on either of our doors."

Nearly an entire year passed. Eddie had been living close to State College, so he could stay close to Elizabeth. Jim moved down south. He had gotten into the habit of having anonymous sex. Just meeting some girl at a club, either going back to her place or taking her to his place and fucking and then that was that. Only he kept thinking about that freak down in Cancun, how she had liked being choked. He kept thinking about how much he'd enjoyed that, how powerful it had felt.

"So I did it to this girl, and she ... she fought me hard. But the harder she fought, the hotter it became, you know? When it was over, I wasn't sure what to do. Now I had this dead woman in my apartment. I thought about getting rid of the body myself, but then I remembered just how good Eddie had been at it. So I called him."

Under the pretense that it was a work emergency, Eddie had driven nearly five hours to Jim's place. There he was met with another dead girl.

"Like a fucking broken record, he said we needed to call the police. I told him he was crazy. He said there was no other option. I said yes there was, we could hide her like we did that other one. He said that was a mistake. I said that if we didn't and something happened to either one of us, you would kill yourself. Eddie said nice try, but he knew better now, and he actually pulled out his cell phone."

What ultimately stopped him was Jim's reminder about what happened down in Cancun. That if Eddie called the police, Jim would confess to that murder and tell them of Eddie's involvement. The whole thing had made national news, the girl's parents being these socialites who painted a picture of a sweet academic who had so much promise. Public opinion was with them so much that if the case were reopened and Jim and Eddie were thrown on the judicial guillotine, both would lose their heads in one easy fall.

"I could tell he hated my guts. I could see it in his eyes. But he had just started his new job, you two had just gotten engaged, so he had too much to lose. He had agreed to help me but told me this was the last time. I promised it was, reminding him that it was just an accident. He said sure, just like the time before. And you know what? That really pissed me off. Like right then, he thought he was better than me."

"He was better than you," Elizabeth said, immediately thinking she should have used the present tense there instead of the past.

"Whatever. The fact was I owned him then. He may not have realized it, but that was the truth. So then another six months passed and I did it again. I'd started driving up and down the coast, picking up these lonely housewives. We'd go to some motel by the Interstate. Their husbands always ignored them or treated them like shit, so they wanted to get back at them, even if their husbands never knew it. I must say, I fucked my fair share. And I tried to restrain myself, I really did. But then one night I couldn't help it. I ended up choking this one woman to death. She was stronger than she looked and fought me pretty hard. Even scratched me a little. I hadn't thought about it at the time, but Eddie apparently did."

Once again Eddie had refused to have anything to do with it. And once again, Jim convinced him otherwise. Jim reminded him of just everything he would lose, and besides, he said, they wouldn't get caught, not as long as Eddie did what he was good at. Again, Eddie went to call the police and words this time would not stop him. Instead, fists did. Jim was careful not to punch Eddie in the face because that would raise too many questions with Elizabeth, but he had pummeled him in the stomach and ribs. He bullied Eddie into realizing he had no other choice but to help him hide the body, and unlike last time, Jim said he wasn't going to stick around. He said he needed to teach Eddie a lesson, so Eddie had to hide this body on his own. And so Jim had left, Eddie groaning on the motel floor, a dead woman on the motel bed.

"That was the first one they found with her ring finger missing. Apparently when Eddie was cleaning the place up, he noticed some flesh under her fingernail. He knew the DNA would match mine. So he cut it off for two reasons. One to keep it as insurance, like you said. And two so it would help start marking the bodies so the authorities would begin to see a pattern."

Elizabeth and Eddie were married two months later. Jim was Eddie's best man. There was nothing between them that suggested any kind of hatred. They both had become perfect actors, playing their roles without fail.

"The next time it happened, Eddie said he was through. He said he wasn't going to help me anymore. I told him that was fine, then if he wanted to turn me in I would make sure you were killed."

"And how were you going to kill me if you were in jail?" Elizabeth asked.

Frank raised his hand. "That would be me."

"You see," Jim said, "I had already hooked up with Frank here. Frank was a state trooper."

"I was also in the service," Frank said. "That's where I learned about explosives. I learned just how effective the right amount of C-4 could be. So that collar right there around your son's neck, the one that killed Reginald Moore, even the one right now around the neck of that FBI agent's kid—those are all thanks to me."

Elizabeth said, "Your mother must be so proud."

"*Any*way," Jim said. "He'd caught me for speeding one night when I was taking a girl to a motel. We were both wasted and he should have arrested me for drunk driving, but he didn't. Tell us again, Frank, why didn't you?"

Frank smiled. "I could tell some serious shit was about to go down."

"So he let me off with a warning. I should have realized then something was messed up about that. He hadn't even made me go through any of the motions, despite the fact I was no doubt way over the legal limit."

Frank said, "I followed them back to the motel and watched them go inside. That woman, she was one fine piece of ass. I'd actually tried hitting on her once at the bar. Got nowhere. And seeing Jim with her, both of them drunk, ready to fuck ... it had pissed me off. So I waited for them for a while and then went to the door. I tried the door and, would you believe it, the drunk asshole had forgotten to lock it. I walked right in and found him almost done choking the girl to death. And you know what, Elizabeth? It was the hottest fucking thing I ever saw."

Jim thought everything was over then. He'd finished and stepped away and there the cop stood, watching him. He'd even raised his hands, which made Frank laugh out loud. Frank asked if Jim had any K-Y Jelly. He asked if he had another condom. Then he went to work.

"So we came up with this arrangement," Jim said. "I'd find the talent and fuck them first, choke them to death, while Frank watched. Then he'd do his thing. Once every couple months we'd drive separately up and down the coast, checking out a few bars and clubs. It was always easy spotting the lonely housewives. And when I did, well, that urge, that hunger inside of me, it just went crazy."

Elizabeth had her hands now cupped over Matthew's ears. It seemed almost fruitless to do so but she couldn't help herself. Remembering all the times she had been alone with the man who had called himself Todd, all the times she had kissed him and felt his hands on her body (not to mention slapped her son a high five or ruffled his hair), made her stomach churn.

"In the end," Jim said, "your husband went along with it because of you. A part of him wanted to turn me in and end this whole thing, but another part, a bigger part, wanted to keep you safe. And besides, he was great at the job. He'd clean those bodies up real well, wrap them in plastic, take them out in the middle of nowhere. Months would pass before they were found. And when they were found, the feds couldn't find any trace evidence on them at all."

Except, of course, the ring fingers would be missing. That would alert the authorities that it was the same killer. The news of the missing ring fingers was never released to the media ("So we had no clue about it at the time, not even Frank, 'cause the FBI was keeping it real hush-hush"). When the bodies were turned over to the families, affidavits were required so each family would not speak to the press. Not until the killer was caught, which the FBI promised would happen soon.

"Truth was, we could have kept going with it forever. But then you became pregnant."

Eddie had finally put his foot down. He said there was no more. If it happened again, Eddie told Jim, he would contact the FBI personally. Jim reminded him about Elizabeth's life, about now the unborn baby's life. And that's when Eddie dropped the bomb about the missing ring fingers. How he'd been cutting them off each victim. How the very first had Jim's skin underneath the fingernail.

"The knowledge of that evidence has been a black cloud over my head these past five years, but now, thanks to you, that black cloud will go away."

"So why did you go into the Peace Corps?" Elizabeth asked. "Eddie was going to turn you in?"

"Actually, no. *I* was the one who put in the anonymous tip to the FBI. But I knew the shit was going to hit the fan very soon, so yes, that's why I signed up. I considered just leaving the country but worried that may cause too many questions. There needed to be a paper trail. I needed to be blameless. And if suspicion of me did come up, then I was already in another country and could make my escape easily enough."

"When did you call the FBI?"

"Remember when you dropped me off at the airport? I made the call right before my plane took off. Put on a hat and sunglasses so the security cameras couldn't see me, even put on a latex glove so they couldn't lift my prints. Eddie wasn't the only one who was smart."

It made sense then, at least to Elizabeth. The FBI got tips all the time, most of them worthless, but they at least had to follow them up. It wouldn't take a genius to track Eddie's movements across the country. They were, obviously, Jim's and Frank's movements first and foremost, with Eddie trailing behind to clean up the mess, but it was Eddie who had landed on their radar and who they one Saturday morning in the summer came to arrest.

For the safety of his wife and son, he couldn't turn in Jim. Not with the threat of another player involved, someone who was either a fed or a cop or someone high in authority. It made sense now to Elizabeth why Eddie refused to speak freely in front of David Bradford. Not because the man was an

FBI agent, but because he feared the possibility he was really Jim's nameless co-conspirator.

"But then you disappeared," Jim said. "Just vanished into thin air. Frank and I kept our ear to the ground. Frank monitored a lot of message boards, especially Clarence's. When that anonymous tip was posted about you being in Kansas, Frank went out there and didn't leave until he found you."

"It wasn't that hard," Frank said. "Jim told me you used to be a teacher. He said you'd loved it. So we figured you'd eventually go back to that."

"That's right. And once we did find you and started keeping an eye on you, we came up with our plan."

Elizabeth said, "Which was?"

"Clarence Applegate," Jim said, and smiled. "We knew from the start he would be our scapegoat. I mean, the guy was a loose canon to begin with, and as obsessed with you as he was, it would make sense he'd snap and start killing a bunch of people."

"He's dead, isn't he?"

Jim nodded.

"He was the one in the passenger seat last night, what I mistook for you."

Jim nodded again.

"Why did he kill Mark Webster?

"He didn't. Fact is, he was aiming for you but the gun was loaded with blanks. I was the one who killed Webster. I pulled him close to me and pulled out my gun and shot him twice in the chest and then slipped the gun back into my coat and laid him out on the ground."

"Clarence didn't realize there were blanks in the gun?"

"He never got the chance to check. We were able to manipulate him pretty well. We knew once your picture started circulating around the news, he'd recognize you immediately and start posting shit on Twitter and his blog and we couldn't have that. We needed you to stay under the radar as long as possible. So we contacted him pretty much the same way we contacted you, with the robotic voice, telling him we had information on you. He didn't believe us at first, but it wasn't difficult to convince him. We even promised him he would be the one who killed you. That was enough for Clarence."

"So when he showed up at the motel, you weren't expecting that, were you?"

"That was a close one. He could have ruined everything. I mean, he fucking shot Frank. I seriously thought that was it then, we were screwed. But luckily you both managed to get away."

Elizabeth said, "Back at Rockefeller Center, he had a different gun."

"That's right. I told him he needed a clean gun if he was going to kill you. Otherwise if he used his own gun it could be traced back to him."

"He was planning to kill me in public and cared about a traceable gun?"

Jim shrugged. "What can I tell you? The guy was crazy. So I left a gun for him, made sure to jam the magazine so he couldn't check. Fortunately for us, he managed to make his escape out of New York a lot easier than you. I followed him back to where he'd parked his truck. Nobody was around, so I killed him and put him under the tarp and drove out of there. Went down to Lanton, stole a car, made like it was my own. He's actually stuffed in that truck right now in some Walmart parking lot."

"What happens when they identify his body? There goes your cover."

"Don't worry. There's not much of his body left to identify."

"So then you killed Foreman, too," Elizabeth said, taking Matthew gently and turning him so his face was pressed into her chest.

Jim nodded.

"What about Van and Harlan?"

"That was me," Frank said, raising a hand. "While you were asleep (I'd roofied your drink), I slipped away to talk to them. Killing them was surprisingly easy."

"Van tried warning me about you."

"Obviously he didn't try hard enough."

"I still don't get one thing," Elizabeth said. "Why kill Reginald Moore?"

Jim crinkled his nose. "Are you kidding me? The guy was a fucking child molester. He deserved to die."

"Right. And you guys don't?"

"It's different."

"Sure it is."

"Besides," Frank said, "we needed to show you we weren't fucking around. Or rather, we needed to show you Cain wasn't fucking around."

"What about David Bradford's son?"

"What about him?"

"Is he alive?"

"For the time being, yes. We knew Bradford wouldn't go through with it otherwise. If he knew his son was dead, he'd bring his people in on it immediately. So I had to give him that slight hope that maybe he would see his son again. It took him longer to get out here than we had hoped. We had wanted him to be here by the time you first arrived in Lanton. Only he had been delayed, and you had gotten it into your crazy head that you needed Mark Webster, and that's why we needed to kill him."

"Because Bradford was the key," Elizabeth said.

"That's right. He's the disgraced FBI agent who always held a grudge against you. And after we're done here, Frank and I are going to track him and his lady friend down and kill them. Make it look like Clarence did it. And Clarence, well, he'll just disappear into the sunset like the crazy cowboy he is."

Elizabeth smiled. She couldn't help herself any longer.

Jim asked, "Why are you smiling? You think this is funny?"

"You could say that."

"Why?"

"Because while you've been blathering on and on, two FBI agents have been standing behind you."

"Bullshit," Frank said, starting to turn, and that was when both Special Agents David Bradford and Julia Hogan cocked their pistols and David Bradford spoke for the first time.

"I'd tell you to drop your weapons, but I don't want to shoot an unarmed man. Now where the fuck is my son?"

62

Back at the cemetery, the hole they'd dug almost refilled, Elizabeth had excused herself, saying she felt ill. Inside the Prius, she had extracted the BlackBerry and wished to whatever god was listening that it allowed text messages. Then she dialed David Bradford's cell number and typed out a text message of where to meet her, the name and general location, and hit SEND.

So she knew they were coming—or at least hoped they were coming—and when she noticed movement behind Jim and Frank, the slightest sight of a gun barrel, she purposely turned Matthew around and buried his head into her chest. She would no longer be able to clamp both of his ears, but it was a sacrifice she had to make, because she didn't want his expression alerting the two men of the federal agents' arrival. Then she smiled and the agents cocked their weapons and David Bradford asked where the fuck his son was.

Both Jim and Frank did not move. They did not blink. They stared back at her, calculating in their heads whatever possible chances they now had.

Finally Jim said, "How much did you hear, Agent Bradford?"

"More than enough."

"And what do you intend to do with that information?"

"I haven't decided yet. Arresting you two is one option. Then again, killing you two right now would save a lot of tax dollars."

Jim kept his gaze steady on Elizabeth. "This storage unit isn't very big. My sister and nephew could become collateral damage if you and your partner did decide to shoot."

"What makes you think we give a shit about tax dollars? Just put the weapons down."

"I'm sorry, Agent Bradford, but you know we can't do that."

It was like they had rehearsed it beforehand, Jim and Frank, the two men almost graceful in their execution: turning toward each other at the same time, stepping away, raising their weapons back at David Bradford and Julia Hogan. The storage unit exploded in a cacophony of gunfire. Cordite filled the air. Elizabeth pulled Matthew even closer to her and turned away, pressing him against the cinderblock wall, her body a shield against the ensuing madness.

It lasted only five seconds. There was shouting, cursing, but she couldn't tell who was speaking because her ears were ringing and Matthew was screaming. She risked a glance over her shoulder and saw the agents were gone, Jim and Frank hurrying toward them. Both were wounded, Jim on his left arm, Frank in the stomach and thigh.

"You take her," Jim said, and Frank grabbed her hair and yanked her to her feet. Matthew cried out again. Jim grabbed him by the arm and pulled him away from her, then settled a grip on his neck and walked him forward. Elizabeth screamed her son's name, trying to writhe out of Frank's steel grip on her arm, pulling her toward the open unit door.

"I'm parked in the back," Jim said. Both men pushed her and Matthew outside at the same time, holding them there for a few seconds, enough time for Elizabeth to see David Bradford down one end of the narrow space, Julia Hogan down the other end, both with their weapons aimed.

"Agent Bradford," Elizabeth shouted, but before she could say anything else, Frank growled, "Shut up," and hit the top of her head with the butt of his pistol.

She bit her tongue, tasted blood, and then she was being pushed forward, Frank slouched behind her, walking her close along the wall, keeping her body between himself and Julia Hogan. She couldn't see Matthew, could only hear him crying, but she knew Jim was using her son as a shield, too.

Elizabeth struggled again, trying to free herself, which earned her another slam on the head with the pistol. The world went blurry for a moment. The strength went out of her legs. She staggered and Frank had to hold her up, shove her against the wall, while Julia Hogan waited at the end of the units.

"You know what I regret?" Frank whispered into her ear as he shoved her forward. "Not getting the chance to fuck you."

She clenched her teeth, trying to fight him, but he was strong, much stronger than she had ever taken him for. She said, "You wouldn't have liked it anyway. I'm still breathing."

"Not much longer you're not," Frank said, pushing her even closer to Julia Hogan, the space between them now less than twenty feet, and, like she had done with Clarence Applegate, Elizabeth leaned her head forward and quickly snapped it back into Frank's face. She could feel the cartilage in his nose give, could feel the warm blood in her hair, and she twisted out of his grip, reached for his head, and shoved it hard against the side of the wall.

Frank went down, but not before he fired his pistol, three consecutive rounds. At least one of them hit Julia, sending her to the ground. Elizabeth was frozen for a moment, not sure what to do next. There was Frank right beside her, Julia Hogan not too far away, and her son and brother at the other end with David Bradford.

Before she could make a decision, though, a hand grabbed her leg and yanked it out from under her. She hit the ground hard, knocking her head against the pavement. She was barely aware of Frank sitting up, the gun still in his hand, but then more gunfire sounded out and two spurts of blood appeared on his chest. He stared for a moment, just stared, and then fell back.

Elizabeth scrambled to her feet and hurried over to Julia. "Is it just you two? Did you call backup?"

Julia Hogan lay flat on the ground. Her face was pale. It was clear the woman hadn't been hit with just one bullet. Blood was seeping from her left arm and her left leg. She nodded, once, and whispered, "Should be here soon."

Suddenly gunfire erupted on the other side of the storage facility. At least a half dozen rounds from two different guns.

Elizabeth went to stand back up, but Julia grabbed her arm. "Don't."

She pried Julia Hogan's fingers off her arm and rested them on the woman's chest. "I'll be right back."

"Don't," Julia Hogan said again.

Elizabeth considered taking the woman's weapon but didn't want to leave her without one. She went to Frank, took the gun away from him, checked the magazine. Only two rounds left. Not a lot, but still two was better than none.

Jamming the magazine back into the gun, she glanced at Julia Hogan one last time before hurrying toward the opposite end of the facility, where the gunfire had gone silent and where she hoped her son was still alive.

Special Agent David Bradford was dead, or at least he looked dead, lying on the pavement, his arms and legs splayed, his eyes closed. Most of his body was covered in blood.

Elizabeth paused long enough to crouch and press her fingers to his neck. There was a pulse, but it was weak.

Bradford's eyes fluttered open. He opened his mouth like a fish, attempting to find speech, but no words came out.

"Shh," she whispered. "Don't talk."

"Leg," he managed in a voice that barely sounded human.

Elizabeth didn't know what he meant at first but then she realized his left leg was twitching. She noticed something near the cuff, a slight bulge, and immediately reached out and pulled back the cuff to reveal the ankle holster. A revolver was nestled there, a Ruger .38 Special, and as gently as she could she slipped it free from its holster.

"Go," David Bradford managed.

Elizabeth set Frank's gun aside, stood with the Ruger, and checked the chambers. They were all full. Five shots, five chances. Five ways this could all go from bad to worse.

She closed the cylinder, started to hurry forward ... but then stopped and stared back down at the gun and the faint glimmer of moonlight reflected off its barrel.

A chain-link fence ran along the back of the facility. She could hear the traffic on the highway, she could hear the leaves skittering across the pavement in the wind, and as she came around the corner she could hear her son sobbing and her brother cursing at him to shut up.

They were at the utility van, a black nondescript thing, and the side door was open and Jim was trying to hustle Matthew inside. The van was maybe thirty yards away. Elizabeth stopped at the rear corner of the unit, raised the revolver, and fired two shots at the van's windshield. The glass spider-webbed and Matthew screamed and Jim went suddenly still. Then, when nothing else happened, he slowly glanced over his shoulder. Elizabeth knew what he saw: his sister standing there with a gun shaking in her hands.

"Let him go," Elizabeth said, her voice hoarse with fear.

Jim just stared back at her. "No."

She closed her eyes and raised her shoulders and pulled the trigger again. Nothing. Just a dry click. She tried it a second time but still nothing happened.

Jim grinned and started to laugh. "You want me to let him go? Fine, here he is."

The moment Jim released his grip on Matthew her son went scrambling toward her. She could see her brother reaching into his pocket when Matthew was twenty-five yards away. She could see her brother bringing out the cell phone when Matthew was twenty yards away. She could see her brother standing there, holding the cell phone up, his thumb on the SEND button, waiting until Matthew had reached her. She could see her brother watching her, and as Matthew neared, she saw something change in Jim's eyes. The smugness had started to fade. A realization had begun to creep in. She watched her brother watch her, as the gun in her hands had suddenly stopped shaking. As her shoulders went back. As the fear in her face disappeared. As she tilted her head slightly to the side.

"No," he whispered.

Elizabeth pulled the trigger one last time and the bullet inside—the bullet she had purposely saved for last, the other two safe in her pocket—exited the Ruger's snub-nosed barrel and a moment later entered Jim's throat.

Before she knew it she was running forward, dropping the revolver and scooping Matthew up as she hurried toward Jim. He had fallen to his knees, his face pale, both hands trying to hold in the blood. He'd dropped the cell phone and it lay beside him, within easy reaching distance. She kicked it away just as Jim made one last futile attempt to grab it. Then he lay there on his side, staring up at her with dying eyes, and Elizabeth, holding her son, turned away.

63

The next several hours were a blurring parade of state police, federal agents, emergency personnel, and bomb squad technicians.

Elizabeth had already taken the explosive collar off her son's neck, placed it in the black utility van—she'd gotten a glimpse of the bed inside, the digital clock behind it, the camera set up on a bolted-down tripod—and she had taken Matthew back to Julia who was severely injured. By that point David Bradford was dead.

The first thing Elizabeth told the authorities when they arrived was about how David Bradford's son had been abducted three days prior. Immediately agents began making calls, attempting to track Jim's movements over the past several days.

She refused to be separated from Matthew. Even after hours of questioning, after telling the same story again and again, after being transported to the nearest hospital for more examinations, Elizabeth demanded she always be in the same room as her son.

As far as Elizabeth knew, she was not under arrest. She and Matthew were put in a room together and a nurse or doctor would come in and check on them regularly, always accompanied by an officer, but so far she had not been read her rights. She wondered if she would need an attorney, and that made her think of Foreman and Mark Webster, and she spent several minutes crying for everyone she knew who had been killed, even Reginald Moore, until Matthew awoke from his doze and touched her arm and asked her what was wrong.

"Nothing, honey." She forced a smile, wiped at her eyes. "Nothing at all."

Her current location had been leaked to the press. She turned on the TV hanging from the wall and saw a CNN reporter standing outside the hospital. All they had now was speculation but the main story seemed to be that authorities had finally apprehended Elizabeth Piccioni.

Just hearing that phrase made Elizabeth's hands tremble. She ended up turning off the television and holding her son until they both fell asleep.

In the morning Julia Hogan came to see her. Her left arm was in a sling and her leg was bandaged. She limped as she moved about the room.

"They found Dave's son," Julia said.

Elizabeth sat up straight in the bed. "Is he okay?"

"He should be. He's scared and dehydrated and exhausted but they have him in the hospital hooked up to IVs and, from what I hear, he should be fine."

"How did they find him?"

"Traced your brother's credit cards. He'd flown out to

Oregon two weeks before. He'd been keeping a close eye on Dave and his son."

"Jim used a credit card for the room he kept the boy in? I would have thought he was smarter than that."

"Oh, he was. For that room he'd paid with a stolen credit card. But the camera he'd set up to take a picture every hour and then send to David's phone, that signal bounced off a local cell tower. They managed to locate that and search all motels in a five mile radius."

The hospital room had that sterile unwelcoming feel to it. It was not a place to be comfortable or even feel relaxed. Beside her in the bed Matthew continued to sleep.

Elizabeth asked, "Am I under arrest?"

"No. At least not yet. You have broken several laws in different states, so that puts you under federal jurisdiction. However, you are now being credited with revealing the true killers behind the Widower Maker Murders."

There was another silence. Elizabeth asked about David Bradford.

"What about him?"

"The relationship you two had wasn't strictly professional, was it?"

Julia Hogan's face flushed. She looked away for a long time before speaking.

"I first met him five years ago when he came to arrest your husband. He was ambitious and brilliant and it looked like he was going to advance in the Bureau. But then you disappeared and his superiors blamed him. It didn't help that he and his wife were having issues, either. One night before he ended up going home we got together at a bar and got drunk and went back to his hotel room. That ... that was pretty much it. Just a one time thing, I thought. Then he'd gotten transferred and his wife left him and he started sending me emails. We'd talk on the phone every night. Sometimes he'd fly out and see me or I'd fly out and see him. We never said it to each other, but we ... we were in love."

"I'm sorry."

Julia wiped at her eyes. "It's not your fault."

Elizabeth didn't want to dispute this claim, though she knew it wasn't true. Everything that had happened was her fault.

"What about my husband?"

"That's another issue completely."

"How so?"

"Does the name Alex Scott mean anything to you?"

Elizabeth thought about it, frowned. "No," she said, then glanced down at Matthew sleeping beside her and paused. "Actually, yes. Before we named our son Thomas, Eddie and I had talked about two other names. Alex and Scott. Why?"

"Alex Scott is the name of the person leasing that storage unit where the fingers were kept. We were able to figure that out pretty quickly—the owner of the place gave us all the information—but the ID Alex Scott had given him was a fake."

"Eddie had a fake ID?"

"Right after he had told your brother about the fingers, he knew he needed to hide them. He knew there was a chance your brother and his partner might come after him, so he managed to get a fake ID, secure a ten-year lease at the storage unit for a fixed rate, and then created a bank account with enough money to pay it off. He set it up so every month the exact amount would be transferred over. He assumed if it came to it, he would go to jail and you would be protected as long as those fingers were safe."

"How do you know all this?"

"Two agents went to speak with your husband first thing this morning. They told him what happened and how you and your son are safe and he confessed everything." Julia paused. "He did all this for you and your son, you realize. He loves you both that much."

Before Elizabeth could respond, there was a knock at the door and one of the FBI agents stuck his head in and gave Julia a look. Julia signaled to him that she would be right out, and his head disappeared and the door closed.

"How much trouble are you in?" Elizabeth asked.

"A lot."

"Will you be fired?"

Julia Hogan ignored the question. She said, "The reason I came in here to begin with was to tell you that the press is outside. They would like you to give a statement. You don't have to, but—"

"No," Elizabeth said, swinging her feet off the bed. "I want to. Now what do you think I should wear?"

Her statement to the press was, she liked to think, short and sweet. She went to stand behind the mini-lectern that had been set up with microphones sticking out like a bizarre bouquet, each with the call letters of the affiliates. She had not changed out of her jeans and wore one of the shirts the hospital had provided. She hadn't taken a shower and she knew her hair was a mess but she didn't care. She felt that her harried look would give her words more impact.

"Right now I don't have much to say about this matter," she told the cameras and the men and women standing behind those cameras and everyone else who was watching what was transmitted through those cameras. "In the next day or so I'm sure the FBI will release their official statement. All I can say right now is that it appears my husband, Edward Piccioni, did not murder any of the women he was convicted of murdering five years ago."

This started a rumble among the reporters, and she raised a hand for silence.

"The real killers were identified late last night. They are now both dead. There were two of them. It's a long story and I'm sure the FBI will tell you everything. Actually, speaking of the FBI, I would not be standing here now if it were not for two special agents. These agents both went above and beyond to protect my son and me and help bring these men to justice. Unfortunately, one of the agents was killed in the line of duty. He was a brave man. The other agent was injured. She seems to be okay now and hopefully soon she will be back on her feet and back on the job that she does so well. They are both your heroes. Thank you for your time. That is all."

Back in the hospital room, Matthew was awake and eating breakfast, a bowl of Honey Nut Cheerios and milk and a plastic cup of apple juice. Julia Hogan sat in the chair next to the bed.

"What did you think about that?" Elizabeth asked.

"You're crazy."

"That should guarantee you at least keep your job. From what I understand, public opinion is a very strong thing." She stared down at her son, then glanced at Julia again. "Now what about my husband?"

"Honestly, I don't know."

"If what Jim said was true, and I now believe it is, then Eddie had nothing to do with those murders."

"He was still an accomplice."

"By force."

"That doesn't mean anything and you know it. Look, the matter is being investigated as we speak."

"Do you trust there will be a fair outcome?"

"I certainly hope so."

Elizabeth stared down at her son again. Matthew chewed his cereal, his gaze directed up at the TV that Julia had now changed to cartoons. He noticed her watching him and smiled at her.

"So you're still an agent, right?"

"Nobody has told me differently."

"I need you to do me two favors. If you wouldn't mind."

"That depends. What are they?"

Elizabeth told her.

Julia Hogan said, "The second one makes sense, but are you positive about the first?"

Elizabeth thought about it for a moment. "I guess I won't know until I confront her about it, will I?"

———

Leaving the hospital was easier than Elizabeth had thought it would be. Julia Hogan made some calls and then told Elizabeth they had the okay. Elizabeth didn't want to leave Matthew alone but didn't want to take him either. Not to the first place she needed to go, and certainly not to the second place. The nurse who had been checking on them since they first arrived agreed to keep an eye on Matthew. Julia talked to one of the cops in the building and asked him to stand guard outside the door.

Despite the bandage on her leg, Julia drove. Neither woman spoke the entire way except when Elizabeth told her to turn here or there. Finally they came to the townhouses. Elizabeth directed Julia to which townhouse and then they were parked and Elizabeth went up the steps and knocked on the door.

Baldy did not answer the door this time. Now it was Sheila, still dressed in her school outfit, the nice slacks and shirt. When she saw Elizabeth her hand went to her mouth.

"Oh my God. I saw the news. Are you okay?"

"I've been better."

"I can't believe it. It's awful."

Elizabeth only nodded.

Sheila's gaze momentarily slid past Elizabeth to Julia Hogan in the parked car. "What are you doing here?"

"Michael's dead."

"I know. You told me last night."

"He was murdered."

"I—" Sheila cleared her throat. "I'm sorry to hear that."

"A lot of people were murdered because of what my brother wanted."

"Wait." Frowning now. "Your brother?"

"If they never would have been able to track me down, none of this would have ever happened. Or at least that's what I've been telling myself."

Sheila's gaze shifted past her again for a second before shifting back. "I don't think I'm following."

"I never told anybody where I ended up. Nobody knew."

"Okay," Sheila said slowly. "Liz, I'm sorry, but I don't understand what you're talking about."

"Nobody knew where I was. I never told anyone. Not even you."

"I know. You had just sent me a message. You never said where you were."

"Right," Elizabeth said, nodding slowly, watching Sheila's eyes, this woman who had once been her very best friend, who with Foreman had helped her escape her old life and start a new one. "I never did say where I was. But you figured it out easily enough, didn't you?"

Sheila opened her mouth but that was it. She didn't say anything. She didn't even frown or make any kind of face. After a very long moment, she said, "I don't know what you're talking about."

"You knew exactly where I was, or at least the general vicinity, and you posted my location on Clarence Applegate's message board."

Sheila pushed her lips together so tight they almost disappeared. The uncertain look she'd been giving Elizabeth had turned into a glare.

"You don't have any proof," she said in a soft voice. "You can't have me arrested."

"Who said I was going to have you arrested? You committed no crime. You simply betrayed me."

"Betrayed you," Sheila snorted. "If anything, *you* were the one who betrayed *me*. We were best friends. We trusted each other. And you ... you got to do something people only dream about. You got to start a new life. But what about me? I've lived in the same town my entire life. I've been teaching at the same goddamn school for fifteen years. My life is going nowhere."

"So, what, you resent me for leaving?"

"You could have stayed. You could have faced everything. But no, you ran away."

"What do you want me to say? I was a coward. I never

should have left. I never should have put you or Michael in that position."

"Michael and I getting together was a mistake. We were completely wrong for each other. But then we had our son and I ... I thought maybe things would be okay. But then our son died. Our son died and three weeks later I get your message telling me that everything is great and you're safe and all that blah blah fucking blah. It literally made me sick. I was furious at you for what happened. If it hadn't been for you, Michael and I would not have gotten together, and if we hadn't gotten together, we never would have had our child. Christ, Elizabeth, I lost custody of my own children because of what happened. And then ... and then you tell me that you're fine, that you're motherfucking fine, and what am I supposed to do with that? How am I supposed to react? I was pissed—I was fucking pissed—and so yes, I tracked your ISP number and then went on Clarence Applegate's board and posted your location. The day after I did it, I regretted it and tried to take it down but he wouldn't allow it. So I tried to forget the entire thing. There now, are you happy? I confessed. Have them handcuff me and throw me in jail. I don't give a shit. My life fucking sucks anyway so you would be doing me a favor."

A moment passed, and Elizabeth said, "To get what I needed to save my son, I had to dig up your child's grave. When I was done we refilled the hole, but you might want to have someone take a look at it and have it redone. I'm sorry for your loss."

And she turned her back on Sheila and walked away.

"So how'd it go?" Julia Hogan asked once Elizabeth was back in the car.

Elizabeth stared through the windshield at Sheila still standing in the doorway of her townhouse. She clipped in her seatbelt and leaned her head back against the seat and closed her eyes.

"It's over with," she said. "Now please take me to see my husband."

EPILOGUE

SIX MONTHS LATER

Edward Piccioni was released from Graterford Prison on a bright crisp Wednesday afternoon in March. There was no preamble to his release, no press waiting outside with microphones in hand, not even a freelance photographer standing with a camera wrapped around his neck and his hands bundled in his pockets to keep warm. Only Elizabeth and Matthew waited outside, watching the entrance tentatively.

The reason for the lack of turnout was all thanks to an agreement between the prison and the FBI. Her husband's official release was not scheduled for another two weeks. Then the prison parking lot was guaranteed to be a circus of news vans and reporters and cameramen jostling for the best shot and opening question. But the FBI had talked with the warden and the warden agreed to release Eddie two weeks beforehand. Only a few people knew the extent of this change in procedure, for fear that someone might leak it to the press and cause an even crazier circus than the one they no doubt already had planned.

Over the past six months Elizabeth had gone to see her husband exactly thirty-nine times. She took Matthew with her only nine of those times. She wished she could have taken him more—she knew Eddie wanted to see him as much as possible, and Matthew had quickly warmed up to the father he had never known existed—but she didn't like taking her son into the prison. Eddie understood, and didn't blame her. Besides, he said, he had the rest of his life to spend with his son.

At 12:47 p.m. Eddie emerged from the entrance doors. He squinted into the light. All he had on were jeans, a gray Champion sweatshirt, and a pair of Reebok sneakers she'd purchased the week before.

Despite the three dozen or so cars parked in the lot, he spotted hers at once. She and Matthew were already stepping out of the car when he started toward them. Matthew reached him first. He ran into his father's open arms and allowed Eddie to pick him up. Elizabeth stood smiling, tears in her eyes. Finally Eddie set Matthew down and turned to her. She stepped into his embrace. She held him tighter than she had ever held him before, kissed his cheek, kissed his lips, and ignored the tears threatening to form in her eyes.

They stood together in the parking lot for at least a minute, just holding each other, before Eddie said, "Ready to go?"

Her head on his shoulder, she nodded.

Despite the short distance to the car, Eddie picked up Matthew and carried him. "Jeez, feel how heavy you are! Is that fat or all muscle?"

"All muscle," Matthew said matter-of-factly, and Eddie burst out laughing.

They got into the car, Elizabeth up front in the driver's seat, Eddie and Matthew in the back. She started the engine and then just sat there, staring at the prison.

"Liz?" Eddie said. "What's wrong?"

"Nothing." She put the car in gear and backed out of the parking space. "Just lost in my thoughts, is all."

Except it wasn't nothing. The past six months had been a continuous onslaught of meetings with FBI agents and lawyers and people from the press. The nice and quiet life she had always envisioned would never exist. She had actually considered running away again—this time all three of them, creating new identities and everything—but she couldn't do that. She wasn't running anymore.

What was worse was she hadn't heard from Julia Hogan in weeks. There had been review meeting after review meeting and Julia Hogan had gone to each one expecting to lose her job. Finally she did. Julia was given a chance to appeal the decision but she told Elizabeth it wasn't worth it. Her career as an FBI agent was over and there was nothing she could do to change that. "Hey, it was a nice run while it lasted," she had told Elizabeth the night of her dismissal over the phone, and then promised to call Elizabeth sometime later when she felt ready to talk. That was the last time Elizabeth had heard from her.

Eddie said, "You know what I want?"

They had just passed through the prison gates and were headed down the drive toward the main road.

Elizabeth glanced in her rearview mirror. "What's that?"

"A Big Mac. A nice juicy and cholesterol-inducing Big Mac. The more calories, the better."

"McDonald's!" Matthew said. "Happy Meal, Happy Meal!"

Elizabeth didn't want to go to McDonald's. She didn't want to use the drive thru or, God forbid, actually park and go inside. What she wanted to do was just go home, be with her family, but still, she wasn't about to deny her two boys.

"Yes, yes, yes," she said. "If greasy food is what you want, greasy food is what you'll get."

Both Eddie and Matthew started cheering and high fiving, and Elizabeth couldn't help but smile. It felt great. No, that wasn't right. It felt even better than great, whatever that was, and as she drove down the drive she glanced in the rearview mirror at her husband and son and, between them, the prison that grew smaller and smaller until she turned the corner and then it was gone.

ABOUT THE AUTHOR

Robert Swartwood is the *USA Today* bestselling author of *The Serial Killer's Wife*, *No Shelter*, *Man of Wax*, and several other novels. He created the term "hint fiction" and is the editor of *Hint Fiction: An Anthology of Stories in 25 Words or Fewer*. He lives with his wife in Pennsylvania.

Made in the USA
Monee, IL
12 September 2023

42610524R00204